Double Star

Cindy Saunders

Illustrations by Laurie Barron

To Mom, for always believing I could fly...
And to Ned, for lifting me into the air.

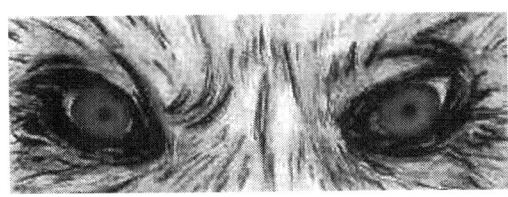

"Dark are the rails of today's twists and turns,
When set in the tunnel of tomorrow's concerns."

Ned Saunders

Chapter 1

Where she was going didn't matter. Where she was, she didn't know. In this run for her life, her focus was to simply get someplace else. Above, the limbs of the great pines held the stars hostage. The only light came from the two moons in the sky. Despite her silent pleas they continued to fall, barely visible through the thick cover of the forest. She knew the darkness concealed many secrets and, from that fact, there was no escape.

Snap. The sound from behind stopped her heart. She dared to turn around. Two glowing rubies, only feet away, rode up and down as the creature advanced on four legs.

Beware the red eyes. The boy's whisper broke through. *They are the eyes of death for you and the ones you love. They will not rest until yours are closed forever.* His image played in her head for only a millisecond, but it filled her with courage. Her heart picked up pace and, with arms out at her sides, hands moving in frantic rhythm, she managed to stay on her feet.

She sensed each passing second could be her last when she heard the creature's rhythmic breathing roll up from her heels. Just then, the red moon revealed an abrupt end to the forest a short distance ahead. In a few steps, her fate would be in the hands of gravity. *Trust!* That was her grappling hook as she threw herself over the edge and tumbled into the darkness below.

The beast followed down the steep embankment and stopped a few feet away. She got to her feet and allowed the wolf-like creature another step. Its red eyes stared up at her. The head dropped between its shoulders. Its weight shifted to its hindquarters. The muscles of hunter and prey simultaneously tensed. The animal growled and exposed a set of long, yellow teeth. Saliva fell in strings from razor-sharp incisors. Unable to move, she watched as it lunged, jaws open wide. She put her hands in front of her and took a step back. Her left foot fell upon air, and then ... she plummeted into emptiness.

1

Chapter 2

"Ally! Are you awake?"

Ally peered out at her clock. The LED display blinked back at her. She groped the nightstand and found her cell phone. 7:17 AM. *Shoot.*

"You're going to be late." Her mother's singsong voice rose up the stairs.

"I'm aw ..." She cleared her throat. "I'm awake, Mom!" *But getting up this early on a Saturday sucks.* She threw off the covers, sat on the edge of the bed and squinted at the opposite wall. The hottest violinist in the universe stared back at her. In David Garrett's right hand was his violin and in his left, his bow. *You can run your bow across my strings any day.*

Yeah, in your dreams—

"Ally!"

"I'm up!" She ripped the tags off the long green skirt and white gauze blouse. Why the hell had she gone shopping with her mom? She looked at the white sandals in the corner and grimaced. Their three-inch heels would put her into the ozone at over 5′11″. No way was she wearing those. She got on all fours and pulled her combat boots from under the bed.

In one quick move, her wavy, light brown hair was contained in a loose ponytail. She grabbed her violin and ran down the stairs.

"The wind must've knocked out the power last night." Her mother fiddled with the clock on the coffeemaker. She looked at Ally and smiled. "I don't know how you do it."

Ally sat at the table. "What'd I do now?"

"You barely touched a brush to your hair, your shirt's untucked, but you make me wish I was seventeen again. I'm so glad I have you ... your beautiful smile."

Seriously?

Mom placed a plate in front of her. "Are you excited about today?"

"Yeah." But excited wasn't the word. Today was her interview with Northern Arizona University's School for the Performing Arts in Flagstaff. The goal? To secure a full music scholarship. Her SAT scores were nothing spectacular, so this interview had to go well.

"You'll do great," Mom continued. "You're an amazing violinist. I'd love to go with you but they'll have my head if I cancel the showing on the Thomas house again. If I sell it," Mom smiled, "I'll buy you a new case. But I want you to take my car. I'd feel better about that long drive."

"And you're going to drive my car?" Ally said, dumbfounded. She couldn't picture her mom driving around in her junky Ford Escort with "If you lived in your car you'd be home now" and "Blessed are the cracked ... they let in the light" stickers on the bumper.

"Why not? You don't have a couple of dead bodies in the back, do you?" Mom chuckled, but then her face became somber. "And ... not that you need it, but I have something I want you to take. For luck. I'll be right back." The words fell backward down the stairs as she ran up them.

Mom returned with a silver chain in her fingers. One Ally recognized too well.

"I can't take that," Ally said. "What if I lose it?"

"You're not going to lose it. Stand up."

Ally held up her hair and a shiver went down her back. This was the necklace her father had given her mother five years ago, on their anniversary. He'd meticulously crafted the setting: The outline of a heart in white gold had been cut into halves, and a pin held a heart-shaped ruby within each. He'd worn one of the halves, her mom, the other. On the lower end of Mom's setting, he'd added a tiny diamond to the white-gold outline.

"Are you sure?" Ally whispered. "You haven't worn this since Dad died."

Mom took her shoulders, gently spun her around and looked into her eyes. "I'm sure. Did you program the GPS?"

"Did it last night." Ally picked up the new Garmin from the counter. A godsend, considering she could get lost before leaving the driveway.

"And Stephanie's going with you, right?"

"Yup." Ally sat down and, in four bites, finished her breakfast. She looked up, but Mom hadn't moved. "What is it?"

"I love you, honestly."

Ally rose from the chair and grabbed her things. "I love you too, Mom."

"Call me later, honey."

Ally's reply was swallowed up by the slamming of the door that led to the garage.

She pushed the button and the morning's light filled the dusty two-car enclosure. She squeezed between her mom's Camry and the garbage cans that occupied the right bay. The left side housed her dad's workshop. One of his hobbies had been woodworking and there wasn't anything he couldn't piece together from a photograph. Bookcases were a breeze and they lined the wall, holding an unthinkable amount of stapled pages and books on every branch of advanced physics.

With a quarter turn the Camry's engine came to life, muffled by the noise of 1430 AM. She poked a preselected station and Thirty Seconds to Mars' "Closer to the Edge" filled her ears.

Ally stifled a yawn. The wind wasn't the only thing that kept her awake last night. The dream. The same dream for the past month. But something in last night's was different.

A boy.

A cute boy.

A cute boy who looked like David Garrett ... with blue-green eyes.

Sure, why not. Anything's possible in a dream. She sighed and tried to clear her head. The piece she'd chosen to play today would demand all her attention, and already she was struggling to focus. But she had to. Otherwise, *buh*-bye scholarship, hello student loans.

Ten minutes later, she flew into Steph's driveway. Steph ran from the house wearing gym shorts and a tank top, her short blonde hair spiked out at crazy angles like some deranged anime cartoon. Her glittered cell phone sparkled in her hand.

Ally stepped from the car. "When I said you didn't need to dress up, I had something a little different in mind."

"Hey, Ally. I hate to spring this on you, but bad news. I need to watch the brat today. Mom has to go to the hospital to see my grandmother."

"Hospital? What happened?"

"They think it was a stroke, but she's gonna be okay."

"Oh, good," Ally said, relieved. *No. Bad.* Steph's brother was seven. Ally only had a Class G driver's license. No driving on a public highway with more than one passenger under eighteen.

"I'm really sorry. I was just about to call you." Steph waved her cell phone.

"That's okay—"

"Hey, let's take a picture." Steph put her arm around Ally's shoulder and held the phone at arm's length. Ally forced a smile. "I just sent it to you, but know I'll be with you today, in here." Steph patted her heart and kissed Ally's cheek. "You'll do great. Call me."

Ally backed out of the driveway. *Crap.*

Well, what was the big deal? It was only a hundred-and-fifty miles. And she had Lady Garmin, the best copilot in the world. No big deal at all.

She plugged in the GPS and laid it on the dash, found the address in her list of Favorites and, without looking back, headed onto West Camelback Road.

"Drive one-point-seven miles then take ramp right." Ally took the exit and went in the direction she was told.

"Drive ninety-four-point-seven—."

The voice of DJ, Young Marc, interrupted the GPS. "A freak windstorm blew through *only* East Phoenix last night and about five hundred residents are still without power. APS is investigating and expects power will be restored by the end of the day. Hey, was Rush Limbaugh visiting the East side, or was it another alien invasion?"

She pulled her iPod from her bag and plugged it into the auxiliary port. Maybe the sound of Rachmaninoff's "Vocalise" would calm her nerves. Her hand touched the heart around her neck.

Could it really have been nearly two years ago? *Don't think about the death, concentrate on the life.* But the memories of her father were beginning to blur, and each new day was stealing the past. She remembered his passion for living, his love for her and Mom, and she smiled. She didn't care that the feeling would pass quickly; at that moment, her soul found a friend on the lonely stretch of road running toward Flagstaff.

"Drive two miles then exit right."

At the Garmin's call, she looked at the dashboard. The display indicated her estimated arrival time was 11:30 AM, in about thirty minutes.

"Huh?" She'd be hitting Flagstaff earlier than she thought and glanced at the speedometer.

"In point-five miles take ramp right."

She looked up. The exit sign advertised Sedona in large white letters.

Sedona? Since when does the road to Flagstaff lead through Sedona?

"Take ramp right."

No time to figure it out. She turned off her iPod and started the descent into the valley. The access road's steep grade, narrow road and hairpin turns could easily put Mom's car at the bottom of the ravine. Fifteen minutes later she drove, white-knuckled, into Sedona.

"In four hundred yards, turn left." She took the turn and waited for the next instruction.

"Drive two miles to destination ... on right."

More befuddled than ever, she glanced at the dashboard. "Have you been drinking? I'm nowhere near Flagstaff." Where was this thing leading her?

She wound her way up Airport Road, past the scenic vistas and tourists taking pictures of the gigantic red rock formations. She glanced to the right. The beauty of the open area was unbelievable as the unseen ground fell to the valley floor hundreds of feet below. On the left, the rocks rose sharply from the road, forming an impenetrable wall.

"Approaching destination ... on right."

Weirder still. The only thing on the right was a lookout turnoff where a man and a young girl were enjoying the view. She pulled into one of the empty spaces and stared at the inanimate device. "Yeah, I think this is where you get off. Let's hope the drop is enough so I can enjoy the scream as you reach *your* 'final destination.'"

Crap. Of all days? Really? She needed to clear the frustration that was beginning to seep into her consciousness. Stretching her legs wasn't a bad idea, either. Ally grabbed the GPS and her bag, in case she needed to reenter the directions, and got out of the car. She placed the Garmin on the hood and tapped the "Recently Found" icon. *201 West University Drive, Flagstaff, Arizona.* After calculating the route, it told her what she already knew. She was in the wrong place.

Her eyes drifted skyward and then dropped to the valley floor below. It wasn't every day she could see something as magnificent as this. She leaned on the hood of the car, closed her eyes and turned her face to the sky. *Dad would have loved this.* And that was enough reason to want the moment etched forever in her mind.

She got to her feet and looked over the guardrail that marked the threshold between this world and the one down there. *This place is ... breathtaking.* In fact, she felt a little lightheaded.

She stepped away from the edge and put her hand on the Camry's hood but the dizziness became more intense. "Deep breaths, just take deep breaths." She needed to get hold of herself before she fell to the pavement. Panicking, she put her hands on her knees, concentrating on the ground, struggling to lift air into her lungs. Her legs were wobbly and she took a few steps trying to regain her balance, but they could no longer support her weight.

And then, it was as if she were being pushed back. Her legs crumpled as two brake lights came at her. *Wait. That's not a car, it looks like two red ...*

The backs of her legs smashed against the metal barrier. A warm, moist breath fell upon the left side of her face.

"Daddy, she's going to fall. What's she doing?" the little girl screamed. The question sounded muffled, far away.

"Hey!" the man's voice shouted, faint, distant.

She lost her balance and reached out for something, anything. A sickening sensation gripped her.

"NOOO!" The scream escaped her lips and then ... an eerie quiet engulfed her as she fell over the guardrail and toward the valley floor below.

"There is no reality except the one contained
within us."

Herman Hesse

Chapter 3

Liam drew his cupped hands from the basin of water and washed his face. "Perhaps today," he whispered. His eyes appeared to float in the reflection. He pulled his long hair aside and confirmed what he already suspected. There was no sign of it changing.

He had just turned eighteen and wondered if Ascencia made a mistake. He was born with the mark: a tiny eight-pointed star just under and behind his right ear. Most boys his age who carried it had already experienced the Shanyo, but his star remained unchanged and the waiting was becoming unbearable.

"Liam, hurry up!" Meg shouted from outside the house.

Today was the Carnival of Ascencia, the Feast of the Beast. Because Meg had reached the proper age, it was her first time to visit the fair, and he was tasked with taking her along. As usual, he would make the trip to Kenyon with Corm and a few of his friends. But because his star had yet to transform, he would be a spectator … again.

"Liam! Let's go! We're going to lose the morning, thanks to you!"

He hooked and twisted the top half of his dark blond hair, tied it with a leather strip and pulled on his boots. "Calm yourself. I am coming."

Meg stood in the front yard, her hands on her hips.

"Meg Cheveyo," he said, "In this world to which you were born, you are to show those you address proper respect, which can only be conveyed with proper English. Why in heavens name are you using contractions—?" He cut his comments short when he saw their grandmother walking in their direction.

"Meg, leave us for a moment," Thea said when she reached them.

"Fine. I am going to get a hat." Meg flounced off.

Thea paused to catch her breath and placed her basket of roots and herbs on the ground. "Liam," she said, "you can and should correct her. By the fire of Hades, you can teach her if you have the time ... and the patience. You will share a future with Meg long after your father is gone but you need to remember ... you are not her father."

"Aye, Thea. But in his absence, I am all she has."

"Focus then, on what is important." She hesitated a moment and pulled a leather pouch from her apron. "Here is something for Cormac's mother. Instructions are inside. It is imperative he follow them."

Liam's mother had been gifted, but the attention his house received came by way of Althea. The medicines she created from her knowledge of herbs and flowers were sought by those beyond the forest. It was unfortunate she could not find the remedy his mother had needed in the short time Fate granted them.

He bent down and kissed her cheek. "We will see you tonight."

"Tell your father to be careful. The wind has changed direction."

He raised his eyebrows. Perhaps Thea was succumbing to the paranoia that accompanied old age. "I will. Come, Pilotte." In an instant, a barking dog was at his heels. He bent down and rubbed the border collie's chin. "I am sorry you cannot come today but, I promise, you will not miss much." Liam led the horses from the barn. Pollux, his black stallion, stood nearly nineteen hands from hoof to shoulder, towering over Meg's gray horse, Shilo.

Meg ran to Liam. He had been distracted earlier and shook his head at her, the frilly white dress and the floppy hat of the same color in her left hand.

"Why must you try my patience?" he said. "Where do you think you are going dressed like that?"

Meg placed the hat on her head, and stuck out her tongue.

"Promise you will not embarrass me." He grabbed the horn of Pollux's saddle and swung himself up. "Let us get this over with."

They rode in silence, communication stifled by Meg's determination to stay ahead and Liam took the opportunity to examine the pieces of his life. The lovely sounds stolen by Death had left his family's house cold. Its visit was tormenting, but brief, and was replaced by Misery, who moved in shortly thereafter and had made herself too comfortable. His father's position in the ministry kept him away from home. Meg was thirteen and it would not be long before she could take care of the household. Soon Liam would be able to … what?

He looked up in time to see his sister entering a dense section of the woods. "Meg! Wait!" He kicked Pollux to a run and caught up to her. The forest of Gilgamesh extended hundreds of kilometers in either direction, but in only a few places did the darkness of night persist so far into the day. For this brief stretch, he listened for any sounds hidden by the trees that might jeopardize their well-being. A few moments later they rode into Crescent Meadow, and had only traveled several hundred meters when a lone horseman appeared out of the grasses behind them to the left.

Instantly, a much larger boy and horse rose up thirty meters ahead of them on the same side. Seconds later, they were joined by another pair of riders who appeared on their right. "Ambush!" one of them screamed.

Chapter 4

The two riders on the right flanked Meg. Liam assessed the situation and smiled, seeing the flaws in their tactics. Rather than stay on the road, he led Pollux into the tall grass, toward the large boy riding ahead of him. His heavy draft horse had come in too quickly and would be the first to tire.

As Liam passed the horse, he crouched low and wrapped his arms around Pollux's neck. A hand found the belt of Liam's pants, but Pollux was past the rider before his fingers could get a grip. The boy did his best to reverse direction but lost distance because of a less-than-perfect turn. With his head tight to the horse's mane, Liam moved fluidly with Pollux, and they galloped down a wide path across the meadow to the east.

"Whoa, Pollux," he called out when it was clear the two would never catch up and brought his horse about. "Corm, I thought you would know better by now."

"That I do, Liam," answered the smaller of the two, "but Shane and I had a wager. He bet me he could catch you in his clever net. Now he needs to make good on it. Aye, Shane?"

"There, now, Beowulf, the fault is not your own," Shane said, stroking his horse's neck and looking at Pollux, his blue eyes in stark contrast to his fair skin. "That is a fine animal, Liam. Admittedly, I underestimated him ... and you."

"Thank you," Liam said. "What did you bet?"

"His hat ... he has the privilege of keeping it," Corm said and flashed a wide smile.

Upon Shane's head was a brightly colored jester's cap. An extensive display of stringy twirls and springs suggested the numerous threads failed to stretch to the full circumference of the wearer's large head. "You will both be jealous when the ladies cannot keep their eyes off me," Shane replied.

"I have no doubt you will be at the center of their attention,"

Corm said as a light breeze moved across the meadow. His loose-fitting shirt billowed, revealing his lean but muscular frame. He pushed his long, brown hair away from his face.

Liam snickered. "Shane, you cannot be serious. What is the purpose of the chapeau?"

"Need to keep them guessing, my boy," he said, and pulled it down tighter. His horse began to shift on all fours, in an attempt to manage Shane's great weight.

"All right, Beowulf, settle down." Shane's eyes focused on the road toward Kenyon. "Corm, are you as nervous as I?"

"How can the grand Shane Carson be nervous about a competition?" Corm replied. "You will be fine, you great bear. It is I who needs to be nervous."

Shane pointed to the three figures in the road. "Is that Meg?" he asked, seeming to notice her for the first time. "I must get reacquainted. Yee-*ha*!" He sped away on Beowulf, with Liam and Corm close behind.

"Ian," Shane said to the rider beside Meg, who was dressed completely in black, "you should have insisted I listen to Oisin with regard to setting this trap."

"You never listen to me." Ian tugged at his long black ponytail. If not for his light green eyes, Ian might have been mistaken for the Dark Ghost with his skin of night.

"He never listens to anyone," Oisin added.

"Excuse me, Liam," Meg said, staring at Shane. "Am I correct that you were worried about *me* embarrassing you?"

"My little Nutmeg." Shane chuckled. "You are looking quite lovely today. First time at the fair is always an adventure. I will never forget mine."

"What happened?" Meg asked.

"My brothers and I snuck into the ale pavilion. Suffice to say there was not a drop wasted that day. My only regret is we were discovered hiding, not all that inconspicuously, behind a keg." "As I recall, you were escorted from the fair that year," Ian said.

"A minor complication for several gentlemen, but little inconvenience to me," Shane said. "Meg, I recommend you stay close, though, to avoid any difficulty."

"Not on your life, Shane Carson! I want to smell the perfumes … see the jewelry … all the girl stuff."

"As a matter of fact, those are the things of interest to me," Oisin replied. His dark, curly hair was kept in place by a bright red scarf tied around his forehead, but it appeared washed out when compared against his red silk shirt. Only the glint from the gold hoop in his right ear was more distracting.

"Please," Meg said, "can we proceed so I can depart this miserable company?"

As they began to ride, Liam handed Corm the pouch. "Here is something Thea prepared for your mother. How is she doing?"

"Not good, I am afraid. Her condition has worsened. I pray this will help."

Liam nodded. "Aye, say it will." Corm's mother had been sick for the last four months, and his father had taken to the bottle to ease his despair. How could Death take one life and leave another utterly broken? It was a question Liam and Corm had discussed on numerous occasions, but they concluded an answer was nonexistent, and both were beginning to realize their dreams would have to wait.

"I have not seen Olivia lately," Corm said. "Have you stopped riding together?"

Liam shook his head. "I do not know."

"Why? What happened?"

What, indeed? Liam had gone over the events of that day more than once. "We were sitting on the bank of the river, sharing an apple. I held it up to take a bite and she leaned over and ... kissed me."

Corm smiled. "Ah. So what is the problem then?"

"The *problem* started when I dropped the apple. She was trying to look into my eyes, but mine were following the piece of fruit as it bounced into the stream and out of sight. She pulled away. I had no idea what to say or do. I have not seen her since. It happened too quickly."

"I did not realize it was something that required a lot of preparation."

"Nor did I. My father gave me advice on the subject of women. He told me, 'The fires of Sirius will never burn like the fury of a woman scorned.' If that is the case, Olivia will not forgive me anytime soon."

"Well, it might make for an interesting day at the fair."

Liam had forgotten about the awkwardness that might come with seeing Olivia for the first time since the fumbled kiss but, with the crowd, he was convinced he could avoid her ... if he wanted to. A mix of emotions flooded his head. Why should he have to avoid her? Why was the construction and maintenance of a good friendship so hard? Friends should be like a barn; once built, aside from the occasional minor repairs, the job was done. But instead they were more like the animals inside, needing constant care and attention.

Oisin slowed his pace to ride beside them. "What are you discussing?"

"The unpredictable nature of ladies," Corm answered.

"Oh, Zeus on Olympus!" Oisin said. "You will not like where *I* stand on matters concerning beautiful women who can steal your heart with hello."

"Oisin," Corm said, "I bet you fall in love by midday."

Oisin's eyes sparked. "We have a wager then."

"Today is my lucky day," Corm replied. "First Shane, and now you. What is it *you* would like to bet...?"

In the company of friends, time passed swiftly and Liam was surprised when he saw signs of the fair in the distance. The tents created a colored patchwork in the valley below, and flags could be seen flirting with the light wind that came in from behind. When the roll of the road was no longer hidden, the sound of laughter drifted toward them.

"Race you," Ian said as he sped away on Nyx.

Corm signaled he would hang back with Meg and, when Liam turned his eyes back to the road, his friends had already covered fifty meters, about a tenth of the distance to the makeshift shelter on the southern end of the fairgrounds.

Liam coaxed Pollux to a gallop and reached the temporary stables first, a length ahead of Oisin. Shane and Ian, however, were a good twenty meters behind. "They will never learn," he whispered to Pollux.

While he waited for the others, Liam looked upon the crowd of people gathered where the road from Pembroke intersected with the North Street of Kenyon. Only one building stood at the T-shaped intersection: the Laius Bros. Trading Post. A sign in front of the building pointed toward the more populous towns to the east and west and in the distance, the snowcaps of the Bellerophon Mountains glistened in the midmorning sun.

Cindy Saunders

Shane let out a sharp whistle. Three young boys ran toward them. The first went directly to Liam's horse and took the reins.

"What is your name?" Liam asked as he dismounted Pollux.

"My name is Perseus," the boy replied.

"From where do you hail?"

"I come from Bristol, sir."

"Very well, Perseus of Bristol. This fine animal is Pollux. Tend to him well and there will be another of these when I return this afternoon." Liam tossed the boy a coin. "If something should go awry, though, the Ministry will see the ferryman, Charon, is paid."

The boy grinned. "Yes, sir. I understand."

"Could you help me down, William Cheveyo of Pembroke?" Meg asked.

Liam rolled his eyes. *Ascencia, give me strength.*

"Allow me the pleasure, my lady." Shane reached up and lifted her from Shilo.

"Thank you, kind sir," she said when her feet touched the ground.

Liam lowered his voice as he bent down, his face level with his sister's. "Meg, it is your first time at the fair and, as much as it pains me to say this, it is my responsibility to guarantee it will not be your last. Please respect my wishes and stay close."

"Liam, I could not *bear* to spend the day with you. I understand Thea would want me to obey your wishes. However, my dear brother, you have yet to inform me with what you are doing your bargaining. Unless we agree to take in a respectable number of the sights I desire, what is to keep my feet from wandering in this direction...?" Meg began walking down North Street.

After five steps, she gasped and waved madly. "Sara! Over here! Sara Acrisius!"

Sara and Meg took lessons together. Liam did not have the patience to provide his sister with the education she needed and Sara's father was glad to have another student.

"Meg! There you are," Sara said. She turned to the man walking next to her. "Dad, can Meg accompany us today?"

"Meg ... Liam, how are you on this fine morning?" Mr. Acrisius said.

"Very well, sir," Liam replied, shaking his not-so-distant neighbor's hand.

18

"Liam, this is wonderful! Do the five of you represent our contingent from Pembroke? What a fine group of young men. We have a fair chance to medal this year. In fact, I am sensing more than one of you will allow me to sport the colors of our stake." He patted the silk flag tucked under his arm with his walking stick. "Indeed, it has been far too long."

"Sir," Liam said while swallowing, "while I agree the stake of Pembroke has an excellent chance to be represented on the podium, I … will not be participating this year."

"Son, you of all people should know the mark you are graced with does not limit your participation to the physical challenges. I hoped you would give those from the eastern port cities a run for their coin in the Contest of Strategy."

"Thank you but, given the quality of participants from the East, a medal in the game of chess would be sure to elude me. And I have no intention of missing Pembroke's greatest moment when we take gold in the physical challenges."

Only three from his stake had ever won medals. Twenty-eight years ago, Ian's father, Lionel Telamon, was the first from the sparsely populated Pembroke to medal in any of the six physical contests. Six years later Sara's father, Ajax Acrisius, took home silver and three years ago, Liberato Fransisco did the unthinkable—he won two gold medals, one in his physical challenge and one in the strategic event. A new hero was born from Pembroke, but the celebration was over before it began, and a mystery took its place. The boy never made an appearance at the festival again and had not been seen since.

"May I have your permission for Meg to join Sara and me?" Mr. Acrisius asked.

"Yes. Thank you," Liam said, relieved for the offer and the distraction from such troubling thoughts.

"We will meet back here after the events then. Good luck."

"Meg," Liam said. When she saw what he held in his hand, he tossed it to her. The coins inside jingled as she caught it and rushed away.

He joined his friends, who had gathered around a piece of parchment affixed to a nearby tree. "The events have been posted," Ian said, pointing. "Cormac, lucky you. You are the first to compete. The Avian Challenge will be in the Far West Pavilion when the bell tolls eleven. I am in the next event, at the Coliseum. Oisin, you will participate in the third contest—at the North Central Pavilion." He turned to Shane, grinning. "And in the sixth and final challenge of the day, we find our little friend, Shane Carson. The Challenge of the Gladiators will take place at the Arena."

"Why is it they always save the best for last?" Shane asked. Before his question could find a witty response, he turned to Oisin. "Any idea on how we should pass the time this afternoon?"

Oisin winked at an attractive female passing by. "My friends, I do not know how we will be spending the time until Shane's moment of triumph, but I suggest we begin moving to the west end of the grounds and soak in the possibilities."

Two dragonheads carved into overhanging tree limbs marked the entrance to the fairgrounds. Tendrils of green moss spilled from their open mouths. The aroma of cedar chips filled Liam's nostrils while the tinny music of a hammered dulcimer could be heard in the distance.

They walked through Hawkers Row, where merchants displayed swords and shields, chainmaille, leather breeches, bows, arrows and quivers. To the left were makeshift shops that sold painted figurines, musical instruments, stoneware and pottery. Peddlers announced their wares while harried-looking vendors maneuvered pushcarts through the crowd, their stress concealed under practiced smiles.

"Ah, yes," Oisin said to Shane. "This is your favorite part of the fairground." Fire-pits lined both sides of the street and all types of meat hung above coals that sizzled as the juices escaped.

"Aye! Franz," Shane shouted to a burly man turning a spit that held an entire pig, one of enormous proportion that could easily feed a hundred guests. The pinkish meat was starting to take on a golden-brown hue. "You have once again made the year worth the wait. When will she be ready, my friend?"

"Patience, Shane, one does not rush the gods' feast. Should be done right around your match time."

"If you promise to save me seconds, you give me sufficient reason to bring a quick end to the contest."

"Do not rush," Franz said. "If you manage gold, I promise the rump for you and your friends. Sweetest part of the whole pig."

"Ah ... a true friend you are," Shane replied and licked his lips.

Franz smiled and basted the crisping skin. "Good luck today."

Beyond the pig pit were tables laden with roast mutton, beef, poultry and spring lamb. As the boys passed, they heard the hungry crowd calling out their requests. The smell of cakes, pies, sweetmeats and fried dough, hot out of the oil, met their noses.

The boys moved into the shadow of one of the grand arenas. A sign directed interested adults down a path to Brewers Lane. There, one could find tents with whiskey, rums, brandy and mead. Kegs of freshly brewed ale lined the row. At the entrance, a bald man wearing a pair of leather breeches, his flesh covered in blue ink, was engraving a likeness of a bird on a young man's arm. The boy's eyes were closed and his mouth twisted with every touch of the needle.

"He is not enjoying that much," Ian said.

"Mine did not cause much discomfort," Oisin replied, and lifted his shirtsleeve. On his upper arm was the head of a wolf. He bowed to three girls who walked by.

"You had a couple of pints before yours, if I recall," Corm said. He nudged Liam and pointed to a sign on the left. "Illusion Alley. You could find out what is going to happen between you and Olivia."

"I am sure I can learn that on my own." What would he say if he ran into her? He did not know, but was beginning to think avoidance might be the best course.

They finally reached the stadium that marked the end of the fairgrounds. A sign on a wooden post read:

Pavilion 1
Avian Challenge
Perception and Perspective – Poseidon's Pool

The modest open-air arena offered seating for at least a thousand spectators. For those wanting to expend the coin, more comfortable accommodations were available in the shade under the cover of the structure's half dome. All seats looked to the west, over an oval five-hundred-meter track where the grass in the center had not been cut since midsummer last year. Liam saw that a few hundred people were already seated, waiting for the competition to begin.

Corm whistled under his breath. "I did not realize there would be this many people."

"Do not concern yourself with them," Ian said, and put an arm around Corm. "You will do fine."

"I noticed Petr Knight on the list of names for your challenge," Oisin said. "His reputation precedes him. Are you ready to compete against his physical abilities?"

"Unfortunately, I doubt it," Corm replied.

Oisin looked into the sky. "I can tell you his Achilles' heel: the lighting. Do not doubt your skills. Never forget where *your* real power lies." He pointed to his right eye.

A short, stout man walked to the middle of the stadium and pulled a scroll from his breeches. "Would all of the Aves please join me!"

Corm exhaled and walked through the gate. He stood next to four boys who embodied similar characteristics: tall, thin, but muscular in their upper torsos.

"Not many of us this year," Oisin said.

"Ah, but more are on their way." Shane motioned to a group of younger boys sitting together.

Ian began his ascent into the stands. "We need to find a seat."

"Ian, I am sure we will be able to secure one," Shane said.

"Aye, but keep in mind, for you we need two."

The man in the center of the arena clapped his hands and cleared his throat. "Welcome, ladies and gentlemen, girls and boys, to the annual Festival of Ascencia."

The crowd cheered and, after a moment, he held up his hand. "My name is Wilford Merrybottom, and I have the honor of being your host for this year's games. This is the Avian Challenge and the contest today involves finding four rings. Two are hidden in the grass to my right," he motioned to the center field. "The largest is made of gold and weighs five hundred grams. It rests on a set of stakes, fifty centimeters off the ground. The second ring is made of silver, and weighs two-hundred-fifty grams. It was tossed randomly from somewhere along the track's edge. The third and fourth rings are constructed from grass cuttings and each weighs less than one hundred grams. One is somewhere on the ground in the center field, the other serves as a halo atop a pine tree within the fairgrounds. A yellow-green ribbon is affixed to the latter ring, to avoid confusion with area nests.

"The winner will be marked based on the following point system: Each ring has a value of twenty-five points and contestants can collect any number of rings they choose. The first one to return to the X at my feet," he pointed down, "receives twenty-five points. The second to return gains an additional ten points and the third, five points. Anyone who finishes after the third party will not receive points, regardless of the number of rings collected. The task will be considered incomplete if one returns to the X without a ring." He paused to take a breath. "Do the contestants understand these rules?"

The five boys nodded.

"When I say to take your marks, be ready."

Corm looked into the stands.

"He looks a bit white, I am afraid," Shane said. "I hope his nerves do not get the better of him."

"Mark!" Wilford yelled. One by one, the boys raised their arms and bent their knees. *"Muutos!"*

In unison, the boys' bodies began to quiver; their features became a blur. There was no flash of light, no cloud of smoke, no clothes fell to the ground but, within seconds and rather simply, four of the five young men were replaced by large birds.

Chapter 5

Rising into the air were a hawk, a falcon, an osprey and an eagle. One boy lost focus in his transition but, within a few seconds, he transformed into a harrier and joined the others above the arena.

Nine months before, Corm's star had changed into the outline of a bird and he assumed his form as the hawk. Liam watched him take to the air. The only contestant that appeared as strong was the eagle, Petr, who climbed to a great height and then vectored off toward East Street.

Corm flew to the shaded area of the field. He sat on the branch of an oak tree and stared into the grass. "Well done, Corm. Use your strength," Oisin said while the others, flying in and out of the sun, were coming up empty in their attempts. After a moment, Corm left his perch and, in his first pass, dropped low and returned to the sky with silver in his talons.

"Atta boy!" Shane shouted and clapped Oisin on the back.

Corm flew to a tall pine on the west side of the track. He screeched and, within a moment, the harrier joined him.

The eagle returned seconds later, holding the grass ring that had been hidden atop one of the trees. "I knew Petr would be the real competition," Oisin said. "He was smart to get that ring first. He would not want to carry the gold around while searching for the others."

"And look how he flies from east to west, into the wind upon his return," Ian said, watching the eagle make a run into the breeze. "His progress is slower, but he can spend more time scanning the grasses." The other birds were circling, but each one's occasional dive turned up nothing.

"Why are they both just sitting there?" Shane asked, pointing to Corm and the harrier.

When a stiff breeze came in, Corm left the branch. The harrier followed, and they flew a few meters above the grass. The eagle flew in the opposite direction more than halfway across the field. Corm let out a screech and looked to the ground. The harrier reached down and came up with the gold ring.

Ian nodded. "Ah, smart move. He kept the eagle from taking the gold, while forcing the harrier to finish. Look." The bird, unable to carry the weight, flew to the X and landed.

The eagle reached the end of the field and turned to start another pass. Corm initiated one as well, and both raced toward the center of the arena.

"It appears they both see the final ring. It is hawk versus eagle." Shane began to shift in his seat.

Corm, the first to extend his claws, grabbed the grass ring and began to climb at a steep angle. The eagle could not pull up in time and his beak made contact with the silver in Corm's talon. Petr dropped the ring he carried before falling toward the ground. The falcon and osprey dove toward the freed article.

Corm spread his wings and coasted to the X. He shook his outstretched feathers and was back in human form. The falcon won the race for the grass ring and landed next to him seconds later. Corm walked to the two men helping Petr to his feet and, when it was clear the boy's only injury was to his pride, he joined the others in the center of the arena. The cheering crowd was on their feet. Under the dome, Ian's father flew the Pembroke flag high. Wilford stepped to the center of the field and held up his hands.

"Well done, lads, well done," he shouted. "Congratulations in opening the games with an exciting first event. I am told that Petr Knight will be fine." He glanced at the scroll in his hand. "The medalists in this year's Avian Challenge are … starting with the Bronze: Thomas Hunter, representing the stake of Greenwich." He placed a bronze medallion around the falcon-boy's neck. They shook hands and he went on. "The Silver is earned by Whitey Fischer from the stake of Waite." He laid a silver medal upon the boy who represented the harrier. "And this year's winner of the gold is …" He squinted and looked at the parchment in his hands. "I cannot read my own handwriting. The winner is …" He looked at Corm.

"Cormac Jeuter," Corm replied softly.

"Cormac Jeuter," Wilford shouted grabbing Corm's arm and holding it high. "From?"

"Pembroke," Corm said, a bit louder this time.

"Representing the stake of Pembroke!" He placed the gold medal around Corm's neck. "Please," Wilford shouted over the cheering crowd, "make your way to the Kenyon Coliseum for the next event, The Sprint of Apollo!"

Ian's father rushed from the stands. "Gentlemen from Pembroke, these games belong to us!"

Shane threw his arms around Corm and lifted him from the ground. "Congratulations!"

"That was for my mother," Corm said when the crowd around him had thinned. He grinned and touched the gold that hung from his neck. In its center was a raised swan.

It was the middle of the afternoon when they exited the North Central Pavilion after Oisin's challenge.

"Why did you refuse the medal?" Ian asked Oisin. They had all been more than surprised when Oisin declined the gold.

"Jonas won the competition. He was the first to return. I decided to relinquish that honor—"

"Excuse me. That was very impressive, rescuing that little boy like you did." The girl behind them looked at Oisin as if he had fallen from the heavens.

"Would you like to know my secret?" Oisin asked with a wink.

"Oh, yes!"

He put an arm around her, and smiled at Corm before he disappeared into the crowd.

Shane looked at them in disbelief. "Why are the lasses attracted to him like bees to honey? I will never understand it." He shook his head. "I have a suggestion. My competition is the last of the day and, while I am saving my appetite for the pig, I could use something to hold me over. I propose we sample some of the lighter fare."

They walked together until they reached Illusion Alley. Liam remembered from past years that the dignitaries' tent would be set up where that footpath ended and East Street began. "I need to find my father," he said. "I will meet you at the arena in plenty of time for Shane's match."

He passed men who breathed fire, swallowed swords and performed magic while their companions called out and requested a few coins in return for the entertainment. Children and their parents looked on, fascinated. Gypsy tents advertised readings into the future or connections to the past. He glanced to his right. A pretty girl stared back at him. "Come in," she said. "Ariana can tell you everything you want to know." The r's rolled from her lips.

Liam read the sign on the tent: "The North Star – What does your future hold for you?" *Ah ... a seer.*

"You have much on your mind. I can see that from here," she said, trying to lure him in. "Care to let me take a peek? Perhaps I can offer advice."

His feet slowed their movement. She was perhaps twenty, and wearing a low-cut peasant blouse. Her curly black hair fell midway down her back. Her skin was light but her lips were dark red and, when he looked into her pale blue eyes, he was hypnotized.

"Why not?" he replied before he could stop himself.

She opened the tent flap and pointed to a chair. He pulled a coin from his pocket and slid across it the table. She looked at the various objects in front of her: a round piece of glass, a mound of colored stones and a deck of cards.

"For you, I will read these," she said, picking up the cards.

Tarot cards. He knew because there was a deck at home. His family had played Troggu, when things were different, but they never used them for fortunetelling.

When the cards were shuffled to her satisfaction, she pulled seven from the top and laid them face down in a semicircle. "You have the Merrow's eyes, very unusual," she said. "They *are* beautiful."

Why had he agreed to this nonsense? He sat back and crossed his arms but, as he looked at her, the intensity of her eyes changed, their color turning to a dark, deep blue ... a seer's eyes.

"These cards," she said, pointing from left to right, "represent your past, present and future." She turned over the first. "The Three of Swords. Your life has been in disorder, and this has left you feeling confused. I see loss and sorrow. So sad to have this card represent your past but remember, pain is necessary in life." She revealed the next. "The Hanged Man. There have been changes but at present you feel ... abandoned. You make sacrifices but to no avail." She looked up at him. "So young to have had so much ..."

She flipped the third card and her face brightened; her eyes shifted and swelled like waves. "Ah, the Ace of Cups. This means new friendship or romance is about to begin. Hard to tell, but I see harmony and balance. Good signs." She turned over the next card and looked at it hard.

"What is it?"

"Odd. This is the Lovers card." It showed a man standing between two women. "This also means beginning of relationship, but more intense than the Ace. This is meant for only the strongest of romance. It signifies trust, honor and deep love. I have never seen them drawn side by side."

"What does it mean?"

She nibbled her lower lip. "It is possible the cards represent the same relationship. Or they could represent two different connections. If that is the case, it could create much discord."

He was thinking about Olivia when she interpreted the meaning of the first card, but were their lives intertwined in the second as well?

"Do you presently have girlfriend?"

He smiled. "I was hoping that was something you could tell me."

She narrowed her eyes. "I will take that as no, but I think that is about to change. How can someone like you be alone?"

"No time," he answered.

"You must make time. Your heart needs nourishment as well as the rest of you. Shall we continue?"

The next card showed two serpents wrapped around a circle. "The Wheel of Fortune. This signifies change, the hands of Fate and Destiny at work. Unexpected events will lead to good fortune or to bad luck and failure. It is up to you."

Was she serious? His future could be good or bad? This reading was so ambiguous, she would be correct no matter what happened.

She turned the next card over. "The Chariot. A journey is in your future. You need to persevere and be mindful of rash decisions. This could lead to defeat and loss."

Well, finally, something he could smile about.

"You seem more excited about the Chariot than you do about the Lovers. Most would look forward to love rather than adventure. You do not agree?"

"No," he replied.

She turned over the last card. On its face was a star, and she hesitated.

"What is it?" he asked.

"The Star is one of the most misinterpreted tarots. Depending on the situation, it has different meanings. Taken into context with the rest of your reading?" She swept her hand over the other six. "I see good things. The light of the Star will lead you on the right path. You will accomplish what you set out to do if you stay true. If you veer and are not strong, I see unfulfilled hopes, immense disappointment and, ultimately … great loss. The Star represents faith, so it is up to you." She looked again at the cards, and caught her breath when her eyes fell upon the last one. "The Star …"

He leaned forward. "Are you all right?"

"Did you not see it? The card changed for instant. It was no longer the Star, but the Ace of Swords. I … I have never seen anything like it."

"What is the Ace of Swords?"

"That card is as powerful as the sword it represents. The sword can serve justice or evil. It depends on who is wielding it. Either way, nothing can stand in its path. I have only heard about the cards changing. I have never seen it. That means the Star and the Sword are connected, somehow." Her eyes were, once again, a pale blue color

He got awkwardly to his feet. "Thank you."

She glanced at his neck. "Wait. You are Shayeen?"

He nodded.

"You must come back. That changes the reading but I need to confer with my aunt to determine the meaning of the cards. Promise me you will do that."

He sighed and, knowing he was not being truthful, agreed. He left the tent confused, a confusion that deepened when he heard a voice call his name.

Liam looked up and it took a moment. It had only been four months since he had seen him, but his father appeared … older. Jon Cheveyo's closely trimmed beard and mustache were now tinged with gray. Even his long dark hair was beginning to show signs of it at his temples.

"William, my son!" His father embraced him and took a step back. "Is everything all right? How are you? Where is Meg?"

"Everything … everyone is fine, Dad. It is good to see you. Meg is enjoying the fair with Sara and her father."

"Ah. I remember my first time at the fair. It is truly an unforgettable experience. Speaking of which … have there been any changes since I last saw you?"

Liam shook his head.

"Your time will come." They began to make their way through the crowd. "Ascencia's mark has never been wrong, but the waiting is the hardest part, no?"

"Aye."

"How is everything at home? How is Althea?"

Liam thought of his feisty grandmother and smiled. "Thea is well. She wanted me to tell you to be careful. The wind has changed direction."

"Thea's premonitions are not to be taken lightly." His father twisted the band of silver on the middle finger of his left hand. "We have encountered a few … complications of late. Nothing we cannot handle and nothing I want you to worry about."

Liam knew it would be futile to press for more, so he said nothing.

"Who is here with you?"

"Corm, Oisin, Shane and Ian," Liam replied."Very good. And how did they fare in their contests today?"

"Corm earned gold, Oisin relinquished gold and Ian … Ian did not medal. Shane has yet to have his match."

"Pembroke secures gold, finally! Shane's contest should be starting soon."

"I am on my way there now."

"Do you mind if I join you?" He put his arm around Liam's shoulders and they walked to the arena. Liam easily spotted his friends outside. It was hard to miss Shane, but there was a new addition. Standing with them was Olivia.

Chapter 6

"Olivia, my love, how are you?" Jon asked and gave her a hug. "Are you keeping my son out of trouble?"

"Oh, yes," she replied with a forced smile.

"And how are your parents?"

Liam ignored the exchange of pleasantries and thought back to the fortuneteller's predictions. Was his relationship with Olivia about to change?

His father turned toward the pealing of a bell. "I am sorry. I must return to the tent. Corm, congratulations today. Liam, please stop by before you take your leave. I need you to carry a letter to Althea."

His friends filed into the Gladiator's Arena, and he and Olivia were left standing alone. The afternoon sun reflected in her long, blonde hair and it looked golden in its light. She was wearing a blue dress that reached her ankles, laced up the front and gathered at the bodice. The wide black belt around her waist accentuated her perfect figure. "Would you care to go for a ride tomorrow?" he asked. "I would like to talk to you."

She hesitated.

"Please," he said, and put his hand upon her arm.

"Yes. I will come by your house in the morning," she answered and, before walking away, she smiled ever so slightly.

The amphitheater was nearly full and Liam took the empty seat next to Corm.

"Ladies and gentlemen," Wilford shouted. He stood inside a large circle painted on the packed earth in the middle of the arena. "May I have your attention? Welcome to the final physical challenge of this year's games. I would like to congratulate all who participated and those who walked away with medals." The audience began to applaud. "As you know, the Challenge of Atlas, or the Gladiators challenge, is often the most anticipated event. This is the test of brute strength. May I have the Ursidae on the field?"

Four boys surrounded him. Shane had always been large compared to Liam and the others but among his own, he was not so intimidating.

"The rules of this challenge are quite simple. When a contestant is forced outside this circle, he is disqualified. Do you all understand?" The boys nodded. "Please, take your marks."

Shane looked into the stands, removed his hat, and a grin spread across his face. His hair had turned lighter when he first experienced the Shanyo, but nothing prepared Liam for what he now saw. Shane's short-cropped hair was pure white.

"Whoa," Ian said. "I think I know why he always wears a hat—"

"*Muutos!*" Wilford shouted.

The four boys changed into enormous bears, but Shane was the only one white in color. Upon their transformation, they dropped from their hind legs to all fours and began to circle one another. Shane was smaller than the rest, and one of the bears moved in his direction.

"Trying to take out the weaker one first, smart move," Ian said.

"Or so they think," Corm replied. "Shane's size might be deceiving."

The bear approached Shane and rose onto his hind legs. He waved his arms in the air and Shane did the same. Within a moment, their arms were around each other, as if they were hugging ... or dancing, while monstrous growls filled the air. Shane peered around his partner at the couple behind him who were engaged in the same intense promenade. He placed his right foot behind his opponent's and gave him a ferocious shove. It caught the bear by surprise. His arms flew to the side as he attempted to maintain his balance. He fell into one of the bears behind him and they both landed outside the circle.

"You are both disqualified!" Wilford cried.

"Unbelievable," Ian said. "He took out two at the same time."

Shane lumbered around the perimeter of the circle and glanced over his shoulder. When he was sure the other bear was following, he picked up his pace. He continued for a few rotations, reversed direction and confronted the bear head-on. Both stood on their hind legs, and then Shane placed both paws under the bear's arms, rubbing up and down with his claws.

"What is he doing?" Ian asked.

Corm's eyes narrowed. "I believe he is ... tickling him?"

Shane's opponent fell on his back and rolled out of the circle. When he morphed into his human form, he was still laughing. He got to his feet and put his arm around Shane's white furry shoulder. The stadium erupted. Shane transformed, picked up his hat and waved it over his head.

"The winner," Wilford said, holding Shane's arm high. "Shane Carson from the stake of Pembroke."

"No one said you *had* to use brute strength," Shane said when he joined them outside the tent, the medal around his neck. "Against the assault of laughter, nothing can stand. Two golds for Pembroke on this fine day. I suspect the Bacchanalia will be quite a celebration for us this night."

Liam and Corm shook their heads at the same time. "I need to get back home," Corm said.

"And I need to return to Pembroke with Meg," Liam said. "That is one aspect of the fair she does not need to experience."

"What about you, Ian? I need someone to revel with," Shane said, his eyes pleading.

Ian bowed. "I would be honored to be part of the attention you will receive tonight."

Shane smiled. "It is settled then. And I propose a challenge of our own tomorrow, at the creek. What do you say?"

"That is an invitation I will accept, but I cannot join you until midday," Liam said.

"Wonderful. To the ale tent, then. First pint is on me ... and then there is a pig's arse that has our names on it." Shane led Ian away. "Life does not get any better than this."

Corm turned to Liam. "Are you ready to make the journey home?"

"Aye. I just need to find my father first."

They took an alternate route to his father's tent so Liam could avoid the North Star. He did not want to hear any more about his future ... or his past.

Two men stood on either side of the entrance to the dignitary tent, looking exceedingly bored. One guard eyed Liam with suspicion.

"I am here to see my father, Jon Cheveyo."

His father walked from the shadows. "It is all right. That is my son."

"Why the need for the sentry?" Liam asked. He never knew the council to require watchdogs.

"Simply a precaution. Thea was right about the winds, but I fear they changed direction some time ago and have developed into a squall. Congratulations on your win today, Corm."

Did he forget praising Corm earlier? It was not like his father to forget.

"Thank you, sir," Corm said.

Jon pulled a piece of parchment from his breast pocket. "Please, give this to Thea for me. And I would find comfort if you and Meg were home before sunset."

Liam took the letter and nodded. "We will be leaving now."

His father put his hands on Liam's shoulders. "William, take care of Meg and Thea. I shall be home soon, until then stay safe. I love you."

Meg was in front of the stables with Sara, her father and two boys. "There you are!" Meg said, seeing Liam. "Where have you been?"

"I was talking with Dad," Liam answered, and smiled at Mr. Acrisius.

"You saw Dad?" Meg did little to hide her disappointment.

"Meg," Mr. Acrisius said, "I am confident your father never could have caught up with us, given all the sights we attempted to see. Cormac Jeuter! Congratulations on your victory." He shook Corm's hand. "Let me introduce my nephews. They kept the girls company while I attended the challenges represented by our stake, but we all took in the final match of the day."

Meg looked around. "Where is everyone else? Are they not leaving?"

"No, they are going to remain," Liam replied. "So it is just the three of us."

"I still cannot believe I did not see Dad," Meg said after they rode a short distance.

"Meg, I have no explanation for his behavior." He did not like making excuses for his father, especially when he was unsure as to

34

why. "He has a lot on his mind right now."

She pouted for a moment then her face brightened. "Shane's match was fantastic, do you not agree? He really is something!"

"Do you know what other match was unforgettable?" Liam asked.

She looked at him, confused.

"Corm's."

She turned around to look at Corm, who was riding behind them. "I know. I am sorry I did not get to see your match, Corm. Although I did hear all about it. Congratulations."

"Thank you."

"Corm, Meg might be interested in seeing some of your maneuvers," Liam said, hoping to keep her mind from returning to their father.

Though he might not have sensed Liam's motive, Corm was happy to oblige.

"Hold this for me, would you?" Corm pulled up next to them and handed Meg his medal. His horse, Lightning, was suddenly without a rider as a huge hawk rose into the air.

Corm's wingspan exceeded three meters and, at one point, his wings stopped beating and he seesawed on the winds.

"Very nice," Meg said as the current took him out of view.

"What did you spend your money on today?" Liam said.

"Oh! I bought a beautiful journal. It even has a lock."

Not necessary. He could not imagine any curiosity about the drivel his sister would write.

"And I bought some perfume for Thea."

Another wise purchase. "Meg, Thea never wears—"

Corm screeched loudly overhead. Liam looked to the sky. Corm circled above the trees to the right, dove into the forest and reappeared a moment later. He continued to cry out and disappeared a second time.

"What is he doing?" Meg asked. "And why is he making all that noise?"

Corm flew into their sight again and Liam sensed it. Corm would not be going to all this trouble to entertain Meg.

"Whoa, Pollux," he said, pulling on the reins. "Meg, stay here."

"But …"

"Stay!"

He jumped from Pollux and walked into the woods, careful to step over the roots of the twisted junipers while he kept his head low to avoid their branches. "Corm!"

"Over here!"

Liam pushed his way through the brush and followed the sound of his friend's voice. A few moments later he stepped into a small clearing. Corm looked at the ground and Liam followed his eyes.

At Corm's feet was the body of a girl.

Chapter 7

"She is alive," Liam said, seeing faint movement in the girl's chest. He looked around and saw no sign of a struggle. In fact, if not for the blood on her face, he might have assumed she had merely paused to take a nap. He met Corm's eyes. "How did you ever see her?"

"The silver around her neck flashed in the sunlight. She has lost some blood and needs to be properly tended to."

Liam glanced back to the ground.

"We cannot leave her," Corm said.

"Aye. Allow me then, since you have done your share of exercise today." Liam bent down and lifted her into his arms.

"Who is that?" Meg asked as she leaped from Shilo. "Is she …?"

"I do not know and, no, she is not dead but she is hurt." Liam laid her on the soft earth along the side of the road.

"What are we going to do with her?" Meg asked.

Liam thought about their limited options. "I have no idea."

"We could bring her to our house," she said. "Thea will know what to do."

But how to get her there? They each had a horse but this girl was in no condition to ride or even be laid across a saddle, by the looks of it. Corm stared into the sky.

"What are you thinking?" Liam asked.

"I could fly back to the fair and get assistance from your father. Or go to your house and come back with the wagon. It will not take long to go either direction, but it will take more time to return."

The celebration of those from Pembroke would continue long after sunset and, though his father hadn't shared them, Liam knew he had pressing matters to deal with. "Go to my house, if you will."

The girl began to stir and then, she opened her eyes.

* * *

The world was on its side. Actually, *she* was on her side. And staring at three pairs of shoes. Correction: one pair of dance slippers and two pairs of boots. Disoriented, Ally turned her head and looked above. Two boys and a young girl were staring down at her like she was from another planet.

"Who're you?" she asked through clenched teeth, trying to keep the panic in her voice to a minimum.

She fought to put this scene into context with the last thing she remembered. Interview ... crappy GPS ... *overlook*. She was standing at the overlook, taking in the view, when she'd fallen over the edge. And then, the images assaulted her.

Her body had cut through the air as she tried to grab onto something, anything. She screamed, struggled to breathe, but couldn't. And then, she defied gravity. It was as though she'd bounced off a trampoline and was no longer falling down, but up! Light had surrounded her before she landed, face first, on the ground. What had happened? And how could she be here, in what looked like a ... *a forest?*

She sat up and put a shaky hand to her forehead. There was blood on her fingers.

"How are you feeling?" one of the boys asked. He was on one knee in front of her, his brown hair fell around his face. His suede pants were not stitched at the sides, but up the front and were tucked into leather boots held up by a long strip of rawhide, tied many times around the boot top. He wore a long beige-colored shirt with wide sleeves. She looked at the two who stood beside him. They were all dressed in clothing from some kind of medieval fair. Well, except the girl. She was wearing ...

"Where am I?"

"You are in the stake of Kenyon," the boy answered.

"The stake of *what*?"

"Are you all right?" he asked.

"No. How'd I get here?"

"We discovered you in the woods."

Woods? In Sedona? She looked past him. Three horses stood in the dirt road. She shook her head and closed her eyes, hoping that when she opened them, this scene would be erased. No such luck.

Where the hell was she?

The other boy went to one of the horses. When he returned, he hunched down in front of her and held out a leather pouch. "Would you care for a drink?"

"Yes, thanks." She looked into his eyes. They were the most amazing color. Not blue, not green …

It can't be.

She couldn't recall the dream, but the eyes. In it, they'd always seemed so unreal. But here they were, looking into hers. The pain in her ankle and the throbbing in her head were much too intense for this to be an illusion.

Okay. Not a dream. Now what? She tipped the pouch and water trickled into her hand. It was cool, wet. Real. She took a sip and her stomach began to flip-flop. *Please don't let me puke.* She turned away and put her head into her hands. A moment later, she heard a familiar cry overhead. "What kind of bird is that?"

The little girl looked to the sky. "That is not—"

"That is a hawk," the boy with the eyes said.

She lifted her head. She remembered hearing, seeing a bird, just before she passed out. "I think that's the second one I've seen today."

"They are quite common in the forest," he replied.

The other boy was no longer with them but all three horses were still in the road. "Where'd your friend go?"

"Corm went to get the wagon," the girl said. "We will bring you to our house."

But where'd he go? Something was off. She could feel it. They seemed harmless enough, but still … "Where's my bag?"

They looked at her and shook their heads.

She must have dropped it somewhere. "Okay. When I get to your house, I need to use your phone. I'll call my mom and she can come get me."

"What is a phone?" the girl asked.

This can't be happening. Was Kenyon so far off the map they hadn't even heard of a phone? She knew some of the Indian reservations around Phoenix couldn't afford nor had use for luxuries of the twenty-first century, but she was sure they had *heard* of them. "Seriously? Never mind." She shook her head and winced. It felt like a gardening tool was impaled in her skull.

"What is your name?" the girl asked.

"Ally … Ashworth."

The girl dipped her pen into a bottle of ink she'd pulled from somewhere, and wrote in a small leather book. "From where do you hail?"

"Where do I what?"

"From where do you hail? Where are you from?"

"Phoenix."

"Phoenix, like the bird," she said. "Well, Ally Ashworth of Phoenix, I am Megan Cheveyo of Pembroke and this is my brother, Liam."

"Nice to meet you." They didn't look like brother and sister. He was tall, rugged, dirty blond hair, blue-green eyes. The girl, on the other hand, was petite, with auburn hair that framed a fair face accentuated by large, dark brown eyes. Ally did her best to smile. It was returned by Meg who went back to writing, but Liam just stared down the road.

Nice to meet you, too. Why were the cute ones always such a pain?

"I hear Corm," Liam said after what seemed like forever.

Ally hadn't heard a thing but felt the ground begin to tremble. "Wow," she said at the same instant she saw a horse-drawn wagon barreling toward them. Corm brought it to a stop and leaped from the carriage.

"A wise choice," Liam said. "Pollux is the only horse faster than Chestnut."

"Thea gave me a bit of direction in that regard," Corm said. "I explained the situation, and she is eager that you bring the girl back."

Meg jumped up and wiped the dust from her dress. "Her name is Ally, Corm."

Corm smiled and bowed at the waist.

"I will hitch up Pollux as well," Liam said. He led a beautiful black horse to the front of the wagon.

"Do you need me to accompany you?" Corm asked. "If not, I will take my leave. I should get home so my mother can begin the medicine."

"No. We will make it home before it gets dark."

Corm took a gold medallion from Meg's outstretched hand and mounted his horse. "Then I will see you tomorrow."

"Congratulations again," Liam said.

"Aye. Thank you."

"Horses, huh? Gas too expensive?" Ally said as Corm rode away. She tried to get to her feet. *"Ow!"* Her right ankle was killing her.

"Let me help you." Liam picked her up and placed her in the back of the wagon. "Push yourself toward the front so you do not fall out."

She nodded and her fingers clenched the wooden sides.

Liam climbed into the seat, and clicked his tongue as he flicked the reins. "Pollux, Chestnut," he said. The horses began to move.

The straw in the wagon was soft and sweet smelling. Ally released her grip and laid back. Where was her car? Where was Sedona? She didn't know, but obsessing about it was making her head hurt. Hopefully, they'd heard of antibiotic ointment around here. They were dressed weird, they talked funny, but she owed them big-time. The thought of spending the night alone in the woods made her shiver. Who knew what kind of animals would be out after dark?

She looked over her shoulder at Liam, at his hair tied in a half ponytail, at the tattoo of a small star under his right ear. Not that noticeable, but it would probably hurt his chance of getting a good job later on. So many companies didn't allow them. *Mom would never, ever let me get one—*

Mom! Somebody should've called by now to tell her that Ally hadn't made it to the interview. Who knew how long it would take to find her car in Sedona. But, when they did, she would have the National Guard combing the countryside. Ally needed to get hold of her before this situation got out of control.

* * *

Barking, Pilotte ran to greet them when they crossed their property line.

"Hush, Pilotte," Liam said. When they reached the house, he went to the back of the wagon and Ally moved to the end. "Do not try to walk." He lifted her into his arms again. "Meg, please open the door, and then put Shilo up for the night."

"Can you not do it?"

"I need to take care of Pollux and Chestnut. Help me for once, would you?"

41

She made a face but ran to the door.

Thea entered the sitting room as he placed Ally on the couch. "What do we have here? You poor child," Thea said. She sat down and held Ally's hand. "Liam, tend to the horses. I will take care of ..."

"Ally," he answered.

"Yes, of course. I will take care of Ally."

He walked outside, unhitched the horses and led them to the barn where Meg was brushing down Shilo.

"What do you think happened?" Meg asked, her forehead lined with creases.

Apparently, she was giving this serious consideration ... unusual for her, but he wondered the same. "I do not know."

"Well, it might be fun to have another girl around here. The heavens know it is not always a delight to be in your company."

He threw her a hard look but she was right. He and Meg used to ride together or play the cards, but since their mother died, they had not shared any time.

"She will not be with us long, I am sure." He removed Pollux's saddle.

"There is something different about her. I can feel it."

"You are correct in that regard," he replied. Her clothing was not unusual, but he had never seen a young girl wearing widow-walker boots. *And her manner of speech* ... "Meg, please do not discuss the Shayeen with her. Something tells me she is not of the forest and I do not know how much we should share."

* * *

Ally looked into the face of an old woman. Wrinkles, like spider webs, lined her blue-green eyes, and her white hair was contained in an unseen bun. When she spoke, it was in a kind and gentle voice.

"My name is Thea. I am Liam and Meg's grandmother. Cormac told me they came upon you in the woods. How did you happen to be there? "

Before Ally could say anything, Thea shifted her gaze to Ally's forehead. "We should clean your cut. Is your ankle sore as well?"

"A little," Ally answered.

"I will be back in a moment."

The living room reminded Ally of a ski lodge. Leather furniture in shades of green and brown faced a massive stone fireplace on the opposite wall. The gray stone mantle was filled with candles and lanterns. Glancing around again, she realized what was missing. Actually, a few things. No lights or lamps, no television, no stereo, no computer. She couldn't imagine what they did around here for fun, but didn't intend to be here long enough to find out.

Thea returned carrying a shallow pan that she placed on a table in front of the couch. "This might sting a bit," she said, and dipped the washcloth she'd brought into the basin. It did burn, but the warm water felt good.

Ally took a deep breath. "I'm not sure how I got here. One minute I was in Sedona, the next I was falling over the cliff. There was no one near me, so I don't know how it happened. Honestly, I'm amazed I wasn't killed. Do you have a phone ... or a car?" She remembered the look on Meg and Liam's faces and braced herself.

"We have none of those things," Thea replied.

"But you've heard of them," Ally said, relieved. "Liam and Meg didn't know what I was talking about."

"They were speaking the truth," Thea said. She placed the bloodstained washcloth on the table, then picked up the bottle beside it.

"I just need to get in touch with my mom. She can pick me up."

Thea shook her head. "I think that would take some doing." She tipped the bottle and let a few drops of bitter-smelling liquid flow onto Ally's forehead. The pain began to fade. "Now, let me take a look at your ankle."

"But how am I going to get home?" *Why wasn't anyone the least bit concerned with that?*

"I do not know, but I have a friend who might be able to help. I will travel to see her tomorrow." Thea stood up and pulled a cloth pad out of her apron. She wrapped it around Ally's ankle and the throbbing ceased. "How does that feel?"

"Tomorrow?"

"It is late. There is nothing I can do now ... except offer to make you a cup of tea." Thea smiled and disappeared.

The front door swung open. "Are you feeling better?" Meg asked and ran toward the kitchen. "Thea, I have something for you."

"Sure, tea would be nice," Ally said to the empty room.

"Why, Meg. Thank you," she heard Thea say. "How sweet, and it smells so pretty."

"Liam thought it was a stupid gift," Meg said as she and Thea walked back into the living room. "But I knew you would like it."

"Here is your tea."

Ally smelled lemon and honey. The cup and saucer were barely on the table when she reached for it.

"Be careful, it is hot," Thea said. "Pay no mind to Liam. He is going through a difficult time."

"He is always difficult. I am going to my room to write. I will see you in the morning," Meg called over her shoulder as she skipped down the hall.

"I heard that, Thea," Liam said from the doorway. "It *is* a stupid gift, and the journal she bought is even more useless."

"Liam," Thea said, "no gift is stupid if given from the heart. You should know that."

Ally sipped the tea. Its warmth relaxed every muscle in her body. She took a few more gulps and her earlier anxiety slipped away.

Liam pulled a piece of paper from his pocket. "Dad wanted me to give you this." He handed it to Thea. "What is for dinner?"

Ally placed the cup on the saucer and rested her head on the pillow. Liam and Thea's voices got louder, as if they were arguing. It was the last thing she remembered before falling into a deep and dreamless sleep.

* * *

Liam helped himself to a bowl of stew. "Do you think tomorrow she will remember what happened?"

"I think she remembers now," Thea answered. "But I suspect she is much farther from home than she imagines. I need to go to Podegar's. She will know what to do."

Podegar's! A day's ride there and back in the wagon. It was not unusual for Thea to visit her friend in Waite, but they usually had time to arrange for Meg to stay with the Acrisius family. If she were leaving tomorrow, he would be on his own with his sister … and Ally.

"Why do you need to consult with her? Can you not send a bird?" They owned three strong carrier pigeons that could make the trip in a few hours.

"I need to speak with her, to be sure of something." She placed the stained washcloth in the pocket of her apron.

"Please, I do not know how to take care of a sick girl, and Meg will be useless," he said. The volume of his voice had begun to increase, but Ally did not stir. "Is she all right?"

"She is fine. I put some chock root in the tea to help her sleep. I do not want her to wake and wander about during the night. Could you put her into your father's room? She will be more comfortable there."

His father's room! At one time it was his mother's as well. "Surely you are joking." He was shouting now.

"No, Liam, I am not, and do not talk to me in that manner. She needs our help and I intend to give it to her. Please bring her into the bedroom, *now*."

More lunacy. In all the time he could remember, Thea never raised her voice. She might have shouted at animals underfoot, but certainly not at him or Meg. Against his wishes, he picked Ally up and carried her down the hall.

He laid her on top of the bedclothes and looked around. Memories of his mother filled his senses and he dropped into the rocking chair beside the bed.

Her sickness had come on fast but seemed reluctant to take its leave. He had never given up hope. Never wanted to admit his mother had already embraced Death. He remembered standing in this room one afternoon, able to do nothing more than stare at her.

She was burning up with fever. Her eyes were closed but, every now and again, her body shook. The fight had left her, but her beauty remained strong, and reminded him that even in defeat there are qualities like courage and love that bring hope.

She had opened her eyes and smiled. "William, my beautiful boy, how are you my love?"

He was close to breaking down so he simply nodded and kept his head high as he sat by her side.

"My time here is not long, I know that. But I need you to remember something." She lifted her hand and, with effort, placed it on the left side of his chest.

"I will always be with you in here," she whispered. "You need to take care of Meg and your father. They will need your strength to get through this and the times ahead. Remember, I love you."

Her eyes left his and she stared at the ceiling. "I will never forget the words the wind spoke to me."

It was the last time he heard her voice, the last time he had been in this room ... until today.

He looked at this stranger in her bed and his resentment began to grow. Thea needed to postpone the trip for a couple of days. He blew out the candle on the bedside table and closed the door behind him.

Thea did not share his reasoning. "Liam, if your concern is the length of time she will be with us, understand the longer I delay the trip, the longer she will remain. I do not think she will find the way on her own. You do not need to worry about her injuries. They will heal quickly."

"I pray you are right," he said, embittered, "about everything."

* * *

Thea shuffled to her room and sat on the edge of the bed. She pulled the washcloth from her apron and looked at it long and hard. "Could it be? Finally?" She placed it in her bureau and read the letter.

"Aye, say it will," she whispered.

Chapter 8

Just a little longer. Ally buried her head in the pillow and tried to obliterate the sun streaming in through the window. She drew in a breath and snapped to a sitting position. Where was she? And then it came back to her, but she didn't recall the crazy events of yesterday ending in this room ... in this guest bedroom, by the look of it. She removed the wrapping from her ankle and stood. Tender but not painful. She touched the scab on her forehead. That didn't hurt either. Whatever Thea used sure was working.

She walked down the hall. "Hello?" The only response came from her stomach. *Bacon.* She followed her nose and found Meg in the kitchen in front of a cast-iron stove. "Morning," Ally said softly.

Meg turned and smiled. "Morning, Ally. Would you care for breakfast?"

"Yeah, that'd be great." What she really wanted was to go home but, for the moment, that was overruled by the empty feeling in her gut.

Meg placed two plates heaped with scrambled eggs, bacon and bread on the table. They sat down and Ally began to shovel the steaming eggs into her mouth.

"You must be hungry. Want some juice?"

"Yes, please," Ally answered between mouthfuls. "This is really good."

"Thank you," Meg said, handing her a cup.

The eggs were neon yellow, the bacon the size of a ham steak, and the bread tasted as if baked that morning.

"Did you make this juice yourself?" Ally asked, looking at the large pieces of pulp floating near the rim of the glass.

"Sure. You do not think Liam would take the time, do you?"

"That's not what I mean. We buy ours at the store."

Meg looked at her.

"You do have stores around here, where you can buy food,

right?"

"We go into town once a week, but we do not purchase those types of provisions. We have everything we need here."

Oh yes. The reality of her situation returned. She was living among the Amish.

"The eggs are courtesy of the chickens, Thea made the bread yesterday, and the bacon came from one of the pigs."

One of the pigs? Ally had no problem with being a carnivore. She never sympathized with vegetarians or worse ... vegans but she'd also never had to witness the food chain first hand. She couldn't think about the pig that sacrificed his life for this meal right now. It was too good.

"Well, it's one of the best breakfasts I've had in a long time." She took another sip of juice and eagerly bit into her bread. "Where is everyone?" she mumbled. The intake of carbs and sugar was starting to take effect, and she felt grounded again.

"Liam is tending to the horses and Thea took a trip. Something about trying to figure out how to get you home. Liam was a grouch this morning so I did not ask too many questions. All I know is I am not going to Sara's for lessons so I can stay here and be with you."

"Stay here and be with me? I need to get home. Can't you take me someplace where I can use a phone or catch a bus?" She appreciated their hospitality ... more than appreciated it. She might be dead if they hadn't found her, but she didn't intend to be here another night.

"Catch a what?" Meg asked, scraping the last of the eggs from her plate.

Ally sat back and rubbed her face. "A bus carries people where they want to go. You have something like that around here, don't you?" It was like she'd been cast in some kooky reality show. And then, a smile came to her lips. Was she being Punk'd? What other explanation could there be? "All right, you can come out now, whoever you are." She began to laugh.

"I have no idea what you are talking about," Meg replied, eyeing her nervously. "I will be right back." She jumped up and ran out the door.

That had to be it, this couldn't be real. These people didn't know about cars ... or telephones. *I guess an Internet connection would be out of the question, then.* She covered her mouth, stifled a giggle and looked around the kitchen. No refrigerator, dishwasher or microwave … just a cast-iron stove and a pump.

Where was the bathroom? She hadn't gone since yesterday and the thought of an outhouse made her shiver. Well, her mother had always said, "Just don't sit on the seat."

Her mom! She'd be insane by now. Ally felt tears begin to fill her eyes when the front door opened.

"She is talking nonsense," Meg whispered as she followed Liam into the house. "She wants to catch a buzz, whatever that is. I do not think she wants to wait for Thea."

Liam walked around the table to face her. He looked upset. *Oh well, join the club.* She wiped her eyes.

His features softened. "What is wrong?"

"What's wrong?" She looked at him in disbelief. "Everything's wrong. I don't know where I am. I don't know how I'm gonna get home. No one here knows anything and I need to go." The desperation in her voice surprised her.

"I have no idea what you would have me do."

The blood rushed to her face. "I want *you* to help *me* get home! *I* have a life! *I* have a family!" She thought of her mother again and then, unable to stop it, she began to yell. "Do you have any idea how worried my mom must be? I need to let her know I'm okay! She probably thinks I'm dead. How would your mother feel if you didn't come home and had no idea where you were? Wouldn't she be worried, or don't you have a mother like that? You don't know anything! All I know is, *I need to get home!*"

He recoiled as if her words were stones she'd thrown at him.

"*We* do not know anything?" he said and began to walk away, but then whirled around to face her. "You do not even know how you got here. Honestly, I no longer care how you get home. I just want you to go!" He slammed the door behind him.

* * *

How dare she talk about his mother like that! She clearly had no sense of … anything. He stood on the front steps, hands clenched into fists and shaking. *Of course* his mother would have been worried about him. She would have set off on her own to find him or Meg, if the situation required it. So … so perhaps he did understand after all.

But he was doing all he could. Which, he had to admit, was nothing. Ally needed to be patient. Thea would have answers when she returned.

"Liam?"

Olivia stood in the front yard, staring at him.

"Olivia. When did you get here?"

"I just arrived. Is everything all right? I have never heard you yell before."

Well, you should have been here last night when I lost my temper with Thea. But she had a point. He was starting to lose control. It seemed Ally's presence was bringing out the worst in him.

He tried to smile. "Really, it is nothing."

"Were you talking to Meg?"

"Aye. You know how Meg is. She thinks she knows everything."

"Believe me, I understand. Remember, I have a little sister as well." She chuckled and mounted her horse, Jade.

"Let me get Pollux." He would apologize to Ally later. That is, if she was still here. But he doubted she would be foolish enough to venture out on her own.

* * *

"I'm so sorry," Ally said to Meg. "I didn't mean to be so rude. I appreciate everything your family has done for me ... a perfect stranger. Well, not so perfect." She looked at the table. "I didn't mean to upset anyone."

Liam's whole demeanor changed when she mentioned his mother. Just how insensitive had she been?

"I am not upset," Meg said, "but Liam ... I have never seen him like that. He has not been the same since our mother died."

"Oh," Ally sighed. "I'm really sorry, Meg, I didn't know."

"How could you? Please do not misunderstand. It was hard on all of us. But it has been more difficult for Liam. I do not know why, but he has been lost since it happened. I miss our mom too ... and our dad. His work keeps him away, and he is rarely home. All Liam and I have is each other ... and Thea. I do not expect you to understand."

Unfortunately, I understand more than you know.

Ally began to pick up the dirty dishes. "When did she die?"

"Three years ago. She got sick. Even Thea's medicines could not help."

Meg took the plates from Ally and put them on the counter. She placed a pot under the pump and began to pull on its handle.

"Many passed on that year. I do not understand why my mom needed to be one of them. We do the best we can, that is all we can do."

How hard it must have been, must be, to deal with life without your mother. Ally was devastated when her father died, but she couldn't imagine how she'd handle it if it were her mom. "Let me help you with these...."

"Thanks, Ally," Meg said after the last dish was put away. "I am going to my room to write in my new journal."

"Hey, Meg, where do you go to the ... bathroom?"

Meg rolled her eyes and pointed outside.

Ally ran to the little structure at the edge of the woods and pinched her nose. She walked out a short time later, relieved it wasn't nearly as bad as she imagined.

She looked around. The stone house was surrounded by tall, gnarly trees. Flowers and bushes in iridescent colors filled the gardens. It reminded her of the Thomas Kinkade print in her mother's bedroom. Mom found its beauty peaceful ... a wonderful place to visit. *Well, here it is Mom, the place you'd love to be. But, I can't wait to get out of here.*

She followed the cobblestone path along the side of the house. A barn, surrounded by small outbuildings, was to her right. Chickens ran around in one pen while two pigs savored a gooey mud bath in another. "You better enjoy that while you can," she whispered, recalling the bacon.

A moment later a dog ran to her side, wagging its tail. She wasn't a dog lover, but this little collie was adorable. He sat in front of her and cocked his head from side to side.

"Who are you?" She bent down and scratched his chin. He answered with a yip. "Come on, let's walk around front." He got up and trotted along the path ahead of her.

The front of the house was as picturesque as the back. An old-fashioned stone well stood in the front yard; a wood bucket hung above it. Made sense. There couldn't be any city pipes around here. A warm breeze carried the sweet smell of honeysuckle. Her father had loved their fragrance, and Ally put her nose to one of the white flowers. Bittersweet memories of the past invaded her senses.

She paused and looked to the dirt road that passed in front of the house. *I wonder* ...

Chapter 9

Liam followed Olivia as she traveled off the main road and down a narrow path. Neither said a word since they left the house, and he was thankful for the silence. After a short distance, they rode into a large meadow.

"First one to the other side," Olivia said.

As Pollux ran, Liam savored the exhilaration. They raced past Jade and Olivia and, when Liam turned to tease her, he realized they'd stopped a good distance behind. "Whoa, Pollux. What is it, Olivia?"

"I am not sure. She seems to be struggling."

"Let us pause then." Liam looked at Jade's leg but did not see anything that caused him concern. They sat side by side while the horses grazed. A single cloud floated in the deep blue sky.

"Liam, I am sorry about kissing you the other day," Olivia finally said.

He took a deep breath.

"Please," she said, sensing his discomfort, "there is no obligation to feel the same. I did not realize how I felt until our lips met."

He took her hands into his. "I am sorry as well. Let us try it again." He leaned over and put his lips upon hers. Her mouth was open and he lingered a moment before he pulled away.

Olivia laughed. "You do not look like you are going to be sick. That is a good thing, is it not?"

He nodded. But it was still not as he imagined. Was it not supposed to be a bit more … powerful? Perhaps those were just stories. Perhaps he was expecting too much.

Olivia looked over her shoulder. "I am afraid I should get her home."

"Ride with me on Pollux to your house, and I will take a closer look."

Liam hoped a visit to Death's Garden would not be necessary. Doc Whitman, Pembroke's veterinarian, had brought him there once to obtain the lethal water hemlock, to assist a sick horse in finding peace. The horse had fought the poison, struggled to remain on this earth and Liam prayed Jade, and Olivia for that matter, would not have to endure that. He knew that poisoning was a most ignoble way to die.

* * *

"Meg! I need to ask you a question."

Meg walked into the living room. "What is it, Ally?"

Hopefully Meg would help her, but if not, she'd go alone. "I need a favor. How far is the nearest town?"

"Pembroke is quite a ride."

She'd been afraid of that. "Do you remember where you found me in the woods yesterday?"

"Sure. Why?"

Ally took a deep breath. "I need to go back there. Maybe I can figure out how I got here or how to get home and I'd never be able to find it on my own. Can you take me?"

Meg bit her lower lip. "I would like to but I am not allowed to go out on my own."

"Well, you wouldn't be on your own, you'd be with me."

"Liam will be mad."

"I'll say I left on my own and you came to find me. We'll make you out to be the hero." Lying didn't come naturally, and she felt guilty about asking Meg to do the same, but this situation required desperate measures.

"Well," Meg said, "do you know how to ride a horse?"

Ride a horse? *Desperate measures.* "Of course."

Meg's eyes sparkled. "Sure, I can help you. What is the worst Liam can do? He went riding with Olivia and then he was going fishing. He will not be back for a while."

"Thank you."

"We can take Pilotte with us. He is a great watchdog."

Ally could see the dog making a lot of noise, but how much protection could he really offer? And why would they need it?

Meg saddled her own horse and one she called Chestnut.

54

Chestnut? Didn't Liam comment yesterday on the speed of that horse?

Ally hadn't lied to Meg, not really. She'd ridden a horse … once. She and her dad had taken a sunset trail ride, on a couple of old mares. But something told her none of the horses in this barn were ready for the glue factory just yet.

Meg handed her a set of reins. "Here you go."

Ally put her left foot in the stirrup, held onto the horn and struggled to throw her right leg over the saddle. When she was safely atop the horse, she pulled her skirt to her thighs.

"Are you ready?" Meg asked, climbing onto Shilo.

Ally nodded and clenched the reins.

"Let us go, then," Meg said. "Come on, Pilotte."

When they reached the road, Meg turned around. "We are going to have to move faster than this if we hope to return home before Liam."

"Okay …"

"*Ayah!*" Meg cried. She dug her heels into Shilo's sides and snapped the reins.

"Hah," Ally said, without conviction. Chestnut lurched forward.

Oh, crap. I'm gonna die. The thought raced through her mind as she bounced up and down. Her ass would be bruised for the rest of her life. But, once she got the hang of it … it was a rush. She couldn't remember the last time she felt so free, so wild. They rode that way for at least an hour before Meg slowed her horse. Ally pulled back on the reins and Chestnut did the same.

"Have you ever ridden a horse before?" Meg said.

Ally smiled. "I don't think I'll be able to sit down for a week."

Meg shook her head and looked into the woods. "This is the location. I remember the cliffs." A high rock formation could be seen in the distance.

Ally looked into the dense forest. Maybe this wasn't such a good idea. "Where exactly did you find me?"

"I do not know. Liam made me wait here." Meg pointed to a group of trees whose trunks twisted up and out of sight. "They came out right there, though."

"All right. But you should stay here again. I won't go too far and, hopefully, I won't get lost."

"Take Pilotte with you. He will find his way back to me."

"Good idea." Ally called Pilotte and together, they began to walk into the woods.

She remembered seeing a hawk fly overhead and looked into the sky. The forest around her was thick; the tops of the trees were barely visible. She pushed her way through thick bushes while ducking beneath low-hanging branches and finally she sat on a large stump. *I have no idea where I'm going.* This whole idea was stupid. "Pilotte," she called, and looked around one last time.

And then ... she saw it.

Pilotte ran to her side. "Good dog." They walked into an open area protected by tall trees. At the edge of the small clearing, she dropped to her knees and picked up her bag.

"*Ssshh,*" she said in response to Pilotte's barking. She heard someone walk up from behind and, startled, Ally glanced over her shoulder. It was Meg, her eyes wide, her mouth open.

"Meg, why didn't you stay—?"

"Ally," Meg whispered, pointing to the woods.

Chapter 10

"Jade has not been herself for a few days now," Olivia said when they reached her house. "I guess I hoped she would magically get better."

"She will be fine," Liam said, refusing to meet her eyes. "I will return later with some of Thea's medicine." He leaned over and kissed Olivia's forehead and began to walk away.

"Liam," she called. "Just so you know, *that* kiss was everything I thought it would be."

What was wrong with him? It was nothing at all as he imagined. Why was it so hard to determine your feelings for another? He prayed Olivia was not aware of his betrayal ... of his confusion.

He found Corm alone at the edge of the creek, fishing pole in hand. "Catch anything yet?" he asked.

"Only a couple of nibbles. Where is your pole?"

Liam whistled for Pollux.

Corm shook his head. "Lightning would only come to me if I held an apple in one hand and a pile of sugar in the other."

Liam smiled and removed two pieces of bamboo from his saddlebag. He twisted them together, threaded the pole and tied a hook to its end. "What are you using for bait?"

Corm pointed to a container. "Earthworms caught this morning."

Liam pulled a worm from the moist dirt and put it to the hook. "How is your mother?"

"The same, but I am optimistic. How is Ally? Are you still graced with her company?"

"Aye, but *graced* is not the appropriate word. Cursed would describe it better."

"Why do you say that?"

Liam sighed. "She is unlike anyone I have ever met. She is so ... so selfish. She has no idea how she came to be in the forest but expects everyone to assist in finding her way home." He tossed his

57

line into the creek. "I would like nothing more than to deliver her there. Where is this Sedona? Thea left this morning to see Podegar. She thinks the augur can help. So, it is Ally, Meg and me for a few days. I will be glad when she is gone and everything is back to normal."

"Yes, because that is *so* exciting," Corm said. "And how was your morning with Olivia?"

Liam pulled in his line and cast it again. "She is no longer angry and, for that, I am thankful. But I am not sure I will remain in her good graces forever."

"Could you gentlemen use a little help?" Liam looked over his shoulder and saw Shane walking toward them. Today, his short white hair was hidden under a black beret. "Allow me to demonstrate the proper technique."

"This is more fun. It gives the fish a chance," Corm said.

"Aye. Using that as bait, you are giving them more than a chance. You are begging them not to bite the hook." Shane tossed his hat on the ground and a white bear stepped into the creek. He stood on a flat rock and looked into the stream as it rushed by. A moment later, he put his snout into the water. When he pulled it out, a large fish flapped in his jowls. He tossed it at Liam's feet and walked back in.

"He takes all the fun out of it, does he not?" Liam said.

"Aye, but we will have trout for dinner tonight."

"That is how it is done," Shane said when half a dozen fish were at Liam's feet. "Should I get more? Where are the others?"

"Not sure," Liam answered. "You were with Ian last night."

Shane smiled and revealed a set of perfect white teeth. "Ah, yes. We met up with Oisin and enjoyed the Bacchanalia. I actually danced ... with a *girl*. I guess notoriety has its benefits."

Shane, dancing? Liam cracked a smile.

"I wanted to tell you, Liam," Shane went on, "Olivia is quite a looker. How was the rest of *your* afternoon?"

* * *

"Don't move," Ally whispered.

Not more than twenty feet away was, what looked like, a huge gray lynx. Had it been there the entire time? The animal hunched close to the ground, and its eyes flicked between her and Meg. Could cats, like dogs, sense if you were afraid? She hoped not. Every reflex told her to run but, she remembered, if you stare down an animal, they might not attack. *No problem. I'm paralyzed right now.* Why had she asked Meg to come along? She'd never forgive herself if anything happened to her.

The animal lifted its hindquarters and shifted from side to side, a cat ready to pounce on the mice it had trapped in the corner.

Pilotte began to growl. "No, stay," Meg said in a low voice.

Ally needed to come up with a plan ... and quickly.

"Meg, I'm gonna cause a distraction. When I do, run as fast as you can." Ally talked in monotone syllables and tried not to move her lips. "Do *not* look behind you. Do *not* stop. Get to the horses. When I count to three, go." Her heart was pounding. She took a deep breath and got ready to throw her bag. She wouldn't be able to move fast with her ankle, and maybe it would take her down first. That would at least give Meg a chance.

"One," Ally counted. "Two ... thr—"

Pilotte bolted as if charging into battle.

"No, Pilotte!" Meg screamed and tried to run after him, but Ally grabbed her arm. Instead of leaping at them, the cat turned his head and looked to its left. Ally's fear was replaced with shock. A second animal lunged into the air, its black coat a blur.

Where had *this* cat come from? Their high-pitched screams broke through her thoughts. As long as the two animals were fighting, she and Meg could try to get away.

"Go!" Ally shouted.

Meg dashed through the brush and Ally followed. "Pilotte, come!" *I hope he knows the way out.* She forgot about her ankle, picked up her skirt and ran while bloodcurdling screams echoed through the woods.

She lost her footing more than once, but they finally broke free of the forest. Ally put her bag onto her shoulder and climbed onto Chestnut. In an instant, Meg was beside her, and they took off down the road.

Once they were a safe distance, Ally brought Chestnut to a stop. Meg pulled on Shilo's reins and came about. "What is the matter?"

Ally wasn't able to believe she just witnessed a scene from Animal Planet. "What happened back there? Where did those animals come from?"

"They live here."

"Oh my god, I'm still shaking. It was a miracle that black cat came along."

Meg looked into the woods. "I hope he is all right."

"You hope who's all right?"

"The panther. Liam will be upset when he learns what happened."

"Well, he won't ... not if we get back before he does."

"Oh," Meg said and grimaced, "I suspect he will know."

* * *

Shane did not interrupt while Liam and Corm told him of their discovery yesterday afternoon, but then the questions came quickly. "How did she get there? Where did she come from? Who is she? Have you ever seen her?"

Liam held up his hand. "Whoa, Shane. One question at a time. But you might save your breath. I do not have answers to any of them."

"Well, where is she now?" Shane asked.

"She is at home with Meg. I should get back and make sure they have not managed to—"

Shane looked past Liam. "What happened to you?"

Liam and Corm turned in the direction of Shane's question. Ian walked toward them, his face covered in blood. Shane rushed to his side and helped him to sit down.

"I am fine," Ian replied. "It looks worse than it feels, I just need to—"

"Take a minute," Shane said. "We will wash off the blood once we are certain you are okay."

Looked worse than it felt? Liam did not understand how that could be true. Ian looked awful. A nasty cut ran over his left eye and a gash the width of his palm could be seen on his upper arm.

Corm ripped the sleeve from his shirt and ran to the creek.

"I was on my way here when I smelled something unusual," Ian said. "I followed the scent and it led me to ... this part might cause you concern, Liam ... it led me to Meg and another girl. They were in the woods, a rather large cat was about to attack them. But it was not a wild animal. It was a fellow Shayeen. I tried to give them the opportunity to get safely back to their horses."

"What?" Liam shouted.

"Pilotte was with them. That damn dog was ready to take on an animal five times its size but he did not have to. I gave whoever it was more than he bargained for."

"You were triumphant then," Shane said.

"You might say that," Ian replied. A smile broke through his bloody face. Corm cleaned the cut over Ian's eye and returned to the stream.

"I am in your debt," Liam said, "and grateful for what you have done. Thank you."

"You are welcome, but you would have done the same for me … for any of us. Who was the girl with Meg, and why were they there?"

Corm rinsed the piece of cloth again and tied it above the wound on Ian's arm. "This will stop the bleeding. Where were you?"

"Not far from Henge Cliff," Ian replied. "Why?"

"That is where we found Ally yesterday."

"Found who?" Ian asked.

Liam whistled for Pollux and picked up three of the fish. "Corm and Shane can provide the details. I need to get home." He wrapped the fish in brown paper and threw them into his bag. "They have some explaining to do. We need to determine who you met today, Ian. Perhaps there is more than one stranger among us."

"Let us take a trip to town tomorrow," Corm said. "Someone must know something."

"Aye," Ian answered. "I will not forget his eyes. They were unusual … black in color."

"Well," Shane said, "I have no intention of allowing you three to go to Pembroke proper without me. I will join you and make Oisin aware of our intention."

Liam mounted his horse and sped away, his anger more intense with each second that brought him closer to home.

* * *

Meg showed Ally how to remove Chestnut's saddle and brush her down. When they finished, she handed Ally three apples. "Here, give her these."

Ally put her hand in front of Chestnut's mouth and they disappeared in one bite. She stroked the horse's nose. "Good girl."

"Come on," Meg said.

Ally sat on the couch, opened her bag and pulled out the jeans and T-shirt she'd brought for after the interview. *Perfect choice.* On the shirt, two hands held a colorful replica of planet earth. "Save the Earth, There is no PLANet B" was written beneath it. "I'll be right back. I'm gonna go change."

When she walked back into the living room, Meg laughed. "A shirt with writing on it? What do the words mean?"

"You're not the problem but I can't believe you've never heard of pollution, global warming, soil erosion ..."

Meg looked at her.

"It means the planet's being ruined with our carelessness."

Meg raised her eyebrows.

"Do you have any idea what I'm talking about?"

"No," Meg answered, "but I am starting to realize I usually do not. What else is in your sack? I have never seen one like that."

"It's a cargo bag. My dad bought it for me because he thought it was cool."

"Cool?"

"Oh, brother." Ally grinned. "It means he liked it."

"I like it too. *Coooool.*"

Ally was about to reach inside when Meg made a face and groaned. "Uh oh, here comes Liam. And I hate to tell you, he is riding fast."

"Well, just don't say anything. Let me do the talking. There's no way he could know."

* * *

How could Ally be so selfish? The question cycled around in his mind during the ride home. It would not take much to sway Meg to do something foolish, although she *should* have known better. He would not allow Ally to disrupt their lives. She needed to either wait for Thea or leave.

She and Meg were on the couch. His anger and frustration simmered just below the surface. All it needed was a push to throw it into full boil.

"Meg! Go to your room. I will have something to say to you later."

Liam's eyes followed her as she ran down the hall. She would no doubt be listening but he did not care.

"What were you thinking, venturing into the forest alone with Meg? You have no regard for anyone but yourself. You put not only your own, but Meg's life in danger. Not to mention that of our dog. For what? Again, I ask, what were you thinking?"

Their eyes met and, despite his anger, he felt something ... slip but before he could continue, she began to speak.

"I'm sorry, Liam. You're right. I didn't understand how dangerous it could be. Meg tried to stop me. I don't understand what's going on. I've gotten lost before but I've always been able to find my way, eventually. I never would have forgiven myself if anything happened. I'm sorry."

His anger began to dissolve and he sat on the couch beside her. "Tell me what happened."

When Ally finished her story, Meg ran into the room. "She didn't tell you how brave Pilotte was. Come in here you brave little puppy." Meg opened the front door and the dog bounced into the room.

"Meg, please watch your manner of speak—"

"But Ally is allowed to speak that way."

"She does not know any better. You do. Make sure Pilotte has a special supper tonight. By the way," he said before Meg could escape to the kitchen, "whatever possessed *you* to think it was acceptable to go out alone?"

"Please, Liam, it's not her fault," Ally said. "She was only trying to help. I'll do whatever I can to make up for it."

"Let me see." A hint of a smile played upon his lips. "Perhaps you could help with the chores tomorrow ... muck the stalls, clean the chicken coop, and milk the cows."

Ally made a face and nodded her head. "A smelly chicken coop along with the aroma of fresh manure? I'm looking forward to it already. By the way, I have a question for you." She followed him into the kitchen. "How do you know what happened? You weren't there. It was only me and Meg and ... Pilotte." She looked at the dog, "And I know he didn't tell you."

"It does not matter." He put two logs into the kitchen stove. "My

Cindy Saunders

concern lies with the animal you encountered. Have you ever seen it before Meg?"

She shook her head.

"We will be taking a trip to town tomorrow, to see what we can find out."

"Town!" Meg began to dance around. "I love going to town. Oh, Ally, you will like it too."

"I will be outside preparing the fish. Meg, please start potatoes and beans."

"You still haven't answered me," Ally said. "How did you know?"

His initial assumption was correct. She would not be asking if she were familiar with the Shayeen. But, apparent as well, she had not been at the fair. How much to tell someone not of the forest? Then, a voice inside his head, clear and strong, spoke to him. *She is not a threat. It is necessary for her to know but use discretion.* It was Thea.

"Come outside. I want to show you something," he said.

Chapter 11

The sun had disappeared and the sky on the western horizon was a beautiful shade of rose. "Do you see those?" Liam asked. His index finger traced a line between four bright stars.

"Yeah?"

"And do you see the six that intersect with them, forming a cross?" Again his finger indicated where he wanted her to look.

"That's the constellation Cygnus," Ally answered, "and, at the head of the cross, is a double star, Albireo and ... Ascencia or something."

"You know the story then?"

"I don't know any story."

Her ignorance continued to astound him. "How can you know about the constellation but not its origin?"

"My father was fascinated with the stars," she said, "the possibilities they held. We used to sit in our backyard and he'd point them out to me."

"All of the groupings of stars tell a unique tale."

"Well, why don't you enlighten me?"

He chuckled. That might take more effort than he imagined.

Patience.

He sighed. "I will tell you the story that I know."

Ally followed him into the barn. She crossed her arms and leaned against Chestnut's stall. Her blue eyes held his but he forced himself to turn away and began to remove Pollux's saddle.

"That constellation is also known as the Swan of the Northern Cross. Long ago, when the gods traveled freely between the heavens and this world, there lived the goddess Ascencia. From her father, who ruled the animal world, she inherited the gift of Shanyo. From her—"

"Shanyo? What's that?"

He turned to face her. "You really do not know."

Ally laughed. "How could I? This is your story, not mine."

"Shanyo is the ability to assume the form of an animal." She opened her mouth in surprise and he continued. "And from her mother, Ascencia received the gift of music. It is said her songs could bring the most brutal beast to its knees."

"I would love to be able to sing like that. I've tried but ... let's just say I should stick to the violin." She met his eyes with eagerness now.

"At birth, Ascencia was betrothed to Cepheus, son of Golan the Hunter. But, as she neared her seventeenth birthday, she realized her true desire was to visit this world, on her own. So, her parents proposed a compromise. She could spend a year in this realm. But, upon her return, she needed to fulfill her obligation to marry Cepheus."

Ally put her hands on hips and looked at him in disbelief. "She had to marry someone when she was only seventeen? That sucks."

Sucks? "I do not know if it 'sucked' or not, but Cepheus was enraged. The marriage guaranteed he would assume the seat on the council held by Ascencia's father, a necessary step in Golan's plot to overthrow Zeus. His impatience was misinterpreted. Ascencia's father assumed Cepheus was merely ... eager to wed, so he offered the boy a gift for his understanding in the matter. The power of Shanyo ... the mark of the wolf and Ascencia traveled to this world, to the forest of Gilgamesh, content to spend a year. But she underestimated what she would discover here."

"Which was ...?"

"She fell in love with Albireo, a poor farmer boy."

"Albireo. Like the double star."

"Aye."

He put Pollux in his stall and took the fish from his saddlebag.

"Is that it?" she asked when he didn't continue.

"Hardly. Come with me while I prepare this, and I will tell you the rest."

They walked behind the house and Liam placed the fish on a flat rock. He pulled a knife from his belt and began to fillet their supper.

"When the harvest moon appeared in the sky, signaling that a year had passed, Ascencia made the decision to stay upon this earth and marry Albireo. The choice to remain here did not diminish her powers, but it did change one thing. She was now mortal … and vulnerable to the dangers of this world."

"She traded immortality for love. How romantic," Ally said. Even in the shadows, Liam could see her smile. She was quite pretty …

"Liam." Ally was looking at him, snapping her fingers. "Earth to Liam."

"Yes?"

"I asked you, what about Cepheus?"

"Aye, Cepheus. He was infuriated by the news. He made the decision to kill Albireo, to take back what he felt belonged to him. He traveled to this world armed with a quiver of his father's arrows and found Albireo at the edge of a pond. He was not aware that Ascencia had taken the form of a swan and was swimming nearby."

"His father's arrows?"

"Yes. The Hunter *never* missed the mark when using the arrows of Golan. But Cepheus chose his words poorly upon releasing it."

"What'd he say?"

"He said, 'Find the one who has stolen my destiny.' And the arrow did as it was told. Its pile and shaft entered the flesh of the swan."

Ally dropped down onto the stone wall beside Liam. "He killed her? Does this story have a happy ending? Please tell me it does."

"It is for Fate to decide if their ending will be happy, or not. Ascencia's spirit was placed in the heavens in her last form, the swan. The animals of the woods protected Albireo, and Cepheus, outnumbered and fearful for his life, changed into the wolf and disappeared."

"What happened to him … Cepheus, I mean?"

"Zeus spared his life but he was banished from the heavens, sentenced to this earth forever, immortal in a mortal world."

Ally looked into the sky. "If they were in love and married, why isn't Albireo's star as bright as Ascencia's?"

Liam followed her gaze. "Some believe it is beginning to die."

"I don't know a lot about legends, but I know the death of a star can have devastating repercussions."

Liam lowered his eyes to the sight of Ally's hopeful face. "Then we need to pray it does not happen. For now, Ascencia's magic is still alive and her light continues to shine on this forest."

* * *

Liam laid out the third fish, expertly slit open its belly, and Ally had to look away. She tried to think about what he'd just said, but her confusion only grew. *It's a great story but ...* "How does that explain what happened today?" she asked again.

Liam finished, put the fish down and wiped his hands on a wet cloth. "Before she died, Ascencia gave birth to a son, half mortal, half god, who grew up in this world."

"And?"

He lifted his hair and she saw the star on his neck. "This is the mark of Ascencia."

"So ... you had it tattooed, out of respect or something?"

"No. I was born with it."

She began to laugh. "And what ... you can change into an animal?"

"No. I cannot."

Whew.

"Not yet. But there are those of us who can. The black cat who saved you yesterday is a friend of mine."

She loved the story, but please. What kind of medication was he on? "Really. And he told you what happened?"

"Yes."

"Okay." He *was* crazy. Not that it mattered. Her goal was to get out of here and find a way home, but she was curious about something else. "Who told you that story?"

The muscles in his jaw tightened and he looked into the woods. "My mother."

Oh. Her shoulders dropped and she swallowed hard. Regardless of his insanity, she owed him an apology. "What I said earlier, about your mother. Meg told me what happened. I had no idea. I'm sorry."

He re-wrapped the fish in the brown paper. "Let us get inside. Meg must be wondering where we are." He stood in front of her and offered his hand.

It was a gesture she wasn't used to but she took it and felt his warmth, his strength, and her cheeks began to burn. She was glad it was dark and when she got to her feet, he released his hold on her and they walked inside.

"That was great. Thanks," Ally said when dinner was over. She cleared the table and, remembering what Meg had done earlier, pumped water into the pot and placed it on the stove. Meg was in her room and Liam disappeared outside. She sat at the table and put her head into her arms. It had all happened so fast. What was the last thing that made any sense?

I was standing in Sedona. But even that was weird. She only wound up there because her GPS malfunctioned, some type of glitch. And then she was falling. Every bone in her body should've been broken, but she survived with no real injuries. And then these kids found her. And what about Liam? She was sure she'd dreamed about him. Maybe she *had* died after all, and crossed over to ... where?

"The water is ready," Liam said from behind. "I have a proposal. I will wash the dishes and you will dry them. Does that meet with your approval?"

She lifted her head. "Sure."

He tossed her a swatch of cotton cloth and rolled up his sleeves. "Thea should be back tomorrow."

Her eyes rested on his broad shoulders. He really was cute. And, although he tried not to show it, passionate and warm as well. *Oh, and don't forget, delusional and crazy.* She pushed the thought aside and took a plate from his hand.

When they finished, she went into the living room and picked up her bag. Liam sat next to her and leaned forward, elbows on his knees. "Tell me, what is in there you were so willing to risk your life for?"

"Apparently not much." She pulled out a small leather pouch. Where did this come from? She opened it and dumped a pile of gold coins on the couch. "What are these?"

"Money," he said. "What do you think it is?"

"I ... don't know."

"It looks like quite a bit of it."

She rifled through the bag for her wallet ... and phone, but both were missing. Maybe when she passed out, someone had stolen them and left this pouch. But why? She had no idea but, in the morning, all of this would surely make sense.

The red moon was bright. She heard movement close by but, when she turned around, it was gone ... or hiding. The gnarly branches of the bush in front of her seemed alive as they twisted in the breeze. Two eyes peered back through the tangled hedge. *It's a trap!* She tried to run, but couldn't. "No!" She began to move forward. "Liam!" He was standing beside her. "Save me!" His eyes changed color; their brilliance began to fade. "No," he said. "It is you who must save me."

Ally snapped to a sitting position, her body covered in sweat. It was light out and familiar surroundings brought her back. *Can you have a dream when you're in a dream ... or a nightmare when you're in a nightmare?* Only one way to find out. She headed to the kitchen, having come to a disgusting realization.

Meg was at the table, a bowl of batter in her lap.

"Morning, Meg."

"Hi, Ally."

"I need a favor."

Meg began to shake her head.

"Nothing like yesterday," Ally said quickly. "Can I take a shower or a bath?"

"Oh. Sure. There is one outside. Let me show you."

"What are you making?"

"Blueberry muffins." Meg dipped her finger into the batter and put it into her mouth.

"Isn't it hard without a mix?"

"A mix?"

Ally sighed. *No, I'm sure it's amazingly simple.*

She followed Meg outside. On the left side of the house was a seven-foot-high roofless, wooden stall, a wooden container was mounted to the house above it.

"You've got to be kidding me," Ally said. "Is that water warm?"

"The sun heats it up during the day. It's not that cold."

I'm never taking anything for granted again. "It's okay. It'll wake me up."

Meg laughed. "Just do it quickly."

Ally stepped inside. A wide spigot hung from the side of the bucket. She reached up, twisted it and released a shower of cold water.

"*Aaah!*" This was going to be *really* quick. She turned off the water and washed up with a piece of soap she found on the shelf.

A towel floated over the wooden side. "I thought you might need this," Meg called.

"You're a lifesaver. Thanks."

It *was* refreshing, and when Ally walked from the stall, she felt better. She dried her hair as she walked to the front of house, and saw Liam in the barn. His pants were tucked inside black leather boots folded over at the knee; the dark green V-neck shirt reached his lower thighs. Very unusual, but hot, in a Robin Hood kind of way.

"Why are you walking in that manner?" he asked.

"Good morning to you, too. I'm a little sore from my ride yesterday."

He grinned. "Was it your first time on a horse? If so, I find it hard to believe you controlled Chestnut."

"You didn't see me riding."

If she never got on a horse again that would be fine, but it was the only way to town so she had to suck it up one more time. He wanted to find out more about the animal in the woods yesterday, she wanted something much simpler. She was going to find a way home.

"I will put an extra blanket on the saddle to protect your … you know," he said. "Do not worry about the chores today. I would not want to be responsible for any more injuries."

"We appreciate that."

"We?"

"Me and my … you know." When she patted her butt, he smiled. *Wow.* Too bad he didn't do that more often. Maybe they *could* be friends. He could visit her in Phoenix. Well, if the 'manner of speak' didn't drive him crazy. Although *that* probably wouldn't be a long ride.

She didn't believe he could talk to animals but, somehow, he knew what happened in the woods. *Come on! You can't be serious,* a sensible voice inside her head said. *Just because you've never seen it, doesn't mean it doesn't exist.* That voice sounded like her father's.

"Meg is making muffins," she said, trying to silence both. "I'm gonna grab one. You want?"

"No, thank you. I have already eaten. The others will be here soon."

"The others?"

"My friends will accompany us. Would you care to wear one of my shirts?"

"Sure, if you think I should."

Cindy Saunders

"Please. Ask Meg to get one for you."

A plate of blueberry muffins was on the table, steam still rising from their time in the oven. Ally poured herself a glass of juice and was licking her lips when Meg walked in.

"Liam wants me to wear one of his shirts. I think he's nervous I won't be presentable to his friends."

"Those clowns? I would not worry about what they think."

"Meg, Liam told me a story about Ascencia. Do you know it?"

"Sure."

"What do you think about it?"

"I think it unfair only the boys get to change. It does not give us girls much to look forward to."

How far from home was she ... really?

She slipped his tan shirt over her own. The neck was loose and the shoulder seams hung midway down her upper arm. She rolled up the sleeves and put on her boots.

"Ally! They are here. Come on!" Meg said.

"Be right there." Ally rummaged through her bag and found her brush. She pulled it through her hair, grabbed her things and walked outside.

Meg and Liam were standing with four boys. Their conversation abruptly stopped but their faces gave them away. They were talking about her.

"This is Ally," Meg said, "and this is Ian, Oisin, Shane and you already know Corm."

Gee. Robin's Merry Men.

They were dressed the same as Liam, but that's where the similarity ended. Ian looked like a Rastafarian; his black dreadlocks hung to the middle of his back. His eyes were a beautiful shade of light green but an ugly scab was over his left brow.

Oisin smiled at her and pointed to her feet. Several strips of rawhide were tied around his wrist. "I like your boots." His curly hair reached his shoulders and a large gold hoop hung from his left ear.

"Thanks."

"Only Oisin would comment on a lady's choice of footwear," Shane said. He could easily take the largest player on the Cardinals football team. Three steps put him in front of her. He removed his wide-brimmed hat, dropped to one knee and took her hand.

"Charmed."

"Oh!" was the best she could manage, seeing that his hair was dyed white. And then, her eyes were drawn to the outline of a bear beneath his right ear.

"Hello, Ally," Corm said.

She jerked her eyes away from Shane's tattoo. "Hi, Corm."

Did they all have a tattoo? Their long hair made it impossible for her to tell.

"Are we ready?" Ian asked.

Ally looked to the road. "Who's that?"

Liam shook his head and closed his eyes. "I completely forgot."

"That is Olivia. Liam's *friend*," Meg said.

Olivia reached them and glared at Liam. "I was worried when you did not return yesterday," she said. "I thought something might be wrong."

"I am sorry," Liam said. "I meant to, but the day got a bit … difficult. There were some issues requiring my attention here."

"Yes, I can see that." Olivia's eyes traveled from Ally's head to her feet and Ally suddenly realized just how out-of-place *she* looked. Olivia's white gauze shirt hung from her shoulders, its wide sleeves reaching below her elbows. Her black silk pants were fitted and tucked inside a beautiful pair of boots. Beveled crystal buttons lined the soles to just below her knees. The belt around her waist, more like a piece of jewelry, draped over her thigh. Ally had never seen anything … or anyone, so beautiful in her life.

Olivia went on. "You never mentioned you had company."

"We do not, or rather —"

"Hi, I'm Ally."

"Nice to meet you," Olivia replied.

Liam hoisted himself onto Pollux. "We need to go to town, but I could stop on the return trip and look in on Jade."

"Where is Jade?" Meg asked.

"Her leg is bothering her," Olivia said, "but … as a matter of fact, I need to go to town myself. Perhaps *I* could join *you*."

Liam hesitated. "I would like nothing more," he finally answered.

Ally smiled. *Take that, Pinocchio.*

Chapter 12

They rode two by two: Olivia and Liam in front, Shane and Meg next, followed by Oisin and Ian, then she and Corm.

Ally glanced beside her. "I didn't thank you for finding me yesterday. I was a little out of it. Thank you."

"You are welcome," Corm answered, "but, if not for your necklace, I do not think I would have found you at all."

"Really." He was cute but in a different way than Liam. Deep brown surrounded the gold in his eyes and his hair was feathered just past his shoulders. "Well, I was lucky. I didn't realize these woods were full of wild animals. Maybe I should thank the black cat as well."

He laughed. "Perhaps you could do that yourself."

"I hope to be outta here soon, so I don't think I'll run into him again."

"Liam was right. You are not from Gilgamesh."

"No, I'm not." She looked ahead of her. "Are Liam and Olivia going out?"

"I have never heard it put that way but I understand your question. I do not know. I am not sure that even Liam knows."

"Why not?" What else could Liam want? She was gorgeous and Olivia liked him. That was obvious.

"He is trying to find himself right now. Sometimes it is easiest to do that when you are alone."

"He told me the story about Ascencia last night, about how he believes there's magic in the forest. Do you believe that, too?"

He smiled. "I know her power is still with us but I sense you deny its presence."

Was it that obvious?

"Look around." He gestured to his friends. "Each of us has a different spirit. Shane represents strength, Ian embodies speed and agility, and Oisin is marked with the traits of cunning and courage."

"And you?"

"I represent the seeker, searching for answers ... or the occasional girl who needs rescuing," he said with a wink. "I am able to see things from a different perspective."

"What about Liam? What does he represent?"

"I am not sure. No one knows for certain until it happens. His time will come, though."

"I ... I, uh, I'm sure it will."

She knew the Indians believed everyone had an animal spirit. She didn't recall they actually thought they were the animals, but maybe these boys took it a bit further. *Well, maybe more than a bit.*

"Ascencia's is not the only spirit alive in the forest. There are others who have left their marks as well."

She gave him an award-winning smile. "Such as?"

He blushed and looked at his horse. "Well, as we share our bodies with the animal spirits, some animals share theirs with the spirits of the gods. Every animal, every living thing has a purpose. I cannot speak for how things are anywhere else, but here there is a delicate balance."

"I thought it was survival of the fittest."

He laughed. "That is a misconception. It is survival of the smartest, and every living thing in the forest knows that to be true. To ensure we continue to exist, the smartest thing we can do is live together."

Ally squinted, thinking. "What about animals like ... the rabbit? Don't other animals eat them? Is that living together?"

He smiled. "Why do you think they multiply so quickly? The rabbit is not only a guide to the shadow world but is a perfect illustration of balance. Butterflies represent change and transformation. If you follow one, it will lead you to joy and happiness. The tortoise is sensitive to the environment. It can feel vibrations within the earth and forewarn of imbalance. The cry of a great horned owl warns that Death will be traveling among us. During the time of the sickness, its cry was heard every day. Certain animals communicate love, power and strength, some call attention to our fragile nature, while others remind us of our dark side."

Chestnut's gait hitched and Ally grasped the reins tight until she settled down. "So you're telling me all animals are good? What about yesterday?"

"There are always exceptions. Consider the wolf, a brave and loyal animal, respected as a wise and cunning hunter. Its intelligence and senses are unmatched, making it a powerful ally—or a deadly predator."

She didn't know why, but she began to feel nervous. "Does the wolf represent good or evil then?"

"It depends. In a pack, they are extremely devoted. Oisin is marked by the wolf, and there is no other I would rather have watching my back. But the lone wolf, unable to connect with others, can be dangerous. There are those who believe they represent evil and bloodshed."

"Why?"

"Cepheus' actions caused many to mistrust the wolf."

"Because he killed Ascencia?"

"That, according to legend, was an accident. It was what he did afterward, because of his desire for revenge and power, which caused many to be afraid of the wolf."

"Liam didn't tell what happened after Cepheus killed Ascencia."

"Do you want to know?"

"I think I do."

Corm cleared his throat. "Well ... after his life was spared by Zeus, Cepheus disappeared, and Albireo raised his son, Deneb. The boy's star-shaped mark beneath his ear was the only evidence he was different from the others in his village. One night, during his sixteenth year, Ascencia sent her son a warning, using the power of the winds."

"Power of the winds?"

"Something else you are not aware of. Trees are considered sacred by the gods. Their branches reach toward the heavens and carry messages between their world and ours. The wind is their way of whispering ... of talking to one another. Ascencia sent an admonition carried on those winds. She told Deneb that Cepheus was preparing to return to the forest ... to take his life. 'Beware the red eyes,' she warned. 'They are the eyes of death for you and the ones you love. They will not rest until yours are—"

"Closed forever."

Corm turned his head to look at her. "I thought Liam did not tell you this part of the story."

"He didn't. But ... I've heard those words before."

Corm shrugged and continued. "Soon after, word traveled to the village about a group of savage marauders moving in from the east, killing any animal or human who crossed their path. Deneb knew it was Cepheus and decided to strike out on his own. But his friends would not allow it. They vowed, made a blood pact, to stand by Deneb and face Cepheus together. It was then each friend noticed a star appear beneath their right ear."

"How did the stars just appear?" Ally said.

"Ah yes, the star ... this was Ascencia's gift to her son, an assurance he would not stand alone against his enemies. They left the village and, after a week's time, came upon a wolf devouring the remains of a deer. Deneb saw the wolf's eyes were the color of fresh blood, and he knew his fate would be realized."

"So the lone wolf was Cepheus?" Ally said, entranced with the story but fearing what would happen next.

"Aye," Corm answered, "but Cepheus was not alone. He was in the company of three men, warriors who carried weapons unlike anything the boys had ever seen. But, as it turned out, the boys possessed a magic of their own. Through the star, they were given the power of the Shanyo, each with the strength of one of the eight. And then—"

Ally gently pulled the reins, slowing her horse, and Corm did the same. "The eight?"

"The traits represented by the eight-pointed star. You do know that eight is a magical number."

"I know that on its side, it's the symbol for infinity."

"Yes, and each of Deneb's friends received one of the attributes associated with the star. Together, the magic within them was powerful enough to defeat Cepheus and, once again, the wolf disappeared."

"Where did Cepheus go?" Ally asked.

"No one knows. Some say they have seen him. His presence can be felt from time to time. The howl of the wolf is a reminder he might be hiding ... waiting. Those who think he is still on this earth believe the Vaki have kept him from entering Gilgamesh."

The others noticed that Ally and Corm had fallen behind and slowed their horses. Ally ignored Liam's curious look and Olivia's annoyed one. "The Vaki? What are they?"

"Not what, but *who*. The Vaki are the guardians of Gilgamesh, tiny man-elves that can enter the body of any animal who threatens the forest, making them quite sick until they are summoned away."

The sound of thunder in the distance made her jump. "So why didn't the gods take care of Cepheus? Kill him or something."

"They were too involved in their own struggle to be concerned with what was happening on this earth. When they finally recognized the danger, it was too late. They were imprisoned, helpless to do anything, or so the tale is told. Why were the words familiar to you?"

"I don't know. I must have heard the story before." And then it came to her ... the freak wind storm ... her dream ... the wolf. Had someone been trying to warn her? *What really happened on that cliff in Sedo—*

"Have you ever been to Pembroke?"

"What?"

"Pembroke. Have you visited it?"

"No," she said and looked ahead of her. "Don't tell me that's it." Although, she should have known.

Chapter 13

She hadn't envisioned Phoenix, but she *had* pictured something a bit more contemporary. A town where there might be a bus stop or a police station. Not some podunk village. *All right, stop being so negative.* It was really quite ... quaint. Stone shops lined either side of the cobblestone street, their roofs varied in color from light pink to brown, and smoke from chimneys trailed lazily into the sky. Windows, made of small panes of stained glass, were framed with colored shutters, and flowers spilled from the window boxes.

As they passed, she looked at the painted signs that hung above the shops. "The Wooden Plank," that advertised, "Custom Casks, Caskets and Barrels," and stated the owner as "Witton Pouncy, Cooper." Whatever a cooper was.

Others were pretty straightforward: "Hermes & Son, Blacksmiths"; "The Pewter Pot, Michael Ferry, Tinsmith"; "Stevens Tack & Livery."

Okay, it's cute. But how do I get out of here?

"Olivia, where is it you need to go?" Liam asked.

"I need to stop by Sophie's for a fitting."

"Okay," Liam said. "Meg, you and Ally go to Stearns. But get only what we need."

"And where will the rest of you be?" Olivia asked.

"We will be at Doc Whitman's. I am curious as to what he is tending to these days. I will ask him about Jade as well."

"I see. I will meet you at the general store when I am finished then."

She rode away and Liam lowered his voice. "I think we should split up. We can cover more ground."

"Aye," said Corm.

Shane grinned. "I suggest starting at the pub. You get more information from those ready to loosen their tongues."

Liam nodded. "You three head to the Black Water Tavern. Corm

79

and I will ride out to Doc's."

Meg dismounted Shilo and began to walk toward a cheery-looking shop. "Come on, Ally."

This sign read: "Stearn's General Store, Everything You Need and More."

Yeah, let's hope so. Ally climbed from Chestnut and looked into the sky. Dark storm clouds were beginning to move in from the east. "What do they sell here?"

"Oh, they have everything, but we cannot buy much since we do not have the wagon. I know we need lamp oil, sugar and flour."

"Okay." *Please, have a phone at least.*

Meg opened the door and a tinkling sound announced their arrival. Ally winced. The store smelled like a medicine cabinet. An older woman was on her hands and knees, wiping a greasy-looking spill from the wooden floor.

"Oh, Meg." The woman sounded relieved. "Not your normal day to come to town."

"Hi, Mrs. Stearns," Meg replied. "We need to pick up a few things. What happened?"

"A bit of an accident, but that should do it." She wiped the floor a final time. "How is Thea?"

"Fine. This is Ally. Ally, this is Mrs. Stearns."

"Nice to meet you," Ally said.

"And you as well. New to Pembroke?" She wiped her hands on her apron.

"Just visiting." Meg disappeared down one of the crowded aisles and Ally looked behind the counter. "I need to use your phone, please," she said quietly.

"My what, dear?"

"Your phone." Ally placed the pinky of her right hand to her lips, her thumb to her ear.

Mrs. Stearns took a step back. "I have no idea what you are talking about."

Great. She thinks I'm going to attack her. Well, that might happen any minute. What the hell was she going to do? She was not leaving this town until she found a way home. "How about maps? Do you have any of those?" she said, hoping to undo whatever damage she might have done.

"No, but if it is a map you need, you should visit Daniel Roberts.

He lives just outside town. He knows as much about the area as anyone. Trying to get somewhere?"

"You could say that." Maybe she could walk or hitchhike. Heck, she was ready to steal Chestnut if it came to that. It was a sad day when stealing was an option she was actually considering. *Hey, whatever it takes.*

She joined Meg, who was holding a long blue quill, awe and longing on her face. "What I would not give," she whispered.

"How much is it?"

"Too much. I look at it every time I come in. One day, I am afraid it will be gone. I am saving enough to buy it."

"Do I have enough?" Ally pulled the pouch from her pocket and dumped the coins into her hand.

"Yes," Meg said, "and then some."

"Well, let me buy it for you."

"Really?"

"Why not? Consider it a thank-you for being so nice to me … and an apology for getting you into trouble yesterday."

"You mean it? Wow! Thank you." Meg nearly knocked Ally over as she threw her arms around her.

"You're welcome," Ally said, and looked over her shoulder. Mrs. Stearns was gaping at them with more than a bit of curiosity. "I'm, uh, going to look around."

She walked up and down the aisles and found soaps, sachets, toothbrushes, hairbrushes and barrettes. Dark bottles with hand-written labels read *Croup Tea* and *Clove Oil – To Relieve the Pain of Tooth Worm.* Tooth worm?

Wooden barrels were filled with flour, oats, cornmeal and spices. Ally finished her inspection and found nothing that could help her. She caught up with Meg at the counter.

"What do we owe you for this?" Ally said.

"Twenty-five drachma," Mrs. Stearns answered.

Drachma? Ally pulled the coins from her pocket and looked at Meg. *Was each of these a drachma?* Meg took one of the silver coins from her hand.

"Thank you," Meg said.

"Please tell Thea I said hello." Mrs. Stearns looked at Ally. "And be careful, Meg."

* * *

Liam and Corm headed to Doc's ranch, which was two kilometers west of town. "You are awfully quiet, Liam," Corm said after they traveled half the distance in silence.

"Sorry. I am a bit preoccupied." He and Olivia had talked during the ride into Pembroke. First it was about Jade and then, the conversation turned to Ally. Liam explained how he and Corm found her, and Olivia asked many questions, to which he had no answers. She was probably confusing his ambiguity with ... what? 'People do not just appear out of thin air, Liam,' Olivia had said. He was aware of that but, when Olivia asked about the sudden trip to town, he thought it best not to tell her what happened yesterday in the forest. He was thankful they did not discuss their relationship. He was tired of weighing the pros and cons as if deciding which saddle to purchase.

They rode into Doc's compound and found him in the barn, tending to a small terrier.

"Liam, Corm, nice to see you."

"What is the matter with him?" Corm asked.

"He was caught in a trap. I thought those were an evil of the past. I would love to get my hands on the one who would set such a thing. Could easily have been a child it ensnared." Doc shook his head in disgust.

Liam squatted beside the little dog. "Will he be okay?"

"He will survive, but he will never be the same. Would you? Ah, but what brings you out here today?"

"Well, I am not sure how to ask this," Liam began, "but have you seen anything ... anyone unusual?"

"You mean other than this? As a matter of fact, I have. I had another visitor today. A boy, a bit older than you, stopped in. He wanted something for fever. When I asked for what kind of animal or where it was, he avoided my questions. I offered to accompany him, but he claimed that was not a viable alternative. I suggested he visit Stearns', that perhaps he could find something there that would help."

"How long ago?" Liam asked.

"Not more than an hour. In all my days, I have never seen anyone like him. His face was covered with tattoos, two small gold hoops hung from his nose … right here." Doc pinched his right nostril. "But the most unusual thing was his eyes. The whites of them were inked and, when he closed them, there was a red eye drawn on each of his lids." The vet shuddered. "Why would anyone do such a thing? Why do you ask?"

"Yesterday, Ian fought with a Shayeen cat … one who was about to attack Meg."

Doc shook his head. "First traps, then Shayeen attacking humans? What is becoming of the world? I can tell you this boy was *not* Shayeen. But he was something."

"Thank you," Liam said. "And good luck."

"Aye," Doc replied.

"Meg and Ally are at the General," Corm said as they mounted the horses.

"I know. Ian said the cat was Shayeen. I am confused."

"Do you think it is the same boy?" Corm asked.

"I do not know, but we should hurry back."

Before Liam reached the general store, Meg was running toward him. "Liam, look what Ally bought me." In her hand was the blue quill.

He sighed with relief. "You finally have it. But you should not allow a stranger to buy such things for you."

"She also paid for the flour, sugar and oil."

Liam climbed from Pollux and nodded to Ally. "Thank you, but it was not necessary."

"It's my way of saying thank you … for your hospitality."

"How *is* Mrs. Stearns?" Corm asked.

"I think I made her nervous."

Corm grinned at her. "That would not be hard to do."

Liam walked into the store. "Oh, Liam. I am glad to see you," Mrs. Stearns said. "Though I am afraid I am going to sound like a foolish old woman," she added, wringing her hands in her apron.

"That is not possible," Liam said. "Did you receive an unusual customer today?"

"Oh, you already know about him." She lowered herself into the rocking chair in front of the potbelly stove. "But there were three, and the most peculiar bunch I have ever seen."

"Three?"

"Yes, and they looked like hooligans. They wanted something for fever. I showed them what I had. At times like this, I wish Ernest was still around." A lock of white hair fell over her eyes and she brushed it away. "Anyway, they had no money. And, the one with the devil's handwriting on his face took a bottle. Before he left, he asked if I had seen a new girl in town. When I told him no, he picked up a tonic and threw it on the floor. The other two did not say a word, but one had cuts all over his face. The boy warned if I mentioned their visit to anyone, they would be back. And then Meg walked in with her new friend, and I was afraid to say anything. Are they looking for Ally?"

"I am not sure," replied Liam, "but I am looking for them. Do you have any idea where they might have gone?"

The white lock sprang out again, and she twirled it around her finger before tucking it behind her ear. "He wanted to know if there were any seers in town. I told him there might be a few of those gypsies from the fair still at Clover Meadow." She looked up at him. "I just wanted them to leave. Did I do the right thing?"

"Yes, Mrs. Stearns. Thank you. Your husband would have been proud."

"Well?" Corm asked once Liam rejoined them outside.

"He was here but not alone," Liam said, thinking. "There are three, and they are leaving quite an impression. They were in search of a seer. Mrs. Stearns sent them to Clover Meadow."

Olivia rode up and began to dismount her horse.

"Hold on," Liam told her. "We are going for a ride."

"You can go wherever you want," Ally said. "Just tell me how to find Daniel Roberts."

Corm turned to her. "Why do you need Daniel?"

"Mrs. Stearns said he's familiar with the area, that he might be able to help me."

"That he is," Corm said, "when he can remember. His farm is in the direction we are heading. We can go together."

"I am a little confused," Olivia said. "Where are Ian, Oisin and Shane?"

"They went to the tavern," Liam answered.

"At this hour?" Olivia's disapproval was clear.

Liam shrugged his shoulders and mounted Pollux. The tavern

was behind the haberdashery on the outskirts of town. If he detoured from Main Street, he might miss the strange trio again. "We can meet up with them on our way back."

Olivia shook her head. "Well, where *are* we going?"

"I need to check on something. It will not take long."

* * *

The shops at the opposite end of town were replaced by houses, and then by farms and fields. Ally was frustrated. The only thing this trip had confirmed was that her situation was beginning to look bleak. This Daniel guy better know how to get back to Phoenix. If not? Then what?

Olivia fell back to ride beside her and Meg.

"I hope Jade feels better," Meg said.

"Aye," replied Olivia. "I have no doubt Thea's medicine will help. By the way, how is Thea?"

"She took a trip to Podegar's," Meg replied.

"Really? Liam did not mention that."

Ally winced. *Oops.*

"He must have forgotten," Meg said.

Olivia looked at Ally with narrowed eyes.

Oh brother. Ally held up her hand. "No worries here."

Olivia ignored her and turned back to Meg. "When is she returning? Perhaps I should come by and look after things—"

"Thank you," Meg said, "but there is no need. She should be home today."

"I will mention it to Liam anyway." Olivia nudged her horse and caught up to the boys.

Meg rolled her eyes.

What does he see in Olivia? One look, though, answered Ally's question. Boys could be so blind sometimes.

A green pasture became visible not more than a quarter-mile away, its color more vivid due to its contrast with a red tent not far from the road. A colorful wagon stood nearby, kept company by two horses and something else ... a cow maybe. Corm pointed to it and Liam nodded. They brought the horses to a stop.

"What are we doing?" Olivia asked.

Liam took a breath. "Ally and Meg were nearly attacked in the woods yesterday by a Shayeen cat. We are trying to determine why. That is the nature of our visit to town today."

"Thank you, Liam," Olivia said. "While I am glad no one was hurt, you should have told me the truth. And what is it you hope to find *here?*" She waved her arm toward the meadow.

"I am not sure."

Olivia shook her head. "Do what you need to do then."

"Corm and I are going to pay a visit to our gypsy guests. The three of you, please, stay here."

The clouds, in the distance only a short time ago, were overhead now, and the first drops of rain spattered on the dusty road.

"And you suspect this might be dangerous?" Olivia asked Liam, her eyes on the sky.

Probably more worried about her hair. Ally stifled a grin. It might be interesting to see what she looked like soaking wet. *Stop it … not nice.*

"Just stay. Do you understand?" Liam said.

* * *

He and Corm left their horses on the road. Near the tent, a campfire burned within a stone circle and voices could be heard from inside.

"Hello?" Liam called out.

"Yes, what is it you want?" a girl's voice answered.

"I need a moment of your time."

"I am busy. You need to come back."

"It will not take long, I promise."

"Please, do as I request."

Liam looked at Corm. His friend's expression confirmed that he felt it as well. Something was wrong.

"Pardon the intrusion," Liam said. He and Corm began to walk away and then stopped. The voices inside picked up, louder this time. It sounded like an argument and, ignoring all he had been taught about respecting the privacy of others, Liam turned and boldly marched into the tent.

It took a moment for his eyes to adjust to the lack of light but he made out a table with two chairs near the center pole, one of them occupied by a young girl. Her face, though, was too shaded to see but her eyes were wide as she stared at them.

Two boys stood behind her, their arms crossed in front of them. Liam followed the eyes of one as he looked to the corner of the small compartment. An older man was on the floor, his hands bound behind his back, his ankles tied in front of him. Seeing Liam, he tried to speak but his lips would not part. The man's eyes darted to the opposite side of the room, accompanied by repeated head thrusts.

Liam looked back to the girl. "What is —?"

"Someone needs to teach you some manners." A third boy walked from the shadows and rubbed his chin, as if trying to come up with a solution to a difficult problem. "Well, Ariana, I had no idea what a popular girl you are. Surprising, given your limited abilities."

"My talents are only limited when trash like you is involved."

"Coming from gypsy scum, I find that amusing."

"Ariana?" Liam said, finally recognizing her as the girl who read his cards at the fair.

"Ah, you two are acquainted," the boy said. "Well, I am going to make my own prediction." He put his hands to his temples and closed his eyes. "You are going to regret your decision to come this way today."

Liam had no doubt this was the boy Doc had described. His long, greasy black hair could not hide his face, which was covered in a maze of black triangles, squares and circles. And, when the boy closed his eyes, Liam saw the bizarre tattoos on the lids, just as Doc had told them.

"I find it pathetic," Corm said, "that you have chosen to intimidate a young girl and an old man. Do you not agree, Liam?"

"I was thinking the same." Liam quickly measured the situation. Three against two. Not impossible, but he could not change into anything that would give them an advantage, and he was unsure how much damage Corm could inflict in his hawk form. If this were to be an honorable fight, they might stand a chance, but he sensed these boys did not abide by the rules of fair play. One look around confirmed that.

Liam assessed the two standing behind Ariana. They were Shayeen. The one to the left was marked with cuts on his face and arms, his eyes red and swollen. *The cat that fought with Ian.* The other was thin but looked strong, and Liam was unsure which form he could assume. Yet if he and Corm could keep them distracted, they might not be able to transform.

The boy with the tattoos glared at Liam. "Take care of them," he said through clenched teeth.

"You might want to move," Liam said to Ariana. She leaped off the chair as Liam lunged toward the boy on the right.

* * *

Ally began squirming on her horse, but not because her rear end was sore. *What are they doing? I just want to get out of here.* But that wasn't entirely it. Ever since Liam and Corm went inside, she kept feeling something was wrong.

Meg must have sensed it too because, before Ally could stop her, she jumped off Shilo and quietly ran to the tent. Ally slipped off Chestnut and followed.

They stood in front of the tent flap and listened. Ally heard a crash and then Corm and another boy rolled out of the tent opening, knocking her to the ground.

She landed hard on her back with an, "Argh!" Meg grabbed her arm, trying to pull her out of the way. A second later, Liam and another boy tumbled out. How did they manage to get into a fight in less than five minutes? The answer was simple. *Testosterone.*

Ally scrambled to her feet and noticed a third boy standing just inside the tent. He narrowed his eyes and held up his palm. "*Incalca,*" he whispered and then ... the features of the boy wrestling with Liam began to blur.

Chapter 14

Ally blinked, and in that instant the boy changed into a ... gray wolf? *Huh?* Liam freed himself from the snarling animal and began to back away. The wolf exposed sharp teeth and moved toward him.

"Incalca," the boy whispered again.

Corm was now facing a gray lynx but he didn't move.

"Corm! Get —" The rest of her warning remained inside. A majestic hawk took to the air. It screeched and dropped, talons outstretched, onto the lynx's back. The cat whirled around and tried to shake him loose.

"Shayeen," the boy in the tent muttered before he began to walk outside. Meg rushed forward and hooked his foot with her own. He fell toward the muddy ground but, rather than land on his face, he put his hands out, pushed himself back and put his feet under him.

"Brave little girl, aren't you." He looked at Meg with contempt as he stood.

Ally looked at the tattoos on his face and then shifted her gaze to his eyes. The whites of them were tattooed with red shapes that moved and shifted.

Oh! What a creep!

She pulled Meg behind her. The boy looked Ally up and down, his eyes stopped at her neck. He stepped closer, a smile on his lips. "What have we here?"

Her heart began to pound and he reached toward her.

She brought her right leg back.

His fingers found her necklace.

She threw her knee between his legs.

He yanked the chain from her neck and fell to his knees. "Bitch," he said and slowly got to his feet.

What now? Ally's breath came in short bursts. She pushed Meg with her as she backed away. What *was* she going to do? She looked around, trying to find an answer, and her heart stopped. Running toward her were a wolf, a panther and a huge white bear.

More? Her fight or flight instinct shut down and she froze. The three animals were almost on them. The panther and wolf ran toward Corm and Liam but the bear continued at Meg and her. Ally turned away and put her hands in front of her face.

"Excuse me, Ally." She opened her eyes and took a step back. Shane was in front of her, and easily threw the boy to the ground. "Stay," he said, his hand upon the boy's throat.

Ally began to shake. She bent down and tried to take her necklace but it was a prisoner in the boy's clenched fingers. "Give it back."

Shane grabbed his wrist. "I will break this if you do not release it."

His hand slowly opened. Ally snatched the necklace and shoved it in her pocket as her eyes returned to the freak show at her feet.

The boy glared at her. *I will be back for you,* he mouthed. *"Alergare. Paianjen,"* he said aloud, and then ... he was gone.

The lynx and gray wolf broke free from Corm and Liam and they ran across the road and into the woods.

What the hell just happened? Ally struggled to breathe. *Slow down or you'll pass out.* She sent the order to her brain and took long, deep breaths. "Where am I?" she asked before her knees buckled and she dropped to the ground.

"Ally ... Ally ... wake up." The faces above came into focus. Shane was beside her and helped her to a sitting position, his arm around her shoulders.

"Are you all right?" Corm asked.

Tears burned behind her eyes. Corm took her hand but she pushed him away. "Please don't." All she wanted was to be left alone.

"I had to change back," Shane said. "I did not want to risk hurting Ally. Where did he go? I had him by the throat. I have never seen magic like that before."

She moved away from him. What was the matter with them? Didn't they understand how crazy this was? She hadn't believed Liam or Corm, yet ... it was true. But hadn't she known something was off all along ... from the moment her eyes opened in the forest?

Amidst her confusion was the memory of a trip her family had taken to the Endless Caverns when she was younger. They'd walked through the underground caves and, once they reached the farthest point, their guide had turned off the lights, burying them in total darkness.

Hearing her terrified whimper, Dad had put his arm around her shoulders and whispered in her ear, "How many fingers am I holding up?"

She couldn't see his hand. She couldn't see anything! She was about to blurt this out when he said, "This business of sudden blindness, a failure of the sense we depend on most for survival, sends the brain sprawling. But think about it. This journey we are on every day takes us places that are certainly unfamiliar, and some days might seem very dark, but there is always a bit of light … hopefully enough to guide us through the caverns and back to the surface."

"I miss you, Dad," she whispered, and raised her eyes. The others were standing around her. Blood from a cut on Ian's arm began to stain his shirt. She looked at his eyes. It was Ian who had helped Meg and her in the woods. That's how Liam knew what happened.

Do you believe now?

Yes. But that realization caused another, every bit as frightening. Where was she, and how was she going to get home? A bus ticket, it seemed, was no longer an option.

"I appreciate what you did, Ally, stepping in to help Meg," Liam said. He looked at his sister. "What were *you* thinking?"

"It serves him right! Did you see Ally? That was quite a kick!"

"It didn't do much," Ally said.

"It caused a distraction so he forgot about Meg," Liam said. "It was not a wasted effort, and I am grateful."

"What were they doing here at all?" Oisin asked.

"I think they were looking for her," said a voice from behind Liam.

* * *

Ariana! Liam had nearly forgotten about her. He stepped inside the tent and shook his head. Most of the furnishings now looked like kindling for a fire. "I am sorry about this. I will replace anything that is broken."

"That is not necessary," Ariana said. "You have done more than enough for me and my father."

"Disrespectful brats," her father said as Corm helped him to an unbroken chair in the far corner. "He put a spell on me so I could not speak. If they are smart, they will never show their face to me again." He put a hand through his curly gray hair, and then to the full mustache that covered his upper lip.

"Why have you remained while the others in your caravan have moved on?" Liam asked. "The fair ended a few days ago."

"My father was ill and not up to the trip," Ariana said. "I insisted the others go on. Times are harsh and our living is made traveling from town to town. I thought if we waited a few days it would be easier for him … and me. The others will wait before heading to next village."

"Tell us what happened," Liam said.

"They did not travel on horseback, so I did not hear them. They walked in without invitation and asked if I could look into the crystal … to assist them." She picked up a piece of glass from the floor. "But I knew the request was formality. They would not accept my refusal. I told them that I only read the cards, that I was not the type of seer they were looking for."

"She underestimates her abilities," her father said from the corner.

Ariana looked at him and smiled. "Even if I could help them, I would not. Caleb, the one with the tracing on his face, said he only wanted to know if there was somebody new to town, someone who did not belong. Asking transients such as ourselves that question made no sense, but he assumed I would use my powers to see. When I would not give them information, they knocked Papa down, bound his hands and used magic so he could not speak. Imagine, three strong boys picking on a sick man. Well, two strong boys. Radik, the cat, is ill."

"I can take care of myself, Ariana," her father said.

"Oh Papa, I know. Then … you arrived. I could hear the one who called himself Caleb when he spotted you." Her eyes rested on Ally. "Tell me, are you the one he is seeking?"

"I have no idea why I would be," Ally answered. "He tried to grab me but broke this instead." She pulled her necklace from her pocket.

Ariana held out her hand. "May I?"

Ally placed it in her palm.

"Where did you get this?"

"It belongs to my mother. She gave it to me for luck. I'm thinking it's not really working."

"Not necessarily," Ariana said. "Although it is beautiful, this chain will no longer do. You need something stronger." She walked to a trunk in the corner and returned holding a black pouch.

"Please, wear it on this." From the pouch, she removed a length of silver.

"It's beautiful, but I can't accept this—"

"You must. I insist."

Ally took it from Ariana's fingers. "Thank you but I didn't think silver was that strong."

"This is very unique metal. Like you, it is stronger than it looks. It will take much for you to lose it."

Liam glanced at Ally. She didn't know where she was, yet there were others looking for her ... those with a powerful magic uncommon in the forest? They must have followed her here. It was the only explanation that made sense.

"Have Liam measure it for you," Ariana said, "but do not trim the excess, leave it intact."

"Thank you," Ally said.

Ariana turned to Liam. "They were already here ... waiting for her I think." Her words matched his thoughts. "The other two will have to leave. The Vaki will see to that. Caleb did not fight, possibly to avoid retribution. I think he will stay."

"Enough talk," her father said. "Introductions are in order. I am Cezar Butacu and this is my beautiful daughter, Ariana, but it appears you two have already met, ya? Where did it happen?"

"Yes, I was wondering the same," Olivia said.

"We met at the fair. She read my cards."

"It appears I was correct about a few things, no?" Ariana said, looking from Ally to Olivia. "But you never returned so I could give you another reading, as promised."

Liam cleared his throat and made the introductions.

Oisin stepped forward. "I do not want you to stay here alone tonight. Allow us to help you pack so you can be on your way."

Ariana smiled seductively. "How kind of you."

They worked together and, within a few hours, the wagon was packed. Cezar climbed into the driver's seat.

"My new friends, until we meet again …"

"Thank you, for everything," Ariana said. She put her hands on Oisin's shoulders and whispered into his ear. He escorted her into the passenger seat, took her hand and brought it to his lips.

"Liam, may I have a word?" Ariana said.

Liam walked to the front of the wagon and she leaned close. "I told you, when I realized you had the mark, the reading changed, but I suspect you are finding that out for yourself. When I see you again, you need to listen to what I have to say."

"If our paths cross, I will welcome the opportunity."

"They will. I am sure of it." Her eyes shifted to Ally and stayed there. "Take care of her."

As if I have a choice. But, he had felt more alive in the last twenty-four hours than in a long time. "I will. You have my word."

Cezar snapped the reins and the wagon lurched forward. It had stopped raining and the sun peeked through the clouds. Could it be, after all that happened today, things were beginning to look brighter? Liam looked at the source of his newfound optimism. Ally leaned against Chestnut and, although she looked tired, something about her glowed. He walked to her. "You wanted to find Daniel Roberts. We can take you there now, if you like."

"Unless he's a magician, I don't think he can help. It's going to take more than a good set of directions to get me home."

"We will figure this out, I promise, but we should head back."

"Sure, whatever." She climbed onto Chestnut.

"Where are your horses?" Meg asked Shane. "And how did you find us?"

"They are at Doc's. We had no luck finding any information in town and were attempting to locate you. Oisin sensed something was wrong. Actually, I think we all felt it, so we took our leave and followed our collective noses. The quickest way here was through the woods."

"I am thankful you showed up when you did," Corm said. "I am not sure Liam and I could have held them off much longer."

Shane looked at Ally. "From what I heard, Ally would have saved your arses."

She returned the compliment with a blank stare.

"All right then," Shane said and quickly walked away.

"We will meet you at Doc's," Ian shouted over his shoulder. He began to jog across the meadow, followed by Shane and Oisin and, in an instant, they were replaced by a panther, a wolf and a white bear.

The ride back to town was quiet. Ally and Corm rode together and Olivia was brooding. She had not said a word since they left the meadow. Meg was the only one talking, going on about what she would write about tonight, with her new quill, in her new journal.

When Liam could speak without being heard, he turned to Olivia. "Have I done something to offend you?"

"Not purposely, I am sure," she answered. "Today I felt … in the way. I am not used to that when I am around you. This girl, Ally," she pointed ahead of them, "appears from nowhere, and now she is staying at your house, wearing your clothes. Her actions were terribly heroic. She put herself in danger to save Meg. But, I feel as though I let you down." The ice in her voice began to thaw.

"You have not let me down," he said. "If you were standing there, I know you would have done the same." But was that the truth? Olivia was too much like … well, like a girl. She would be the one in need of saving, not the other way around.

"I am sure I would have," she said quickly. "It is the way you looked at Ally earlier. I was … jealous."

How could she be jealous of Ally? Here was the perfect moment to tell Olivia about his hesitation. It might be less painful if she thought it was due to his affection for another. It would hurt, but she would look outward at the cause rather than at herself.

But he could not lie. "She will not come between us. I promise you that."

"I apologize for being so emotional. Will you still come by and look at Jade?"

"Of course," he said, but his thoughts were somewhere else.

When they arrived, Doc was surrounded by Ian, Oisin and Shane. Their animated gestures and Doc's shocked expression indicated they were telling him what happened. Liam dismounted and walked over.

"Liam, I knew there was something about that boy. Do you need any medical attention? Ian has refused, although I think he should allow me to stitch his arm."

"Doc, it is only a scratch," Ian said.

"Well, I am going to pass the word about these outsiders. We will drive them from the forest and back to where they came from."

"Keep in mind two of them are Shayeen," Liam replied.

"Well, they have forgotten who they are, what they represent. They should be ashamed."

"Liam," Ally called softly. "I'm going back to the store. I need to get a few things."

"Allow me to accompany you," Corm said.

* * *

As they rode, Ally regretted saying yes to Corm's request. She needed to think this through. She was farther from Phoenix than she ever imagined. The shock had worn off and was replaced with unease. These boys were different, and it frightened her. What other type of magic did they possess? Could they make *her* disappear? At home, she wasn't the most outgoing or the smartest, but at least she was on equal footing with those around her. Here, she was vulnerable and helpless.

She ran her tongue along her teeth. Maybe she should pick up a toothbrush ... and some shampoo. *And how about a loaded gun or a lethal dose of sleeping pills. I wonder if Mrs. Stearns sells either of those.* She needed something to end this nightmare: now. She looked over at Corm and had to give him credit. He knew when to keep his mouth shut.

"Would you like me to wait out here?" he asked when they reached the store.

"Yeah, I've got this."

"Forget something, my dear?" Mrs. Stearns said.

How do you tell someone you forgot to tell your mother goodbye? That you forgot your rational mind on the side of the road in Sedona?

"Yeah. A few things." Ally walked down one of the aisles and picked up a toothbrush and a piece of purple soap. "What do you have to wash your hair?" Mrs. Stearns joined her and handed her a bottle. *Rice husk and merang. Yummy.*

They walked to the front of the store and Ally put two coins on the counter. "Is this enough?"

"Yes, more than enough." Mrs. Stearns pushed one of the coins back.

"Keep it."

Corm was waiting beside Chestnut and extended his hand to help her, but she was afraid to even touch him. "Thanks, but I'm okay."

They caught up with Liam and the others just outside town.

"Drachma for your thoughts," Corm finally said in a low voice.

She tried to stay strong but a tear escaped and trickled down her cheek.

"A gold coin would not cover it, eh?" he said with a slight smile.

"I guess I thought ... as stupid as it sounds now, I'd be home tonight. You might find this hard to believe, but boys changing into animals, people disappearing, it doesn't happen where I come from. It's got me a bit freaked out. It's not normal. You aren't normal."

"It is the norm around here."

"Where is here? Where am I? I keep thinking this is a dream and, if I don't wake up soon, I'll never wake up at all. I'm scared. I'm alone. I'm afraid I'll never see my mom or my friends again. This isn't where I belong."

There, she said it. She waited for him to make fun of her, to tell her how crazy she sounded.

When he spoke at last, it was slow and deliberate. "I cannot offer any explanation for your situation nor can I predict your future, but I will tell you what I do know. You are not in a dream. I am real, not a figment of your imagination. If that was the case, I hope I would be more handsome."

Before she could stop it, she smiled.

"I believe everything happens for a reason," he continued, his gaze cast down. "I have to. To assume the struggles we experience each day occur by chance and not for greater purpose would make this existence unbearable. I found you and you are here for a reason and, you will return home, if that is what is meant to be. Think about what might have happened if you were found by Caleb and his friends." He lifted his head and looked into her eyes. "You are not alone, nor will you ever be as long as I am around. Do not forget that."

She swallowed the lump in her throat. He was right. She did

believe in fate. It was just easier when good things happened ... easier to justify why you deserved it. It was different when it was something bad, like her father dying, or something scary, like being here. What was the explanation then? But, because of his words, of their truth, she began to feel better.

"Thank you," she said. "I want you to know, as ungrateful as I seem, I appreciate everything you've done for me. You're not like the others, are you?"

"Liam and I have much in common. The others," he said, "know these things to be true, but they do not spend time dwelling upon them. I, however, cannot help it. It is part of who I am. One of my strengths is that I recognize my weaknesses. And, although we do not always agree, my friends accept me for who I am. That is enough, is it not?"

Yes, it was, and she realized, despite everything, how lucky she'd been. "You're really amazing," she said.

"So are you." He told her about his family, his mother's sickness, his father's drinking, and his constant battle with the forces that threatened to destroy his family. The clouds that filled the sky earlier were a distant memory, but the fresh smell of rain still hung in the air and moisture dripped from the trees.

At a fork in the road, Liam held up his hand. "This is where we part company. I need to look in on Jade."

"Then, if my services are no longer required," Shane said, "I am going home. My body requires sustenance. Would anyone care to join me for a slice of my famous meat pie?"

"You mean your mother's meat pie and, yes, I accept," Ian replied.

"Aye, I will as well," Oisin said.

"Corm?" Shane asked.

Corm shook his head. "Thank you, though," He looked at Ally. "Take care of yourself."

"Thanks Corm ... for everything."

When they reached Olivia's house, the front door opened and a tall, slender woman stepped onto the porch. "Olivia. I was worried. You told me you were going to Liam's and coming back. That was over six hours ago."

"I am sorry. We went into town and I visited the dress shop."

Her mother shook her head. "Liam, Meg, how are you both?

And why are you so dirty?"

"Hi, Mrs. Banister," Meg said.

"We are well," Liam replied.

Mrs. Banister looked at Ally and smiled. "Who are you?"

"A friend of the family," Liam said. "Ally, this is Mrs. Banister, Olivia's mother."

"Nice to meet you," Ally said.

"And you as well. You will stay for dinner, I hope. There is a side of beef smoking on the hearth."

"Thank you, but we need to get home." Liam dismounted Pollux. "I wanted to take a look at Jade. How is she doing?"

"The last I checked, she was the same. I am sorry, Olivia."

Olivia leaped from her horse and they followed her into the barn. She entered the last stall on the left.

"What is the matter with her?" Meg asked.

"I am not sure," Liam said. "Her knee is swollen, and, now it appears she has fever."

"What are we going to do?" Olivia said.

"We will start with Thea's salve. I need a warm wet towel."

Olivia took his hand. "Come, I will get you one."

The brown horse was on her side. She grunted and tried to stand, but couldn't. Her eyes were milky. Puss oozed from their corners and discharge flowed from her nose. "Poor thing," Ally said. At the sound of her voice, the horse lifted its head.

Ally walked into the stall, knelt down and put her hand on the horse's nose. Her fingers ran the length of her muzzle. The horse was burning up and whinnied at her touch. "Where does it hurt?" She looked into its eyes and moved her hand from the horse's nose to its neck. Her hand was drawn across Jade's shoulder and down her front left leg. *I wish there was something I could do.* Ally shut her eyes.

"*Aaah!*" she cried a moment later. She gripped the horse's knee and an awful sensation traveled up her arm. The animal cried in protest. Ally's arm went numb and her body began to shake.

"What are you doing?" Olivia screamed from behind. "You are hurting her!"

Olivia's voice shattered the connection and Ally's arm fell to her side.

Olivia strode into the stall. "Get out of the way."

"I don't know what happened. I'm sorry." Ally got to her feet and ran outside. Her arm was tingling and her knee began to ache. *Perfect.*

Liam rushed toward her. "What happened? I heard you scream. Are you hurt?"

"I ... don't know," Ally said. "I wanted to help Jade. She's in so much pain. Will she get better?"

"I do not think so. The infection has spread. I need to tell Olivia how often to change the dressing and we can take our leave."

"Tell Olivia I'm sorry. I wasn't trying to hurt Jade."

"I am sure she knows that. It has been a long day for her," Liam said before he disappeared into the barn.

Seriously? Try walking a mile in these boots, baby. Ally stretched her leg, trying to loosen the muscles in her knee, but the pain was getting worse.

* * *

Caleb liked being in his other form. In fact, he preferred it. It was easy to go unnoticed ... to hide ... to eavesdrop undetected by most. The big oaf did not see him tunnel underground and he slipped away while they were in the tent. He was incredibly quick when eight legs were guiding him. Yes, he accomplished that with little effort, but had failed at something much greater. Fate put the girl within his grasp and, just as quickly, took her away. He had not sensed her outside the tent, and she caught him unaware.

But, the day's misfortune was not entirely his fault. She had not come through where the Master anticipated, and Caleb lost valuable time reaching her new destination. Two from the forest had been persuaded to detain her until he arrived, but even that did not go well. How she had fallen in with the Shayeen so quickly was a mystery, but she wore the necklace. There was no mistake she was the one. He did not believe the superstition about the Vaki, but had not wanted to chance it. It had been wise to leave the fighting to the other two. Now they were ill and had left the forest. If he got sick as well, the Master would have been terribly disappointed.

I will ensure she leaves Gilgamesh and comes to us, the Master had said, with uncharacteristic calm given the circumstance. *Do not let her out of your sight.* Caleb could not see him but knew the Master smiled when he added, *This is turning out better than I imagined. You will be rewarded upon your return, you have my word.*

Caleb shadowed the girl, and those around her, out of town and to this house. He would not lose her again. He would stay with her until the Master told him what he needed to do.

She stood, alone, just outside the barn and Caleb crawled closer.

* * *

Still reeling, Ally had to lower herself to the ground.

Meg appeared beside her. "I know you were trying to help. What happened in there?"

So it wasn't her imagination. "It was strange," Ally answered, staring at the grass.

"Well, Olivia is not pleased, but ... what are you looking at?"

"That spider, see it?" Ally pointed to a spider not more than five feet away. "Look at the design on its back."

"That is a fiddlehead," Meg said. "But I have never seen one like that before. Its fangs almost resemble a wolf spider's. They can give a painful bite if you are not wary of them. Nasty-looking thing, is it not?"

"I think it's kinda cool. Scary, but cool."

Meg brushed her boot in its direction and it skittered out of sight. "Living in the woods, you need to know which ones to avoid. Definitely, stay away from that one."

Chapter 15

"Thea's home!" Meg shouted, and urged Shilo to a gallop.

Thea's horse was still hitched to the wagon, Liam noticed, but she wasn't there. It was not like her to leave the horse unattended. Before he could dismount Pollux, the front door opened and she rushed outside.

"Where have you been? I was worried."

"We went to town," Liam answered. He looked at Meg, Ally and then himself, took in their filthy appearance. He had been able to avoid Mrs. Banister's question on the subject, but knew Thea could not be put off indefinitely. "When did you get back?"

"A short time ago," she replied. "Why are you all covered in mud?"

"It is a rather long story," Liam said.

Meg hopped off Shilo and led him to the barn. When Ally attempted to do the same, she grimaced in pain. "Let me help you," he said. "Remove your feet from the stirrups and turn to the side." She slid into his arms and he placed her on the ground beside him.

"I need to talk to you about something important," Thea said. "Liam, when you finish with the horses, please come inside and make sure Meg is with you. Come, Ally."

Liam unhitched Thea's horse and walked into the barn, followed by Chestnut and Pollux.

"Why do you think those boys were looking for Ally?" Meg asked.

The question had been preying on his mind as well. "I do not know."

"I like Ally. I do not want anything bad to happen to her."

"Aye," he said in response to both statements. He was impressed with how Ally handled herself today. Very brave and very selfless ... for a girl. He would have expected that from Corm or any of the others, but from someone who hardly knew them? Although Meg tried his patience, he would do whatever was required to keep her safe. Despite his complaining, he admired her. She did not take herself, or most situations, too seriously. It balanced his nature to focus on the negative, to obsess about things beyond his control. He was, indeed, indebted to Ally, more than she would ever know.

He put the horses up for the night, grabbed the hamper from the front seat of the wagon and looked into the sky. The first stars twinkled against the dark backdrop; Ascencia and Albireo shimmered side by side. There was no time to tarry so he hurried inside.

Thea was on the couch by herself. Liam brought the basket to the kitchen, and she stood when he reentered the sitting room. "Liam, before you say anything—"

Ally stepped from the washroom. Something about her looked … familiar.

"I hope you don't mind," Ally said. "Thea insisted and I'm really grateful." In her hands was a basin of dirty water.

He inhaled. "Lavender?"

"Oh, that's the soap I bought at the store."

That was one of his mother's favorite scents, but it was not the only reason memories of her washed over him. Ally wore a pair of her black riding pants and her favorite embroidered tunic. He had no idea what happened to his mother's clothing. Thea had seen to that and, on any other day, even this morning, the sight would have incensed him. But at this moment he was surprisingly at ease with it.

"I had forgotten about those." He took the basin from her hands and placed it on the table. "You look … nice."

"Liam," Thea said. "Close your mouth and come sit down. Meg, please join us."

Meg ran in and sat at Thea's feet.

"What I am going to tell you needs to stay here, for now. Once I explain, you will understand why. The world in which *we* live," Thea said and looked at him and Meg, "is not the only one that exists. There is another, similar but not the same, that travels in parallel to our own. An unseen but strong force holds them together. Many centuries ago, our world was linked to the heavens but, over time, those passageways were sealed and others created in their place, doorways to another world through which travel is uncommon but not unheard of."

She turned her eyes to Ally. "That world belongs to you."

Ally stared, mouth agape, at Thea, and then dropped her head against the back of the couch. "A parallel dimension," she said softly.

Thea nodded. "Those secret corridors allow the spirit gods to travel between the two worlds. But, an indiscretion has led to their use by other beings causing the fabric that holds them together to become compromised. It has developed tears within the seams where the energy wavers. I do not understand why you made the journey, Ally, but it is not the first time a human has traveled between them."

Thea gave an uncharacteristic sigh. "I am telling you this so you can understand what I am about to say. There are some who believe the ability to cross between our two worlds, despite the consequences, will give them great power. However, their greed will only serve to destroy us all."

Liam got to his feet. "How long have you known, Thea?" He could understand the subject not coming up in day-to-day conversation, but why had he never heard so much as a rumor?

Thea shook her head. "Liam, are you so vain as to assume yours is the only world that breathes life?"

He began to pace. "I have never given it a thought—" His feet stopped. "If what you say is true, what makes you think Ally is from this other world?"

"I sensed it the moment I saw her. That was the reason for my trip to Podegar's." Thea pulled a washcloth from her apron pocket. "This is stained with the blood I wiped from Ally's forehead." She unfolded the rust-colored rag. In its center was an area where the blood was not visible. "Podegar poured tama juice on this. When the blood disappeared, it confirmed my suspicion. It is slightly different from our own."

"That would explain it," Ally said.

Liam looked at Ally. "How can you simply accept this?"

"You haven't been listening," she answered. "I told you I wasn't from around here. You thought I was crazy. Trust me, I questioned my own sanity when I saw what happened today. People don't change into animals where I'm from. Not literally anyway."

"Ah, you know about the Shanyo." Ally nodded at Thea's statement.

"If what you say is true, Thea," Liam said, "could the location where Corm and I found her be one of those passageways?"

Ally's body tensed. "Yeah, why can't I just go back the way I came?"

Thea's expression washed over with sympathy. "The portals allow movement in a single direction. The one you traveled through leads into the forest, not out of it. In order to return home, you must find the correct one. It is true that certain spirits can travel at will between the worlds. The gods before us could do it quite easily. Yet, even then, the journey changed their powers, either diminishing them or making them more powerful. Certain objects are able to travel to and from as well. Some change. Some simply do not make it through at all."

"So how do I find the right passageway home?" Ally asked.

Thea shook her head. "You traveled through unintentionally. Great care must be taken if you journey through again. I learned a great deal during my time away. The opening of certain doors can result in dire consequence. Almost seventy years ago, in your sense of time, a spirit traveled from this world and allowed Chaos to enter yours. It had also happened twenty-seven years before, with a similar result. Prior to your arrival, the last time someone from *your* world traveled here was three years ago." Thea looked at him and Meg. "The time of the sickness that took your mother."

Liam asked, incredulous, "Who would *do* such a thing?"

Thea looked at him but did not speak. Ally began to count on her fingers.

"What are you doing?" he asked her.

"The math. Seventy years ago was 1941. Twenty-seven years before that was 1914. Huh. I know those dates. We talked about them in Hist—" Her mouth dropped open. "Are you kidding me? World War I and World War II? Are you saying something from *over here* caused those wars?"

"I cannot say if the passageway was traveled before or after the trouble began. I do know that evil takes root when people have given up hope. I suspect the timing of such things is not chance but seen as an opportunity. I am sad to say, within the past year, the door into your world has opened again. Forces here tried to prevent that, to no avail. Tell me, is your world experiencing anything unusual … anything of consequence at the current time?"

Ally nodded. "Yeah. Wars and terrorism are spreading, there are tsunamis, earthquakes, natural disasters. And oh, the world economy is about to collapse … to name a few 'unusual' things. Everything's falling apart."

"If your world falls, ours does as well," Thea said.

"Why was I not aware this was happening?" Liam asked.

"Because you have been self-absorbed for the past three years, Liam."

Meg had spoken quietly from her spot on the floor. He had forgotten she was even in the room. He began to open his mouth, but was unsure of what he wanted to say.

"Well, it is the truth," she said. "I have sensed it. I have even written about it. You have been in your *own* world since Mom died. Have you not noticed that the last three crops have failed, or that the winters are more bitter? Not to mention what happened to Mom. The same thing is happening to Corm's parents. Have you not noticed how more and more people are leaving Gilgamesh each day?"

He gritted his teeth. She was right. He had been oblivious to everything going on around him. The cut that formed when his mother died had never healed. It reopened every day. He always thought if he had been home, instead of on a hunting trip with Corm, none of it would have happened.

"You still feel guilty about Mom," she said. "It was not your fault. And, if what Thea said is true, it had nothing to do with you."

"Don't blame yourself, Liam," Ally said. "I know how easy that can be."

"How could you possibly know what this is like?"

"Because I lost my father two years ago. He got sick, too." Ally jumped to her feet.

"What is the matter?" Meg asked.

"I just remembered my mom. What does she think happened to me? She must be crazy by now."

Thea took Ally's hands within her own. "Podegar's visions are not always detailed but they are never wrong. I asked her the same. She said your mother knows you are alive and that you are doing everything within your power to return."

"How does Podegar know that?"

"As I said, I trust Podegar and, therefore, so should you. Your mother is a strong woman. You take after her in that way."

"Thank you." Ally bent down and put her arms around Thea.

"You are welcome. I am going to send a bird to your father, Liam." Thea got up from the couch. "He needs to be aware of the situation. Until we hear from him, it is best we stay close. Meg, bring me parchment and a quill, please—"

"What is that doing in here?" Liam was looking at the floor, where a large black spider was in the shadow of the couch. He got to his feet and followed it as it raced to the hearth and up the chimney.

He had thought their house was spider-proof. Pilotte was keen at discovering an unwanted visitor of that size. It suddenly occurred to him there had been no welcoming committee barking at his heels when he arrived home. "Thea, have you seen Pilotte?"

"I have not."

Liam rushed from the house and into the front yard. "Pilotte!"

No answer.

A sinking feeling made its way to his stomach. He entered the barn and Pollux whinnied from his stall. And then, a whimper came from the farthest corner. Liam followed the sound and looked into a pair of sad brown eyes. When had Pilotte crawled in here?

The dog tried to get to his feet, but could not. Liam touched the fur on his back and Pilotte bared his teeth. "Okay." He stroked the dog's head and, when he was confident Pilotte would not bite his hand, he tried again. His fingers came upon a welt and the dog howled in protest.

Meg gasped from behind. "What is the matter with him?"

Liam was able to see the wound now, and the sight filled him with terror. "I am afraid it is some sort of a bite. He is having a bad reaction to the venom. Where is Thea?"

"She is in back with the pigeons."

Ah yes, sending a bird to his father. What would she have written? *Dear Jon: Just wanted to inform you a girl from another world is in our midst, Shayeen are attacking those in Gilgamesh, and Pilotte has been poisoned. How are things with you?*

He shook his head and lifted Pilotte into his arms. "Let us get you in the house."

* * *

Dear Jon,
The malakai is among us. She found your son as we hoped and feared. It is time you travel to the Elders.
Althea

Thea rolled the parchment tightly and slipped it in the tube fastened to the bird's leg. Raya was the swiftest pigeon in the coop, and the darkness would not deter her. "Give us strength, Ascencia. To Jon!" She tossed the bird into the air. It lifted its wings and headed east, into the night.

Chapter 16

Ally sat on the bed. *Why me? Why? Why? Why?* An answer, one that made sense, eluded her.

Thea had explained it was a five-hour flight to the ministry. Once the pigeon rested, she'd make the return trip and should be back first thing in the morning. *Boy, do we take things for granted.* Her cell seemed like a huge luxury now. Too bad it didn't come through. Although who would she call? To make the whole phone-thing work, you needed someone on the other end. Maybe something in her bag had changed into a teleport device. She began to look through it again.

She opened the zippered compartment inside the lining and tossed a tattered book of matches, a reminder of her one attempt at smoking, onto the bed. *What's this?* She pulled out a gold compact mirror. It was decorated with sparkling rhinestones and, when she opened it, a piece of paper fell into her lap. She unfolded it and recognized her father's handwriting.

Look into this and remember, you can do anything you put your mind to. The key is to realize where you are standing. Take in the view. Find patience in your search for truth.

When had he put this in there?

The irony brought tears that stung her eyes. She had done her senior physics project on parallel dimensions, and most of her research had come from her father's papers. When he was alive, they talked for hours, speculating how many worlds existed. She just enjoyed the time with him, had never really believed it. But Dad always explored the possibilities, was never afraid to travel down an unknown road.

Her family purposely got lost, took alternate routes from time to time, "Lost Boy Rides" Dad called them. They'd drive around without a thought as to where they were going. *Yet somehow, we always found our way back—*

A thought ... no, more of a revelation ... came to her. Was this any different? If Podegar was correct, her mom somehow knew she was okay. Ally missed her, but obsessing about it wasn't going to get her home any quicker. So, wasn't this the craziest Lost Boy Ride ever? She looked into the mirror and then at the piece of paper in her hand. *This is more than a Lost Boy Ride,* a sane voice argued. She hated that voice but it meant the other was close behind. *It's a Lost Boy Ride, all right. How many others have ever had this opportunity? Make the most of it. Experience everything.*

She usually listened to the voice of reason; it was her nature. But for crying out loud, she was in a place where boys could change into animals! How amazing was that?

She needed to stop feeling sorry for herself and being afraid. This wasn't a fairy tale where some knight in shining armor was going to rescue her. She needed to save herself, take control of her own destiny. She stood, excited by her newfound attitude, her newly discovered independence, but was pulled from her epiphany by Liam's voice.

He was shouting for Thea.

Pilotte was on the couch, shivering. "What happened?" Ally asked.

Liam pointed to the dog's back. "He received a bite, spider or snake perhaps. We need to draw the poison."

Poor Liam. Her life hadn't been the only one flipped on its side. Her arrival had done a number on him, too. "What can I do to help?"

"He might act strange if you get too close. He growled at me earlier."

Thea walked in from the kitchen and handed Liam a steaming towel. "This has been soaked in plantain. You need to place this directly on the bite."

Liam took it and leaned closed. Pilotte, in turn, exposed his upper teeth. Liam threw his hands in the air. "He will not allow me to do this."

"Let me try." Ally sat on the couch and looked into Pilotte's eyes. "Let Liam help you." She put one hand under the dog's chin and the other between his ears. "Do it now."

The dog whimpered but didn't move. "Don't be afraid, Pilotte. We're here," she said over and over until Liam touched her shoulder.

"All done," he said.

"Did it work?"

"We will have to see."

"Ally and I saw an odd-looking spider at Olivia's today," Meg said. "It looked like a fiddleback but uglier."

"That sounds similar to the one I saw in the house earlier," Liam said.

"Yuck! Do not tell me one of those is in here," Meg said. "Do you think that is what bit Pilotte?"

"I cannot be sure, but it might be a new breed. If we see another, we need to bring it to Doc Whitman. Perhaps he knows something about them."

Ally stood. Sudden nausea forced her hand over her mouth.
Weird.

"Are you all right?" Liam asked.

"I think so," she answered. She took a few breaths and, when her stomach settled, she put her hand into her pocket and pulled out Ariana's silver chain. It shimmered and seemed to move in her hand. She reached into the other pocket and took out her broken necklace. "Can you fix this? I'm not sure how it's going to fasten. There's no clasp or hook."

"I think she wanted me to melt the ends together."

"How're you gonna do that?" The image of a blowtorch on the back of her neck made her cringe.

"I can heat a clamp and seal it together." He walked into the kitchen and returned a moment later. "It is warming on the fire."

"Meg, I could use your help with dinner," Thea said. "Podegar sent fried chicken."

"Yummy!" Meg said and ran from the room.

Liam turned to face the fireplace, his hands on his hips. She looked at him ... his half ponytail, his broad shoulders, the muscles in his arms and, although she couldn't see them, she envisioned his beautiful eyes ... and sighed. He was actually very cute. *Cute? He's hot!* As if hearing her thoughts, he turned around.

"I want to tell you that I am sorry," he said and looked at the floor.

"About what?"

"You spoke the truth about not being from this world, and I did not believe you."

"Then I should apologize, too. I didn't believe you, either. And there's something else."

He lifted his eyes. The intensity of his stare caught her by surprise and it took a moment to regain her composure. "I've been thinking ..."

His expression became expectant.

"First," she said, "thanks for all you've done for me. You're the one person I haven't said it to yet, so ..." She walked to him, stood on her toes and gave him a hug.

His face flamed red. "You are welcome. You said 'first.' Might there be something else?"

"Yes. I don't know how long I'm gonna be here but, while I am, I want to know everything there is about the forest, about how you live. It's so different from what I'm used to. That is, if you don't mind."

"I am flattered you find all this interesting," he began and then stopped. "I apologize. I do not mean to be so rude ... I cannot help it sometimes. I would be honored." He bowed at the waist. "Now, let us get your heart back where it belongs."

She smiled but it quickly faded when he came back into the room. In his gloved right hand was a metal clamp. "What are you doing?"

"Put the chain around your neck with the heart in the back and the ends in the front."

"Okay."

"Now, cross it where you want the length to be."

She held the necklace together where the heart would hang perfectly.

"Are you sure? Once I do this, it cannot be undone."

"I'm sure, just get it over with."

He stepped closer and she felt the heat from the iron. "Please don't set me on fire." She closed her eyes and heard him laugh. "I'm not kidding."

"I have no intention of setting you afire, not unless you move."

She heard the sizzle of the metal and held her breath. He stepped away and she opened her eyes. There was a crease where the ends were melted together.

"Can I touch it?"

"Yes."

She tried to turn it around, but it was tangled in her hair.

He put the clamp in the fireplace. "Allow me."

"Thanks." She lifted her hair and, when his hands brushed the back of her neck, she shivered. *Please, he has a girlfriend. Don't forget about Olivia.* "Okay," she said harshly.

"What? Does that hurt?"

"No." *But it could, couldn't it?*

Meg giggled.

"Compliments to the chef?" Ally said after she couldn't stifle the burp that had escaped her. The fried chicken was delicious. Podegar also sent fresh bread and baked beans. Ally picked up her plate and walked to the kitchen. She filled the wash pan with warm water and began to hum. Halfway through the first stanza, she realized it was "Lost" by Coldplay. *How appropriate.*

Liam walked in and cleared his throat. She sang louder, horribly off key, and he raised his eyebrows.

"What? No one sings around here?"

"Nothing that sounds like that," he said. He picked up a towel and took the clean plate from her hand.

"If I had my iPod, you'd hear a lot stranger."

"What is an eye pod?"

She kept forgetting technology didn't exist here. "It's something that plays music. You pick songs you like, put them on the iPod and play them back, hear them whenever you want."

"It does not seem like much fun. Why would you not play the music you want to hear?"

"On an instrument?"

"Yes, why not?"

"Well, not everyone knows how to play. And you might not be someplace where that's an option. But, the main reason? I guess it's easier."

"Aye, but not nearly as much fun."

"You're right. I wish I had my violin."

"We do not have a violin, but we have a fiddle."

"Do you play?" she asked.

"I play the guitar. Meg plays ... or rather, Meg massacres the flute. But the violin and fiddle are similar, are they not?"

"Yes." She finished the dishes and picked up the basin. "Could you open the door?" Her fingers were pruned from the dishwater, and it reminded her of what she really needed. "I could use a warm bath."

"I will make a deal with you," he said, taking the pot from her hands. "If you play for me, I will show you how to take the bath you so desperately want ... and need."

She laughed. "We call that blackmail where I come from, but I accept."

He stepped back into the kitchen, pulled a piece of kindling from the neatly bundled pile in the corner and touched it to the embers in the oven. "After you," he said and opened the door.

"No lantern?"

"No need." He pointed to the sky. "Full moon. Follow me." The moon was bright overhead, more brilliant than she ever remembered, and its light cast shadows on the ground.

"It's beautiful tonight," she whispered when a warm breeze caressed her face and caught the trees overhead. The leaves rustled softly, as if agreeing with her. They reached the shower stall and she was still looking into the sky.

"Are you going to pay attention so I do not have to show you again?"

She scowled and looked to where he was pointing. A circle of rocks surrounded a hole to the right of the shower and he placed the burning stick inside it.

"What did you just do?"

"I lit the coals that line the bottom of this trench." He pulled on a rope and a metal barrel floated down from the sky. It stopped a foot above the ground and he tied it off to a clamp on the side of the house.

"Yeah, and ...?"

"The coals will heat the water in this barrel by morning. Make sure you use the mitts in the kitchen, and pour the water from this barrel into the underground trough." He pointed to a pipe in the ground. "Then go to the bath and pump the water into the tub."

"All this, just to take a warm bath?"

"Now, it is time to make good on your part of the bargain." She could see him perfectly in the moonlight as he smiled.

Back inside the house, she sat on the couch with Pilotte. His nose was on his paws and, already, he looked better.

Liam descended the ladder from the loft. What song would she play?

"Will this do?" he asked.

Her eyes widened. She'd heard the jokes about fiddles. 'What's the difference between a violin and a fiddle? Answer: about ten thousand dollars.' Or, 'When you're buying it, it's a fiddle, when you're selling it, it's a violin.' She examined the ornate carving on the scroll. It was more beautiful than any violin she'd ever seen. He handed her a bow.

"Real horsehair?"

"What else would it be?"

She was used to playing before a group, but playing to one? She pushed her anxiety aside and decided on Rachmaninov's "Vocalise," the piece she'd planned on performing at the interview. She plucked at the strings while turning the pegs on the fiddle's scroll. When it was tuned to her satisfaction, she placed the rest under her chin and began.

The similarity between this fiddle and her violin was amazing. She lost herself in the song; her arm moved back and forth as the bow connected with the strings. The piece came to life with little effort. Her body moved to the music and, at the crescendo, she was on her toes. She'd never felt so inspired. As she played the last note she opened her eyes. Thea and Meg stood beside Liam.

"That was beautiful, my dear," Thea whispered. "It has been too long since we have heard music in this house."

Liam nodded. "You are quite talented."

"Thanks. I love that piece but I think we need something a little lighter. How about this?" She began to play one of David Garrett's rock symphony pieces, Aerosmith's "Walk this Way." The bow flew over the strings. Meg's head bobbed up and down, Liam tapped his foot and even Thea looked like she might begin to dance. When Ally finished, Liam got to his feet and they all began to clap.

"Thank you, thank you." She took a bow. "That felt great. Thanks for letting me play it." She handed it to Liam.

"Keep it for now. I think I have found my bargaining chit."

Ally sat on the bed and looked at the fiddle. It really did have an awesome pitch. She turned it over in her hands and something on the back caught her eye. She leaned close to the lantern and held it at an angle. Carved into the wood were the words:

William, always remember the power
and the magic of music
Love, Mom

William, she mused ... Liam. So he did play the violin ... fiddle. His mother had given this to him, yet he so easily handed it to her. She didn't know him well, but knew enough to understand the complexity of the gesture. He really was a nice guy. So were his friends.

Where would they fit in, in her world? Shane, intimidating but good-natured. Defensive end or class clown. Either way, he'd attract friends like a magnet with his easygoing nature. Ian? He was harder to read than the others. Quiet, but brave and smart. Honor club maybe, or quarterback. Something that required brains and brawn. Oisin. She smiled. He'd fit in with the pseudo-hippie crowd, trying to sniff out a good time wherever he could find it. He'd hang around the school, ditch class and chase girls.

Then there was Corm. A member of the poetry club, surely. Soft spoken, but not shy. He wouldn't pretend to be something he wasn't just to fit in. He'd avoid all the drama. The girls would love him but he wouldn't get involved unless it was something special.

She put the fiddle beside her. What about Liam?

He'd fit in anywhere. He was smart, had a sense of humor, when he let his guard down. The girls'd be all over him, but she didn't see him as a flirt. Which brought her to Olivia. In a different place, could she and Ally have been friends? Would Ally have been friends with any of them back home? She didn't think so but, there was *one* thing she was sure of. She felt safe with them. They'd choose the right path, regardless of the consequence. A virtue that was, sadly, lacking in her world.

* * *

Liam was anxious to hear from his father. The misuse of the portals had led to dire circumstance. He had never thought about such things before. Living in the forest did not bring those kinds of ideas into focus. His father had certainly been distracted at the fair. And what, if anything, did this have to do with Ally?

The thought of her caused something inside to stir, like dry leaves lifted by the wind that slowly settle back to the ground. She was quirky and unpredictable but she had made the fiddle sing, something he had never been able to do. He would allow her to hold onto it while she was here. He thought his mother would have approved. In fact, he knew she would have.

His mother loved music. When she was alive, there was rarely a time when their house was not filled with its sound. She often told him music lifts the soul, that a song in your heart will make even the darkest of times bearable.

That was a bunch of rubbish. Was she carrying a tune all the way to her death?

Stop it, Liam. Live your life. His mother's voice caught him by surprise, but he listened. *Fate stepped in and I could not get out of its way. The time is approaching when you need to be strong and put this behind you. I will always be with you, to give you strength.*

He laced his hands behind his neck and stared at the ceiling over his bed. "I will try, Mom." In good conscience, he could not commit to anything more.

Chapter 17

The bird was strong and flew at a swift pace. Caleb held on, and a few hours later, she entered her hole. How long before someone realized there was a visitor ... or two? He heard footsteps on the stone stairway and disappeared in the shadows.

A man struggled to catch his breath. "Raya," he said. "What brings you at this late hour?" He removed the canister from her leg and, after reading the note, let out a heavy sigh. He slowly walked down the stairs, leaving Caleb and the bird alone again.

Caleb changed into his human form and looked around. An empty burlap bag was in the corner, "Property of the Council of Gilgamesh" stenciled on the fabric. *Ah, so this is where I am. But why?*

The boy's father, the Master said, breaking into his thoughts. His sudden appearance startled Caleb. *This will work to our advantage.*

"How?" Caleb said. "The girl wants only to go home."

Leave that to me. Return with the bird, but make note of your location. You will not be carried when you return here again.

He and the bird arrived back in Pembroke at an early hour, and Caleb entered the house through a tiny aperture in the eaves.

* * *

Yawning, Ally stretched her limbs, and then did both again. She hadn't slept that soundly in a long time. *I didn't even get undressed last night ... not that I've got anything to change into.* She needed to do laundry and made a mental note to find out where, and how, they did it here.

After she filled the reservoir outside, she slipped into the washroom and began to pull on the pump. Warm water splashed into the large tub but, despite her efforts, trickled to a stop when the tub was only half-full. Well, better than nothing. She got in and draped her arms over the sides.

"*Ssshh*, Pilotte," she said half-heartedly when the dog began to bark. It would take more than that to get her to rush right now. She stared dreamily into space until slight movement in the corner of the room caught her eye.

"You again?" A large spider crawled down a silk thread. "Shoo!" She splashed water toward it and covered herself with her hands. It was only a spider, but something about it gave her the creeps. It was like it was watching her.

* * *

When Liam heard Ally at the back door, he descended the ladder from his loft and joined her outside.

She was sitting upon the stone bench in the garden. "Raya's back."

"I can see that." He pulled the canister from the bird's leg and read the note from his father.

"What does it say?" Ally asked.

"He is leaving Gilgamesh to gather more information. He requests we remain here until we hear from him."

Her hair, still wet, hung in ringlets around her face. The rose color, high in her cheeks, was nearly the same shade that defined her lips, and her blue eyes sparkled.

"What's your father like?" she asked.

He walked to the bench and sat beside her. "He was actually quite a bit of fun, until my mother fell ill. Then, he became relentless in his search for answers. Because of his passion, the council offered him a position. He is supposed to represent our best interests, to watch over us, but he was not even here when she died ... nor was I. We see him occasionally, but it will never be the same."

Ally nodded but remained silent.

"What are you doing out here at this early hour?"

"I came outside after my bath, which was awesome by the way," she said. "I can't believe how beautiful this is. It was so quiet, I thought I heard the trees singing. It sounds crazy, but everything seems so alive ... the way the dew glistens on the ground, the color of the flowers. It's really intense."

He knew what she was referring to. In the right frame of mind, you could hear more than just the trees. The forest had affected him that way when he was younger but, over the years, it lost its magic. Why had he allowed that to happen?

"It is beautiful," he said.

"The air smells so clean," she turned up her nose and inhaled loudly. "Oh, speaking of clean, I really need to wash some clothes. How do you do laundry?"

She was still wearing his mother's pants and shirt, and something fell into place. "After I cook breakfast, I will show you," he said and got to his feet.

He made them each a three-egg-and-cheese omelet with fried ham and, when he looked up, her plate was clean. "Are you not going to burp? You will offend me if you do not."

She took in a breath and belched.

He smiled. "Pack the clothes you need to wash. I will meet you outside." As he walked toward the barn, Meg ran up from behind.

"Where are you going?" she asked.

"Ally and I are taking a ride."

"I want to come."

"You may join us as far as Sara's. It has been nearly a week, and they will be wondering what happened to you. You need to get back to your lessons."

"Cool!"

Cool? What did that mean?

Liam led the horses from the barn and handed Ally the reins to Chestnut and Shilo. "I will be right back." He went to his room, unsure of where they would be but, under his bed, he found the tin. Most of the charcoals were dry and would no longer serve their purpose, but he found a piece that was still soft and placed it in his pocket.

He stopped in the kitchen on his way out, and saw Thea busy chopping roots.

"Are you off somewhere, Liam?" Her eyes twinkled, a faint smile on her lips.

"Aye," he replied. "Here is the note from Dad."

She took it from his hand. "And here is some lunch for you and Ally."

"How did you—?"

"Ally mentioned you were taking her to clean her clothes."

"Aye." He smiled and kissed her cheek.

"Tell my daughter I said hello."

Liam watched Ally as she mounted Chestnut.

"Why are you making that face?" she asked.

"I need to show you how to ride in the proper manner. It is no wonder you are sore. Look how I sit in the saddle. See how I am aligned? Keep a straight line from your shoulders to your hips to your ankles."

She stiffened and sat up straight. "Like this?"

"Yes," he said slowly. "Keep only the balls of your feet in the irons. Pull yours out a little. If you get thrown, which is highly unlikely on Chestnut but possible, you do not want to get caught up and break your ankle."

"Highly unlikely but not impossible ... great." She slid her feet out of the stirrups.

"Good, now push your heels down, your toes should be pointing up."

She looked at him and rolled her eyes. "How did I manage to stay on at all without all this instruction?"

"She told me she knew how to ride," Meg said.

"She obviously lied, Meg. Look at her."

"Shush, you two. Let me get the hang of this."

He gave Pollux a gentle nudge. "Now relax and let your body flow with the horse. We will take it slow so you can get accustomed to the feel. Once you are comfortable, we will try a trot or a canter."

By the time they reached the Acrisius family's house, Ally was looking more at ease in the saddle.

Sara ran into the yard. "Meg! I hoped you would come by today."

Mr. Acrisius walked from the barn and opened his arms to Meg. "You have missed a few days," he said.

"May she spend the night, Dad?" Sara asked. "Please."

Mr. Acrisius tipped his hat. "Liam."

"Nice to see you again, sir."

"I hope you will allow Meg to stay for at least a day. Sara has missed her and, if Sara is missing her, I am missing her, if you take my meaning." He winked.

"I do and that would be fine, although she did not bring a change

121

of clothing."

"Yes, I did, Liam," Meg said.

Mr. Acrisius smiled. "It appears they had this planned all along."

"I apologize," Liam said. He turned and introduced Ally. She was trying to remove her left foot, which had become wedged in the stirrups.

"Nice to meet you," she finally said.

"And you as well." Mr. Acrisius walked over and withdrew her foot. Ally smiled at him and shook her head. "Do not worry, my dear, it could happen to anyone."

"When would you like me to return for Meg?" Liam said.

"I think two days should be enough. That should provide ample opportunity for them to get reacquainted, and to allow Meg to catch up on her studies. She is a bright one, Liam."

"Of that, I am well aware, sir."

"We will bring her home in the evening. Please give my best to Thea." Ally was now attempting to disentangle the reins. "And good luck."

"Aye. I am afraid I might need it."

* * *

Following Liam's lead, Ally concentrated on riding properly. He slowed Pollux and waited for her to join him.

"We can temper our pace for a bit," he said once she was by his side.

"It's just so beautiful … the forest … the sky … the color of the mountains in the distance. I'm sorry I'm slowing us down but I'm too busy looking around."

"Do you not have any of this where you are from?"

She sighed. "We do. I suppose that's the problem. I don't know how things are here, but in my world there's a lot of distractions. I became too busy to notice. I forgot about things like this."

"I, too, am guilty of allowing distractions to blind me to my surroundings. I regret losing focus."

"Let's rediscover it together then," she said and lifted both arms to the sky. "*Wooo Whoo!*" she shouted, and laughed. "That's been dying to get out."

"Really?"

122

"Go ahead, try it."

He took a breath and a half-hearted scream escaped his lips.

"Oh, come on. Look at the size of you. You can do better than that."

He closed his eyes and drew in his breath. "AAHHH!" he shouted. His voice echoed off the ledges on either side of them. He looked at her and grinned. "How was that?"

"A little more intense than I imagined, but you get a ten."

"A ten?"

"You know, on a scale of one to ten, that's a ten."

"I have no idea what you are talking about, but you are right. It felt good." He pointed to a path that led into the woods. "We are going to turn off the road up here. There will be hanging limbs and branches, so be careful. And please, for now, look where you are going."

"I meant what I said about enjoying the ride, but all this way to do laundry?"

"No. We typically clean our clothes at the house or at the creek, if the weather permits. But this is a special place … one I have not visited in a long time. I think you will like it."

The path was difficult, but she managed to stay on Chestnut. "Is that Corm?" she asked when a large bird flew overhead.

He laughed. "No."

"I like him. It's too bad he's going through a rough time."

"I regret that as well. But Corm keeps his perspective about such things. His emotions do not control him. He sees things as they are, not as he wishes them to be, regardless of the circumstance."

"I like all your friends. You're lucky."

"Please," he said, "do not tell me you are without friends."

"I have a few … not many. Actually, only one. Kind of like you and Corm. Her name is Stephanie." With the mention of her name, Ally realized just how much she missed her friend. She needed to remember every detail so she could tell Steph all about this place when she got home.

"There's magic here, isn't there?" she asked.

"It is always present, but you will not see it if you do not look."

Perhaps, but she *could* feel it. She had sensed it all morning and it was … wonderful.

The path ended at the edge of a meadow the size of ten football fields, and it was full of tall, beautiful flowers in every shade imaginable. It looked like a giant rainbow and above them were hundreds of butterflies, their wings brilliant with color.

"This is so cool," she whispered.

"Cool? Meg said that earlier. What does this 'cool' mean?"

She chuckled. "Cool means … wow, unbelievable, fantastic."

"I see. Then it is very cool. I felt the same way when I saw it the first time."

"Wait!" she called when Pollux began to move forward.

"What is it?"

"I want to remember this and I don't have a camera." He looked at her, confused. "Never mind. I need to draw a picture with my mind, with all my senses. Then, when I'm eighty years old, I'll be able to remember what all this looked like, what it smelled like, even you."

She closed her eyes, cleared her mind, and then looked out on the meadow. She saw how the colors of the flowers faded perfectly into one another ... red, orange, yellow, green, blue, purple and white. The butterflies. One came close and she saw the intricate detail on its wings. The sun, high in the deep blue sky, golden and full of warmth. The breeze that caused the flowers to sway in unison and brought their fragrance to her nose. A long moment later, she inhaled deeply and allowed all this beauty to travel to her brain for safekeeping. "What kind of flowers are those?"

"Lupine. They bloom but once a year. Our timing is perfect."

She nodded, listening to the birds. One in particular caught her ear. It would sing the same song four times then switch to a different tune. "What is that?" Ally asked after at least five different calls.

"That is an Ardana. There is one in that spruce."

She looked at the small bird and, when it finished its chirping, it changed from blue to purple and began to sing again.

At her shocked expression, Liam explained, "He changes color each time he finishes a pattern. He knows seven songs, one for each color of the flowers you see."

"You're kidding."

"This is the meadow of Patalena, and it is full of magic. If you follow a butterfly, it will lead you here. Once the lupine is passed, the daisies are in bloom, followed by the sunflowers. We need to cross this to get where we are going."

"This isn't what you wanted to show me?"

"I thought you wanted to wash your clothes. There is no place to do that here."

"I did—I do. I forgot. We have to cross through this? I don't want to kill anything. It's too pretty. Couldn't we just go around?"

He smiled and looked out upon the meadow. *"Voida me viettaa!"*

What was he doing? And then, the flowers began to part.

"No way."

He motioned for her to go ahead. "After you."

Halfway across, she looked over her shoulder. Behind her the path had disappeared, as if it had never been there at all. "What did you say back there?"

"I asked Patalena if we might pass. Her answer was obvious."

"What if she said no? It's not like we couldn't do it anyway. It's only a field of flowers."

"Then you would not want to attempt it."

"Why? What would happen?" The lupine brushed against her leg and she began to get the willies.

"I have never witnessed it, but my mother told me those who cross the meadow without permission will do so with great difficulty. These flowers can change into long branches full of sharp thorns. It would be painful for even horses to ride through against her will."

"How does Patalena know what your intentions are?"

He shrugged. "She just does."

"Where to now?" she asked when they reached the other side.

"We need to travel into the forest again for a short distance, and then we are there."

She didn't think anything could top what she'd just seen. She was mistaken.

Chapter 18

They rode out of the forest and up a small incline. Liam was in the lead and stopped when he reached the crest. She joined him and stared into the field below.

The deep-green landscape was dotted with wildflowers and long timothy grass. A lake, surrounded by enormous weeping willows, shimmered in the sunlight. But there was one thing in this meadow that was not in the last ... something that made it more beautiful. Half a dozen children, dressed in white, ran barefoot through the grass, pulling kites shaped like butterflies. Their long blonde hair wafted behind them.

"I have not been here since my mother died," Liam said softly. "I had forgotten how beautiful it is."

The wind carried an erotic fragrance. "What do I smell?" she asked.

"Jasmine."

Her body began to tingle and the sound of laughter brought back memories of her own childhood ... the fun, the freedom. It seemed like forever since she felt that way.

Liam wiped his eyes with his right hand. "We have been spotted."

The children pointed at them and, one by one, their kites drifted to the ground.

She and Liam rode down into the meadow and, when they reached its edge, he got off Pollux. One girl broke from the group and ran to him.

"Liam!" she cried. "It is about time."

He lifted her off the ground. "You have grown since I last saw you, Laurel," he said.

One by one, they surrounded him. "Where have you been?"; "Why have you not visited?"; "Where is Meg?"

Ally hid her shock. He hadn't been here since his mother died? The pain of coming back must have outweighed the pain in staying away … until today. "Looks like they missed you," she said.

"Yes, it has been too long. This is my friend, Ally."

These children were beautiful. Their skin was the color of whipped cream and their cheeks were a shade she'd never seen without the help of makeup. They ran to her and, one by one said, "I am Casidy," "Christian," "Kaytlin," "Patrick," "Fiona," "Laurel." She might forget their names, but she'd never forget their faces … or their eyes. They were all the same shade, a deep blue-green.

"Play with us, Liam," Laurel said and picked up a kite.

He grinned. "I will if Ally will."

"Okay, just let me take these off first." She removed her boots and socks, and wiggled her toes in the grass. Patrick handed her a spool of string.

Ally began to run, letting the line unravel a little at a time. She looked over her shoulder. The kite caught the breeze and tugged at the string as it tried to break free. She glanced to her right. Liam's kite played in the air as he laughed and ran beside her. Her heart swelled, and she struggled to keep it where it belonged. She had never dreamed she could feel this happy again.

Why?

Because dreams can be dangerous. What if you imagined your life traveling a different path, only to find that place was out of reach?

But what if you never try?

She picked up the pace and cut to the right. Liam did the same but stopped when a woman stepped from the willows. His spool fell to the ground and he walked and then, ran toward her. They threw their arms around each other and Ally's feet came to a standstill. She began to wind the string, not wanting to stare but found she couldn't help herself. Liam pointed to Ally and they walked in her direction, arm in arm.

"Ally," Liam said, "I would like you to meet my Aunt Neala."

Aunt?

"Ally, how wonderful to meet you. I am overjoyed you brought Liam to see us."

"I can't take the credit for that. He brought *me* here," she said, and handed Laurel the kite.

"Oh, I suspect you had something to do with it. Come." She put her arm around Ally's shoulders. "We are family."

"We are in need of using the lake to wash Ally's clothes," Liam said.

Neala smiled. "Ah, the nature of your visit is not strictly social, then."

Liam jogged to where Pollux and Chestnut were grazing and returned with their bags.

"We have missed you, Liam," Neala said. "Why have you stayed away so long?"

Liam took a breath. "I was unsure of how this would affect me, of how I would deal with the memories this place would awaken."

"Do not be reluctant to remember something wonderful, for those are reminders of what we need to keep close. The important thing is you are here." Neala squeezed his shoulder. "You have become quite a young man. Your mother is proud of you."

His face stilled. "Do you not mean 'would have been proud'?"

"No. Look around you, Liam. She is here, and is always with you."

He looked at the ground, silent. "Meg was right. My head has not been in the right place for a while."

"Ah." Neala laughed. "How is dear little Meg…?"

* * *

Caleb was entwined in the horse's tail but leaped to the ground before they joined the children flying those silly papers. He waited in the high grass above the meadow while they made fools of themselves. Their laughing would be over soon enough. He did not understand how they could be having so much fun. It was meaningless child's play, but still he watched, unable to turn away.

* * *

The lake was an incredible shade of aqua and the sun created brilliant diamonds on its surface. The smell of jasmine was strong here, and Ally began to feel giddy. She squinted against the glare of the sun at the blue-green surface and saw a beautiful girl walking from the water toward the shore.

Her dress and long blonde hair were dry. How could that be? She looked to be the same age as Ally but this girl was in better shape. Much better. Taut muscles defined her arms and legs. In Ally's world, the girl might be accused of using steroids, but here?

"Cousin, I thought that was you," the girl said and hurried to Liam.

Liam smiled. "Deidre, it is great to see you."

"I am surprised you can remember my name after so much time." She gave him a hug, looked at Ally and raised her eyebrows. "I see you brought a guest."

"Yes, this is a friend of mine. Ally, this is my cousin Deidre."

"Hi," Ally said.

They shook hands but Deidre didn't immediately let go. Instead, she gripped Ally's hand tight, her eyes widening with surprise.

"What is it?" Liam asked.

"How did you two meet?"

"I should have known you would see," Liam said and shook his head. "Corm and I came upon her in the woods a few days ago. Apparently, she is a long way from home. Lost, you could say."

Deidre folded her arms. "A long way from home? Yes. Lost? I am not so sure. I felt something when I touched her." She began to smile. "Someone from the other side, finally! I must know everything!"

"Deidre," Neala said, "it has been too long since we have seen Liam and, while I am curious about that as well, now is not the time. Let them enjoy the day. Liam, I suggest Rooster Rock. It will allow you to reacquaint yourself. And please see me before you leave."

The silver sand of the beach was like fine powder, warm between Ally's toes. "How did they know?" she asked once they'd left the others behind.

Liam rolled up his pants and walked along the water's edge. The waves gently lapped the shore. "Deidre and my aunt can see things through their touch. It is a trait I did not inherit."

"Well, I'm glad about that," she said and smiled nervously. "Hey, is it okay if I put my feet in?"

He laughed. "Would I have brought you here if it was not? But, it might be unlike anything you have ever experienced."

She hitched up her pants and stuck her toe in. It was warm. She stepped forward and bent down. The water trickled between her fingers and, she realized its color had nothing to do with the reflection of the sky. It really was blue-green. It felt oily but, when she lifted her hands, they were dry. She looked at Liam, confused.

"Magic," he whispered.

"Jasmine," she replied and smelled her hand.

"Yes, but be careful, its powers can be quite ... interesting."

He carried her bag as they walked side by side; the beach in front of them stretched out forever. Perspiration glistened on his arms. The thin blond hairs stood out against his tan skin. Even his feet were perfect. *Please, get a grip.*

She forced herself to look forward and, about a half-hour later, he dropped their things in the sand. "This is it."

Rocks of all shapes and sizes littered the beach. One in particular had three jagged edges on top and one to the side.

"Rooster Rock?" she said.

"Aye." He sat on a flat boulder and leaned back on his hands. "Well, you better get started."

She threw him a sarcastic smile. "You know I have no idea what I'm supposed to do."

"I believe you have enough information to figure it out."

She thought about it and pointed at him. "Aha! Tell me, *before* I do this, if I'm wrong." She began to walk into the water and looked over her shoulder. "Nothing's gonna bite me, right?"

"Not unless you want it to."

She glared at him.

"I am only teasing and, yes, you are doing it correctly."

She walked until the water was chest-high. Its warmth felt good and she dropped down, onto her back. It was so dense it took no effort to stay afloat. She pinched her nose and went under and, when she stood, her hair and clothes above the waterline were dry. She laughed. "Gives drip-dry a new meaning, doesn't it?"

He looked out at the lake.

Probably has no idea what I'm talking about, as usual. "Well, these are clean." She sniffed his mother's blouse and her arms. Aromatherapy was fantastic. "Where can I change?"

"You can easily wash the rest of your clothes without having to wear them."

"Yes. It would be easier ... but not nearly as much fun."

He smiled and pointed behind him to a willow on the shore.

"Okay." She stepped through the yellow cloak of branches that hung to the ground. Insects danced in the narrow shafts of light while she slipped out of his mother's clothes and into her filthy jeans and t-shirt.

"Would you care for a sandwich?" Liam asked after she stepped from the lake a second time.

She nodded and sat on the beach beside him. He handed her a cloth napkin that held two thick slices of bread filled with ham and put two brown-glass bottles in the sand. "Beer?" she asked.

"Hardly. Cider."

She took a bite and looked up the beach. "They're different from us, aren't they?"

"They are the Merrows and, in a way, I am one of them."

"Merrows?"

"A unique people who assume a Neptunian form while in the water and a human form when on land. Thea is a Merrow. When my father stumbled upon this place, he met my mother and, although it was unusual, she left the water and married him. I was born two years later. She went into labor during a visit here, but there were complications. To save my life, and hers, she gave birth to me in the lake. The power of the Lake Lorwyn is truly amazing. They continued to frequent this spot as I grew, and I became close with Aunt Neala, Deidre, and her brother Luukas. I loved coming here. Meg was born four years later, at home."

"That's why your eyes are this color and Meg's aren't."

He nodded. "Thea came to live with us twelve years ago, after my grandfather's death. She began to experiment with medicines and potions. When the sickness came … none of the Merrow were affected. But my mother … there was nothing anyone could do."

Ally tried to think of something positive to say but she had nothing. Her father's death had taught her that grief was a private matter.

"My father never forgave himself," Liam went on. "Had she not left the water to be with him, had the magic not left her blood, she might still be alive. I thought if I ignored this place, the pain would disappear. I was wrong." He raised his eyes to hers. "Thank you for accompanying me. It is something I needed to do."

She finished her cider and placed the bottle in the sand beside her. "I wish I could've met your mom. Being here, hearing you talk about her, I know how special she was." She got to her feet. "One more to go. I'll be right back."

Ally put on the last of her dirty clothes … the skirt and blouse *her* mom had bought for the interview. Homesickness threatened to consume her and she ran into the water, swimming hard, trying to stay ahead of it, when something brushed against her leg.

She put her feet under her as a large fish swam past. It turned around and started back. Liam was getting something out of his bag and she was about to scream when Deidre's head appeared beside her.

Ally heaved a sigh of relief. "You nearly gave me a heart attack."

Deidre spit a mouthful of water at her and smiled. "Care to go for a ride?"

"What are you talking about?"

Deidre motioned behind her. Under the water, her body was that of a fish nearly six feet in length. "Get on."

Lost Boy Ride.

"Okay." Ally lifted her skirt, put her leg over Deidre's body and wrapped both arms around her neck.

They began to swim toward the middle of the lake. It gave riding with the dolphins a new meaning … and it was a blast!

A fish swam alongside them and leaped from the water. As he arched through the air, he was in his human form and then, he disappeared into the lake.

"Can we do that?" Ally asked and pointed as he rose into the air again.

"I was hoping you would ask," Deidre shouted. "Hang on!"

Ally held her breath. They went under and up. As they traveled through the air, she was straddling a girl. They reentered the lake but, before she could close her mouth, some water slipped down her throat. It tasted sweet and, once it settled in her stomach, it made her feel … strong. Her thighs gripped Deidre tighter as they headed for the far end. When they reached the other side, a fish swam up from behind.

"Luukas, I thought you would never get here," Deidre said.

The boy smiled. Long blond curls framed a handsome, slender face that reminded her of Liam. "You were lucky," he said.

"I am carrying a passenger; luck has nothing to do with it. I am stronger than you. Admit it."

"I will admit nothing of the sort." He looked at Ally. "Hi, I am Luukas."

"I'm Ally."

"Would you like another chance to prove it?" Deidre asked.

Again, they reached the shore well ahead of Luukas. Ally climbed from Deidre's back and stood in the water.

"Luukas, you will never learn," Liam called out and shook his head.

"Aye, you are correct on that account, cousin," Luukas replied.

"You had good instinct upon my back," Deidre said, and then a bit louder, "almost as good as Liam."

"Thanks," Ally said, "and thanks for the ride." She walked from the water and sat on the sand. Liam was leaning over a piece of paper on the flat rock in front of him, drawing. She sighed and laid back. This day was like a fairytale.

When she opened her eyes and sat up, the sun was no longer overhead. Her throat was dry and, with effort, she got up and walked to the water's edge.

"I would not do that," Liam said, as she scooped up a handful and put it to her lips.

"Why not? I drank some earlier, by accident. It made me feel stronger, that was about it."

He grinned. "Then you should definitely not do that. Among other things, the water is an aphrodisiac. Here." He handed her what was left of his cider.

She took a gulp. It wasn't cold but it was wet.

"I must've fallen asleep," she said, still in shock she'd gone out so easily.

"Yes, you did. We should get ready to leave. The sun will be going down soon."

"Please, wait. I need to remember this." She closed her eyes, and opened them, took in the water's extraordinary color, the purple mountains in the distance, the yellow willows and silver sand ... the strong scent of jasmine ... the laughter of the children ... and again, Liam. She would never think about this place without remembering the boy she'd shared it with.

"I'm ready. I've got it all up here." She pointed to her head.

"Well, just in case you forget." He picked up his sketch and handed it to her. She did little to hide her surprise when she looked at it. He'd captured the entire essence of the day, including her sleeping on the beach. It was done in black and his style, his talent, was unbelievable.

"I could not draw the snoring," he said and smiled. "All my color charcoals are dry. I was lucky to have this one. I hope you like it."

"Like it?" she said. "It's beautiful. Thank you." And, before she could stop herself, she stood on her toes, reached up and put her arms around him. She was about to step back, embarrassed, but he put his hands upon her waist and, for a brief moment, held her tight. *Oh, yeah* ... She looked up, into his eyes, and his arms dropped to his side.

"I think you swallowed more than a mouthful," he said.

"By the way, I don't snore." She rolled up the drawing and picked up her empty bottle. "I would like to take a little of the lake's magic. Is that okay?"

"Yes, but cover it quickly or it will evaporate."

Their walk back was quiet, but the silence wasn't uncomfortable. He certainly was more than she'd ever imagined.

* * *

The children raced down the beach to greet them. "Can we fly kites again, Ally?" Laurel asked.

"I don't know," Ally said and looked at Liam. "Do we have enough time?"

He nodded. "I need to speak to my aunt before we leave."

Ally ran off, the small group close behind, and he wondered who was having more fun as he walked to find Neala.

"Liam, will you and Ally join us for dinner?" Neala asked.

"I have no doubt we would both enjoy staying longer but I would not want to worry Thea."

"How is my mother?"

"She is doing well, given her age."

"Please, tell her I will stop by in a few days." When Thea had left the Merrows, Neala visited on occasion but only once since his mother died.

Neala took his hand. "I want you to know, Ally brings out the best in you."

"Today, she brought out the child in me."

"Sometimes, that is the best part of who we are. She is a long way from home. You need to watch over her, Liam."

Ariana had told him the same. "What do you mean?"

"The doorway into the forest is one that rarely invites a guest. She has found you and, until the reason is clear, you must be careful."

His eyes went to Ally and then back to Neala.

"News of problems in the East has reached our ears," she said. "Deidre is determined to travel that way but knows her place is here for now. However, that might change very soon."

Deidre. Of course she would want to set out and discover what lay in the eastern stakes. Her will was formidable and equally matched by her fortitude. At one time, he had been stronger than his cousin. Now, he was not so sure.

"I love you, Liam," Neala said. She reached out and squeezed his hands. "It is wonderful to have you back."

"You have seen some of my world today. I would like to know more about yours," Liam said after they crossed Patalena's Meadow.

Ally shrugged. "It's not nearly as interesting as this one. Trust me on that."

"I find that hard to believe."

She explained all the devices, all the technology in her world, which made life easy … and yet so complicated. It was hard to imagine. But she had made the transition into his world with relatively little effort. If the situation were reversed, he was not sure he could have done the same.

They rode into the yard before the sun's nightly disappearance.

"I will take care of Chestnut," he said.

"I can do it. Meg showed me how."

"Well, let us see if Meg provided the proper instruction."

She smiled. "You underestimate her … and me."

He kept a watchful eye and was impressed at how competently she put Chestnut up. She even finished before he completed the nightly ritual with Pollux.

Ally placed her saddle on the stand. "Perhaps *you* could use some assistance?"

She was correct in that regard, but she had done more than her share today. "I think I can manage, but thank you … for everything."

Once finished, Liam sprinted up the steps and into the house. He detected the smell of roast pork, unfortunately mingled with the bitter aroma of roots. He walked quietly up behind Thea, who was stirring the source of the pungent smell, and kissed her cheek.

"Oh, Liam!" She turned around and gave him a warm smile. "The light has reentered your eyes."

"That it has." He picked up an apple from the fruit bowl and bit into it loudly. "I think it is safe to say Ally shares my affection for the lake. Where is she?"

"She went to her room."

"Aunt Neala looks well. She will be leaving the lake to pay you a visit."

"Very good. By the way, Olivia stopped by. She was upon Jade and thanked me for the salve. She feels the horse will make a full recovery."

Jade was going to recover? Yesterday he doubted if she would survive the week.

"What did you use, Liam?"

"A remedy I found on your potion shelf. It smelled like a serum."

"Odd. I did not have any left. I used the last of it on Ally. That is what I am preparing now. I just need to acquire some wild root to complete it."

"That is impossible," Liam said.

"If memory serves, a jar of burn ointment has disappeared. If that is the case, whatever helped Jade had nothing to do with me."

"Did you tell Olivia that?"

"I did not feel the need. The horse is better, that is the main thing, is it not?"

"Aye. I suppose it is."

After dinner, Thea ticked off what was needed in town when he and Corm made their weekly trip in the morning. "Tomorrow, I will be up with the sun in search of wild root. This is the only time of year it can be found. I could always use another set of hands. Would you be interested, Ally?"

"Sure," Ally replied. "And oh, if it won't bother anyone, I'd like to go outside and play the fiddle."

A few moments later, the sound of the strings filled his ears. Liam had an idea but wanted it to be a surprise. He grabbed a lantern and slipped into the supply shed. He picked up a leftover plank from the barn repair he undertook last year. Trimmed, it would work nicely. A neatly folded pile of his mother's bed sheets lay on the table in the corner. He smiled. These would be perfect. He picked up the materials and walked to the barn, close enough to hear her play but removed from prying eyes.

The music stopped an hour later and, after he was sure she entered the house, he went to his room and retrieved his last usable piece of charcoal.

Chapter 19

Corm usually arrived early on Wednesday, and Liam was up before the sun. He had just finished in the barn when he spied Ally and Thea walk from the house. Ah yes ... in search of the ever-elusive wild root. Which reminded him: Despite the fact they were out of Thea's salve, Jade had somehow regained her strength and fought the infection. Liam was pleased but something about it bothered him, some connection he was missing.

He walked from the barn as Corm rode into the yard. His friend jumped from the wagon and smiled wide as he greeted Ally and Thea. Given the circumstance, Liam was surprised to see Corm in such high spirits. Perhaps his mother was feeling better. He hurried to catch up with them in the backyard.

"Liam," Corm said, "How does the day find you?"

"Morning, Corm ... Thea ... Ally," Liam said, looking from one to the other, his eyes lingering on the last. "The day finds me well.

Corm turned to Ally. "I would like to hear more about your trip to Lake Lorwyn," he said. "Perhaps you could tell me when I return?" He gave her a warm smile, his eyes full of life, and Liam began to feel uneasy. Corm's upbeat mood might be due to something ... or someone, other than his mother.

"Has Ally remembered anything further?" Corm asked after they traveled a short distance from the house.

"Actually, Thea was able to provide quite a bit of information on the subject. An amazing amount."

Corm whistled under his breath when Liam finished. "The concept is overwhelming, do you not agree? And how is she to find the correct passage that will deliver her to where she belongs?"

"I do not know. We are awaiting word from my father. Apparently, he has knowledge of this. We are the only ones who have been left in the dark."

"There *is* something about her. Can you feel it?"

"Aye," Liam answered, and looked at Corm from the corner of his eye.

"I believe she found your day at the lake extraordinary," Corm said.

"It was." Corm waited for him to go on. Liam had intended to share his feelings for Ally with Corm, but he could not do so now. His best friend liked her. And who could blame him?

Liam told Corm what he wanted to hear instead, and finished as they arrived in town.

They acquired what was needed and rode out to Doc's. They found him in the barn, wrapping the leg of an injured bull. "Liam, I have kept a watchful eye, but there has been no sign of those ruffians since the other day. Have you seen them again?"

"No. I came to ask you the same."

"Well, if I should, I will be prepared." Doc picked up a heavy walking stick.

"Aye," Liam answered, but he doubted if a piece of wood would be sufficient. "I wanted to question you on another matter as well. Pilotte received a poisonous bite. His condition is fine now but, I have to admit, I was very nervous until we drew the venom. I noticed a spider, unique from anything I have ever seen. It appeared to be a combination of a fiddlehead and a wolf spider. Have you come across anything like it?"

"I cannot say I have but I will keep my eyes open. Are you sure you removed all of the venom?"

"Yes, Ally assisted ..." and then the connection he was missing earlier fell into place.

"What is it?" Corm asked.

"I ... am not sure."

* * *

Ally followed Thea along a well-worn path into the dense woods. They each carried a basket and spade. Thea pointed out roots and herbs and, occasionally stopped to pull one from the ground.

They broke from the path where a knee-high stone wall rambled through the woods. A short time later, Thea pointed to a cluster of purple flowers. "Ah, here it is. It never grows in the same location twice and can be quite difficult to find." Thea dug around one of the flowers. "Now, my dear, delicately pull the root. It cannot be separated from the bloom. There will be a bulb at the end."

Ally gingerly tugged and succeeded in extracting an egg-shaped mass from the soil.

"Wild root," Thea whispered and took it from her hand.

"How much of this do you need?"

"Thirty plants should be sufficient."

Ally put the tip of the spade into the soft earth and began to carve out another root. They filled their baskets and, when they returned to the house, Thea showed her how to prepare them for boiling. They were just about done when she heard the wagon pull up outside.

"You are a very quick learner, my dear," Thea said, "and your assistance was invaluable today. These old bones do not always do what I ask of them anymore."

Liam and Corm walked into the kitchen, their arms full.

Ally began untying her apron. "Need help bringing anything in?"

Liam placed two sacks on the counter. "No, thank you."

Corm dropped a small wooden keg on the floor. "When we are done unloading, would you care to take a ride?"

"Sure," Ally replied, and looked from one to the other. "Where do you guys want to go?"

"I need to attend to a few things here," Liam said and walked outside.

"Okay," Ally answered slowly. "Let me just grab a shirt."

She joined Corm in the barn. "I know how to take a saddle off but I'm not sure how to put one on. Can you show me?"

"Of course. This is the most important part of the lesson." Corm straightened the saddle. "If it is too tight, it will bother the horse ... too loose and it will bother you." He demonstrated how to cinch it and attach the bridle and, when he was done, handed her the reins.

They rode through the woods and stopped the horses where a rushing creek cut through the landscape. Corm's eyes sparkled in the water's reflection.

"Tell me about Liam. You're his best friend," Ally said once they dismounted.

"Liam? What is it you would like to know?"

"I don't know. He seems a bit … complicated."

"Why are you asking?"

"Curious, I guess."

"Something tells me you never ask a question without reason."

She didn't answer, and he laughed softly. "*Mmm*, I am a bit naïve."

"You might be a lot of things, but *naïve* isn't one of them," she said.

"I have a blind spot when it comes to certain things. I should have known." He was quiet for a moment. "Let us take a walk."

They stepped on the flat rocks embedded in the shallow water at the creek's edge. "I have known Liam since we were both young. My mother and his were good friends, so we spent much time together. He is smart, compassionate, honest … and a good friend. There is nothing I would not do for him."

"I know he feels the same about you." Ally picked up a flat stone and threw it into the water.

"Lately he is more distant than usual," Corm said. "I know he is eager for his mark to change." He looked at her. "And then, you entered our world."

"Not by choice, believe me. But I want you to know, the two of you will always hold a special place in my heart."

"Speaking of which, I see that Liam fixed your necklace."

"Yes." Ally fingered the silver chain. "It sucks that Caleb broke the one my father gave to my mother. He actually made a matching one for himself that fit into this one. He said his heart wasn't whole without her, and he wore it every day, until he died."

"I now understand why it is so important to you. I am sorry," Corm said.

"Thanks," Ally said and touched the heart, "but that's why I can't lose this. It's one of a kind."

* * *

"Liam," Thea said when he walked into the kitchen, "Ally's stay in this world might not be indefinite. Once we hear from your father, events may be set in motion over which we have no control. Do not live your life with regrets about what might have been."

He thought he had hidden his feelings. "You are right, Thea. I will not allow that to happen." He went to his room and looked at the diamond-shaped piece of cloth on his worktable. The sketch on the cover was nearly finished. The carved spine and spar were fastened together with fishing line, and he had stitched a pocket along each corner of the sail. No regrets. He picked up the kite and shoved it under his bed.

Jade *was* fine. He knew Thea would not lie but needed to see it with his own eyes. "Thea's potion worked," Olivia said. "Thank you." She hesitated. "When I stopped by yesterday, she told me you went to Lake Lorwyn. I am disappointed you did not take me when you finally decided to visit. Why is that?"

"Aside from looking in on Jade, that is why I am here," he said, unsure of how to go on. He shoved his hands into his pockets.

"What is it, Liam?"

"I finally understand the nature of our relationship and I need to be honest. I do not share your feelings. I am sorry. It would be selfish of me not to speak the truth."

"It is that girl."

"This has nothing to do with Ally. I cannot give you the affection you want, what you deserve. It would not be fair to either of us."

She sighed. "I supposed I had already sensed this. Yet I feel closer … more comfortable with you than I do with anyone. I thought that meant something."

"It does. I can always be myself when around you and never have to worry you will not like me because I am not the person *I* always want to be. That means more than you will ever know."

"Can we go back to the way it was then?"

He lifted grateful eyes to hers. "I would like that."

It was dusk when Liam rode into the yard, and he went directly to the barn with Pollux. Curiosity burned within him to know what happened between Corm and Ally, but he was not sure she would tell him, was not sure he even wanted to know. Corm was like a brother, and he could not interfere. He removed Pollux's saddle and began to brush him down.

"Hey, Liam."

He turned around. Ally stood in the doorway and she looked …

beautiful.

"Did you have a nice ride with Corm?" he asked, unable to help himself.

"Yeah, it was a lot of fun."

He stared at her but remained silent.

"Liam, is something wrong? You haven't been the same since you got back from town."

She walked into the barn. Her blue eyes looked into his and his heart raced.

"Have I done something to offend you?" she said.

He found nothing at all about her offensive and, when he began to walk toward her, he did not consider Corm. He did not think about anything other than what his heart was speaking. He stood in front of her, slowly raised his hand and put it upon her cheek. He leaned close. Her breath fell upon his face. He closed his eyes and covered her lips with his own.

And then hers were moving, searching out his, not willing to let them part. Something inside of him, asleep for far too long, awoke. He lifted his head, but she placed her hand on the back of his neck and pulled him closer. The brush, still in his hand, dropped to the floor, and he wrapped his arms around her.

He held her face within his hands and put his mouth over hers. He tasted the sweetness of her breath, felt the softness of her lips and, reluctantly, allowed them to part so he could bury his face in her hair, kiss her neck. It was more than he ever dreamed. It was unbelievable. *It was ...*

"Cool," he whispered in her ear.

* * *

Not exactly the word I would have used.... Ally pulled back and looked into his eyes, trying to catch her breath.

"Liam, Ally, dinner!"

Thea's voice startled them both and she laughed. "Well, that's one way to ruin a moment."

He cupped her face and kissed her forehead. "It is a moment I will never forget."

During dinner, Thea was busy talking about the roots and herbs they'd found today. She and Liam answered her questions but said little else except what transferred through their eyes to one another. She'd known it from the moment she saw him … the boy from her dream. Nothing had ever felt so right and, when their eyes met, she knew he felt the same.

"How about a duet, if you're not too tired?" Ally asked once they finished clearing the table.

"If you are sure you do not mind playing with a novice such as myself," Liam replied. "It has been a while but, because *you* asked? Of course."

He returned with an acoustic guitar as handsome as the fiddle, and she sat beside him while he put it in tune. "Give me a moment." He continued to play with the pegs while the wind howled outside.

"Take your time. I'm not going anywhere." And then, very slowly, she began to smile. For the first time since arriving in this strange place, it wasn't a statement that made her sad.

* * *

Liam walked from the chicken coop, a basket of eggs in his hand. The wind from the previous night brought in dark storm clouds and the morning light was murky. How would he tell Corm about Ally? As his friend rode toward him, he realized the truth was the only place to start.

"I did not expect to see you today," Liam said. "Is everything all right?"

Corm dismounted Lightning. "I have some news for you."

"I need to talk to you as well." Liam shifted his weight from one foot to the other.

Corm held up his hand. "Let me speak first since it was I who rode here at this early hour. I am not sure how much of this was spoken in confidence, so I will relate only what is necessary. There is something compelling about Ally. I have been attracted to her since we first met, but her heart lies with you."

"I am aware of that as well, and I am sorry."

"There is no need to be sorry. I am disappointed, but it was not meant to be," Corm said softly. "But, I need to be honest. There is a bond between she and I, and it is one I cannot ignore. I suspect, given enough time, she and I will become good friends." Corm smiled.

"Now, what is it you wanted to talk to me about?"

Liam returned the smile. "Never mind." Corm followed him inside and watched while he placed four slices of bacon into one skillet, dropped a piece of butter into another, and began to crack the eggs.

Corm sat at the table. "Shane, Ian and Oisin are planning to venture into the forest for a few days to perfect their skills. They want to prepare themselves for the next competition."

Ally walked into the kitchen. "Morning," she said cheerily.

Butterflies invaded Liam's stomach. "Good morning," he answered, turning around, finding it difficult to take his eyes from her.

"Morning, Ally," Corm said and pointed to the stove. "Liam?" The butter had started to burn and smoke began to fill the kitchen.

"You're cooking again?" she asked.

He smiled. "If you can call it that. Please, have a seat." He poured the egg, cream and cheese mixture into the skillet.

"They would like for us to join them," Corm continued.

Liam looked at Corm, confused, and then recalled what they had been discussing. "And what would I concentrate on?" But the question was not accompanied by the bitterness he was accustomed to.

"Moral support?"

The back door opened and Thea walked in. "Liam, your father's bird was with the others this morning." She handed him a piece of paper.

William,

Meet me in Portsmouth at the Davenport Inn in five days' time with our guest. I have learned that her journey home will begin here. Will explain when I see you.

"Portsmouth?" Liam asked.

Ally stood. "Home?"

"Will you be traveling east then?" Corm asked.

Liam closed his eyes. "Aye ... I believe we are."

"Allow me to accompany you, then."

145

His father had knowledge of how Ally could return home? Liam glanced at Thea, but her face revealed nothing. He looked at Ally. She appeared excited by the news. But why should he be surprised? She did not belong here. And she certainly did not belong to him.

"Thank you, but that is not necessary, Corm."

"Aye, but you have no idea what awaits beyond the borders of the forest. Remember what transpired at the gypsy encampment."

That was true. He was not worried about himself, but would not take a chance that might put Ally in danger. "Perhaps you are right."

"I will leave Lightning and fly home to make my parents aware of my intention. I will return with Magic. Another horse will be required to carry supplies," Corm said and hurried out the door.

"Liam, allow me to see your neck," Thea said.

He lifted his hair.

Ally raised her eyebrows. "That's different."

"Come." Thea motioned for Liam to follow her. He walked into her bedroom and looked into the mirror.

His star had changed into the outline of a sword.

Chapter 20

Caleb finally felt a sense of purpose. He was tired of waiting and wanted his worth realized. They would be leaving the safety of the forest with the girl. Once she was in his capable hands, he could dispose of the other two in any manner he chose. The Master would be pleased. He needed to move quickly, but it was going to be too easy. After all, it was only a girl and a boy and a Shayeen hawk.

* * *

Cepheus stared out the window of his chambers. "Maelyn, the boy is weak." He turned to face the witch.

"I was told Caleb must be the one to deliver her. The oracle was clear in that regard." Maelyn stared at him with her right eye. The left was missing, the upper and lower lids stitched together.

"Do you have any idea how long I have been prisoner in this miserable world? How long I have waited? For your sake, I pray you are correct. It would be a pity if you were to lose your sight altogether."

She was his most trusted advisor. Her ability to see the future was more reliable than any other in this world. Her talent at seeing the present had been powerful at one time as well, but that gift had betrayed her. The source of her misinterpreted vision, her right eye, had been removed and found a home, with his other charms, on the locket around his neck. There was no reason to doubt her, she knew what was at stake, but he had sensed Caleb's vulnerability when the boy had been at the lake.

"I loathe the fact my ability to use him, to see through him, has been compromised," he said.

"The forest has always been difficult for you, my lord," Maelyn replied.

"It appears difficult for you as well." She flinched, but he knew she spoke the truth. His sight had always been limited in Gilgamesh but, upon his return from the other world, he could barely glimpse anything, as if the girl was interfering with his powers. He needed what she possessed. The final piece of the puzzle had been revealed and his intent was to simply take it, but that was proving more difficult than he anticipated.

The winds pulled her out of his reach and into the only place he felt … vulnerable. He could not risk entering the forest again, not without consequence. The council was aware of his existence and was preparing to stop him. Not that they possessed the ability or the imagination to do so, but there were forces within the forest that threatened him.

And there was another matter. There was something, recognition perhaps, in the girl's eyes when he approached her on the other side. Had she been forewarned? "Impossible!" Maelyn had told him. "The trinity's alliance is pure. I am confident the others have not betrayed you."

The Chaos in her world had exceeded his expectation, and he longed to linger a bit, but he was powerless there … for now. Soon, the only door that mattered would be unsealed, the one that would allow him to travel across in human form, to transport anything he chose between the two worlds. Then, he would possess what was necessary to destroy the forest and those who threatened him. The girl held the key … of that, he was sure.

"Leave me," he said.

Caleb had to accompany the girl out of the forest, but two of his most powerful warriors would escort her the rest of the way. *Soon, my boy, you will get the reward you deserve.* He sent the thought to Caleb and smiled at the boy's response. Pulling his cape around his shoulders, he descended the tower stairs. He wanted to inform his prisoner that his child was on the way.

Chapter 21

"The sword?" Liam heard how his voice shook with the question.

"What does the sword mean?" Ally asked.

Thea took Liam's hand. "It means that Liam has been blessed with the gift of strategy. That is why he has always been more successful than others from Pembroke in the game of chess. It is one of two traits of the star not often seen."

"The traits ..." Ally said. "Corm mentioned those to me. We studied mythology in junior high. I remember now. The eight qualities deemed vital by the gods. Strength, Shane. Swiftness, Ian. Courage?"

"Oisin," Liam replied.

"Of course. Perception, Corm. Strategy, Liam." Ally continued. "Camouflage and determination. That's all I remember, but that's only seven. What is the eighth?"

"A virtue you possess, my dear," Thea answered. "You are the reason Liam's mark has changed. The eighth trait is inspiration."

Surprise coloring his features, Liam looked at Ally and then to Thea.

"Liam," Thea said, "the feelings inside that Ally has brought to life have made you whole, have made you strong. The passion, which has found life in your soul, has allowed the sword to be revealed."

Thea pulled an envelope from her bureau drawer. "Your father left this for you. He suspected he might not be here on this day."

Liam took it from her hand; saw that it was marked with the Cheveyo family seal. He opened it and read the letter silently:

My Dear Son,

I hope with all of my heart you are well. I am saddened I could not be with you today but my responsibilities dictate my place is elsewhere. Your destiny has come to light and you, and the others who come of age, must do what is necessary to secure a future for the forest. As our time is less each day, the weight you carry increases. You have been given an earthly reward. Bear it well and with honor.

I am indebted to you for assuming the duties of the household in my absence. I know it has not been easy and I apologize for not being there, perhaps when you needed me most. I could never have asked for more.

I give you all the blessings that a good and tender father can give to his son. Your beloved mother and I are proud of you.

Your father,
Jon Cheveyo

Liam put the letter on the bed and his head into his hands. The sword suggested his place might be on the council. Some born with the sword had even taken positions as great statesmen outside the forest. He thought about his father. What had public service done for him? Nothing, except take him away from his family. It was a thankless position and one Liam refused to even think of assuming.

"Why, Thea? Why the sword?" he asked.

"One cannot choose one's destiny, Liam. Your father took his seat upon the council because of your mother, because of his love for the forest. However, it is up to you to determine how to use the gift you have received. But, your first order of business is to travel to your father. Upon your return, we can—"

The front door slammed. "Liam, Thea, Ally!"

What now? Liam rushed from Thea's bedroom and collided with his sister. "Whoa, Meg," he said and put his hands upon her shoulders. "What is the matter and where is Mr. Acrisius?"

"He accompanied me to the gate. I told him I needed to come home right away ... after my journal spoke to me."

"What in heaven's name are you talking about?"

Meg pulled the leather book from her bag and handed it to him. "Read the last entry."

He fumbled with the clasp. "It is locked." She removed the rawhide strip with the small key from around her neck. He opened it, found the page and read the words aloud:

The cat, the hawk, the wolf, the bear,
With Ascencia's blood—the magic rare
And this land's breath—The Malakai
The inspiration from elsewhere.

With The Bumon, his strength, his might
His sword is ready to see the light
The time grows short, they must depart
The forest and beyond their sight.

Vulnerable this six will be
In the days ahead on their journey
No concealment or unremitting body
To carry them to their destiny.

Thea peered at Meg. "Did you write that, dear?"

"No ... I mean yes. The quill was in my hand, but the words flowed to the page on their own."

Thea took the journal from Liam. Her fingers traced the faded "S" engraved on the cover. "Where did you get this at the fair?"

"We were walking along Illusion Alley, and a woman called to me. She had two journals for sale. I preferred the red, but she insisted I purchase the green."

Thea's hands tightened on the book. "The Diaries of Seshat," she whispered. "These were thought to have been destroyed." A smile came to her lips. "The wind was strong last night. Messages were being sent from above ... to you, Meg."

"What do the words mean?" Meg asked. "It mentions the Bumon but I know of no one born with that symbol."

"Your brother now bears the marking of the sword," Thea answered.

"Let me see," Meg said and ran to his side.

Liam lifted his hair.

Meg touched his neck. "Cool! And *'the inspiration from elsewhere'* in the poem? That must be Ally. Are you taking a trip then?"

"Aye," Liam answered. "Ally, Corm and I are traveling to see Dad. He has requested we meet him in Portsmouth. He knows how to return Ally to her world."

"It mentioned the others, I think—Ian, Corm, Oisin and Shane. Are they going as well?" Meg asked.

Liam shook his head. "Perhaps the diary was incorrect on—"

There was a loud knock. "Hello. Is there anyone home?"

Liam opened the door. Shane walked in, followed by Ian and Oisin.

"Ha!" Meg said. "It was right!"

Liam looked at the journal and then back to his friends. "What brings you here?"

"Corm stopped by and declined our invitation into the forest," Oisin said. "He said you three were planning to travel to Portsmouth. So we would like to accompany you, instead."

"Ally, I knew there was something different about you the moment we met," Shane said, "but another world? I had no idea. How amazing!"

"Aye," said Ian. "Corm provided a brief explanation but I have more than a few questions."

"I will do my best to answer them," Thea said. "But, let us wait for Corm to arrive. There have been a few additional ... discoveries since he left."

Once Corm joined them, Thea told of the appearance of Liam's mark, and Meg eagerly shared her experience with the journal.

Shane put his arm around Liam. "The sign of the sword? Impressive."

"Indeed. Congratulations," Ian said.

"Thank you," Liam replied. "And, although the diary has foretold of us journeying together, I do not want you to feel any obligation."

"Liam, surely you are not serious," Oisin said. "I love the forest but I think I can speak for all of us when I say, we are more than ready to adventure beyond its boundaries."

Ian looked over the words again. "Aye, but this mentions we might be vulnerable once we leave. Again, the journal is correct—outside the forest, we can no longer change into our animal counterparts."

"Yes, that is true," Thea said. "You will retain the characteristics you have inherited, but the magic of the transformation lies entirely within Gilgamesh."

Shane held up his fists. "We will not be vulnerable as long as we have these."

Ian shook his head. "Aye, but the diary might help warn of any potential danger, if that is its purpose. If the legend is correct, Thea, the messages are only delivered to the one it has chosen."

Thea nodded her head. "It will only speak to Meg, true. But it has been placed in our hands for a reason."

"Then I need to go, too," Meg said.

"No," Liam answered. "You need to stay here and help maintain the household. Thea could not possibly attend to all the chores on her own."

Thea turned to Corm. "I have an idea."

She and Corm went outside and when they returned Corm was smiling. "Raya and I have made a connection," he said. "She will find our location and deliver any messages Meg receives, regardless of where we are."

A clap of thunder shook the house, followed by the sound of rain on the roof.

"We should delay our departure until that subsides," Oisin said. "It would only slow us, and at this late hour, we would not get far."

The look of disappointment from Ally was obvious but Liam had to agree. "It would be irresponsible to neglect Fate's hand in these matters. We will take our leave in the morning."

"I will sleep in the barn," Shane said after they finished dinner. "Liam, I would like to set up a target to brush up on my archery skills, if you do not mind."

Meg shook her head. "Shane, please do not impale one of the horses."

Shane picked up his bag. "Meg, you disappoint me."

"I will join him," Oisin said. "Something tells me that 'brushing up' might not describe the task at hand."

Ian pulled an armful of books from the bookcase and began to separate them into two piles.

Corm sat beside him. "What are you doing?"

"Research. None of us has ever left the forest. I have done more

153

than a bit of reading, but it would be useful to possess a chart or map to help guide the way."

Liam looked at his friends. All of them were excited, impatient even, to leave. His star had finally changed. Everything he longed for, all his dreams, were beginning to come true. Why was he not happier?

He reached out and took Ally's hand. "Please," he said, and motioned to the ladder that led to his room. "I have something I would like to give you."

* * *

Ally carefully stepped over the last rung. *Wow!* Drawings hung from the walls of his room, some in color, some in black, but all in the same style as the one he'd given her at the lake. "These are amazing."

"Thank you," he replied. "Please, sit down."

She sat on his bed and he reached beneath her feet.

"I made this for you," he said and handed her a piece of cloth. "I thought you might enjoy it. You had so much fun at the lake."

She unfolded the material. "A kite? You made this?" Drawn on the sail was the outline of ... "Is this a butterfly?"

"It began as that, but it is now something more, as you have become to me." He picked up his charcoal and drew a circle above the body. It now resembled an angel.

"I love it," she whispered. "Thank you."

He sat on the bed beside her. She leaned over and kissed him.

"Perhaps I should make something for you every day," he said as he looked into her eyes.

She smiled. "Perhaps you should...." His expression was serious ... sad almost. "What's the matter?"

He took her hand. "I have been waiting my entire life for the star to change. The mark of the sword dictates that the greater good should be one's focus. What if I am not able to do it justice? What if I let my father down, or the others of the forest?"

"You won't. I know that much about you. Don't let pressures of what others expect you to be, change who you are."

"That might be easy, if you were to remain by my side, but ..."

No matter how she tried, he refused to say more than that. When she awoke during the night, his arm was curled protectively around her. They had talked for hours until she fell asleep. He was special. She'd known that from the beginning. She wound her fingers through his and pulled his arm closer. His grip tightened, even in his sleep. She envisioned him making the kite ... tried to imagine his hands creating the delicate treasure.

She and her mom had gone through her dad's study after he died. Inside a shoebox, they found some of the cards and drawings Ally made for him when she was younger. At the time she couldn't understand why he saved them. But now, she knew. There really was nothing as precious as a gift from the heart.

* * *

Liam opened his eyes. His left arm was wrapped around Ally. He held her close, wanting to prolong the moment, wanting to remember the smell of her hair, the softness of her skin, the taste of her lips ... Why was life so complicated?

He kissed the back of her head, reluctantly slipped his arm from around her waist and headed out to the barn, where Shane and Oisin were saddling the horses.

"Top of the morning, Liam," Shane said. "Where are the others?"

"They are still asleep."

Oisin looked at Shane. "Aye, I am certain sleep comes easily when the noises of the barn are absent."

"Oisin," Shane said, "the horses were responsible for the foul noise this morning, not I."

Liam saw the target Shane had constructed on the wall at the far end of the barn. Arrows surrounded the bull's-eye but none were within its center. He walked over and began to remove them. "Did either of you even come close?"

"I could have, if Shane had removed the covering from my eyes," Oisin said.

"You did this blindfolded?'

"Surely you do not think my aim would have been so careless had I been able to see my target?"

Liam *had* actually thought that for a moment, but forgot with whom he was speaking. He was not aware of anyone who possessed greater skill than Oisin with a bow.

Liam handed Oisin the arrows. "How are you able to focus, put the goal in your sights, when the objective is hidden?"

"I do not understand it myself, but it has become a sixth sense."

Liam removed his quiver from the wall. It was blanketed with a layer of dust, a reminder of another interest neglected for far too long. He set an arrow into the bow and focused on the center of the target. When he released it, the arrow hit well to the right of center.

Oisin took the bow and held it to his eyes. "You have some drift. This needs to be adjusted. Bring it, and I will take a look when we stop tonight."

"Corm, it is about time," Shane said, seeing Corm enter the barn. "You slept soundly, eh?'

"That I did," Corm replied. "Liam, I hope you do not mind that I slept in your father's room. It appeared no one was going to sleep there."

Liam felt the color rise to his cheeks. "Ally fell asleep in my bed and I did not want to wake her."

Thea stepped into the barn behind Corm. "Liam, I need a moment. Please come with me."

He followed Thea into the house and to her bedroom. "This belongs to you," she said. On top of the bedclothes was a sword.

He swiveled his head to meet her eyes. "Where did you get this?"

"It was given to your mother. She knew it would benefit you one day. I believe that day is upon us. Deidre brought it to me during the night. It has been called by many names over the centuries, but you know it as the sword of Nuada."

"The sword of Nuada?" Liam pulled the sword from the long metal sheath. It was beautiful. The steel cross guard of the hilt was decorated in red and black; the grip and pommel held intricate carvings. A red jewel was embedded in its center. Carved within the blade was a labyrinth of symbols. He was in awe of it … the way it fit so easily in his hand.

"You will learn how to use it in time," Thea said. "It will serve you well but you must keep it close."

"How did my mother come upon it?"

"It has passed between Ally's world and ours, has fallen into the wrong hands from time to time, but it was delivered here, to

Gilgamesh, before your mother died. She went to great lengths to ensure it was safe until you needed it."

* * *

Ally admired Liam's artwork while she packed her things. His drawings *were* unbelievable, and one sketch caught her attention. It was of his mother, gazing toward the sky. He'd used color and it ... she, was beautiful. As Ally stared at it, the drawing began to move. His mother lowered her head, looked at Ally and smiled.

I'm still half-asleep, that's all. Ally shook her head and closed her eyes. When she opened them, the picture was as she remembered, but she glanced at it from the corner of her eye while she dismantled the frame of the kite and wrapped it inside the sail. She looked around the room, and at the drawing of his mother, one last time. "I'll take care of him. I promise."

Ally stepped down the ladder, and Meg ran in from the kitchen.

"Something smells good," Ally said, putting both feet on the floor.

"Thanks. Breakfast is almost ready." Meg smiled. "I want you to have this." She handed Ally a length of braided string. "It is a friendship bracelet. See, I have one, too." Meg displayed her wrist. "I made it from extra pieces of thread."

"It's great," Ally said, and held out her arm so Meg could tie it to her wrist. "I'll think of you every time I look at it."

"I am going to miss you," Meg said when she finished pulling the ends together.

"Me, too." Ally remembered, not that long ago, wanting desperately to leave here ... to find her way home. In her heart, she sensed this trip might lead to that. *Well, I'm getting my wish.*

So why wasn't she happier?

"Where is everyone?" Ally asked.

"Liam is with Thea in her room and the others are in the barn. Could you tell them breakfast is ready?"

Ally walked into the barn. Ian was kneeling on the floor in front of a piece of paper. "I copied a map I discovered in one of the journals," he said. "It might be outdated, but I determined the distance we could travel each day in conjunction with the towns we will pass through." His finger moved along a bold black line. "These

X's indicate where we can stop for the night. And this is the boundary of the forest." He pointed to a spot almost off the paper.

"So," Ally said, "based on that, how long 'til we get to Portsmouth?"

"Traveling eight hours a day should put us out of the forest in three. Portsmouth is an additional two-day ride from Gilgamesh."

Five days, riding eight hours a day? *Liam better put more than an extra blanket on Chestnut.* She rubbed her face. "Oh, Meg wanted me to tell you breakfast is ready."

"I hope she prepared enough for all of us," Shane said and hurried out of the barn.

Ally helped herself to a plate of pancakes, bacon and fresh fruit and was about to sit down when Liam walked from Thea's bedroom. A sword, concealed within a sheath, hung from a belt around his waist.

Oisin pointed to it with his fork. "New piece?"

"You could say that. It is a gift from my mother," Liam replied.

They stood in the front yard. "I will send Raya when the diary speaks to me," Meg said.

Liam bent his knees to meet her eyes. "Know I am counting on you to help Thea until I return."

Meg put her arms around his neck. "Hurry back," she said and kissed his cheek.

"I will, I promise."

"Thank you, Meg. I'll never forget you," Ally said and wiped her eyes. When she got home, she'd never look at things the same way. And that was good. Now she could really *see* what was around her. She touched her necklace. Dad would have been proud.

Thea took Ally's hands and whispered into her ear, "Safe travels, Malakai."

Ally looked into Thea's eyes. "I've heard that word a few times. What does it mean?"

"Angel, my love, it means angel."

Liam helped Ally mount Chestnut. She held his hand tight, not wanting to let go. She looked at Meg and Thea, closed her eyes and committed their faces to memory. She didn't want to forget because she began to sense she'd never
see either of them again.

Chapter 22

When the group entered Pembroke, Ally and Corm volunteered to go to Stearns' while Liam and the others rode out to Doc's. They found him in the yard, not tending to an animal but kneeling over a bed of flowers, pulling out weeds. "Good to see you again," he said, eyeing the straw hat on Shane's head. "Are you off somewhere?"

"Aye, that is the reason for our visit," Liam answered and dismounted Pollux. "We are headed to Portsmouth. I wanted to ask if you might check in on Meg and Thea if you are out that way."

"I will be glad to. I have to pay a visit to the Brickman's day after tomorrow, and will travel by your house." He got to his feet. "Portsmouth, eh? I have not visited there in a long time. It is quite an interesting town, quite different from Pembroke. Many ships pause in her port as they travel north. There is a lot of activity and not much law, which only adds to the excitement."

Shane nudged Oisin and smiled.

"We are headed to the Davenport Inn," Liam said. "Have you heard of it?"

Doc thought for a moment. "I cannot say I have, but where are you staying before you reach Portsmouth?"

"I determined we could stay in Constance tonight," Ian said, "and then a pause in Exeter and Berwick. Once we leave the forest, Hollis and Fredericksburg."

"Find the veterinarian in any of those towns within the forest. Tell him 'The pig is wearing long johns.'"

Shane laughed. "What does that mean?"

"It means you will secure a warm, dry place for the night."

"Thank you," Liam said. He assumed they would camp and, although the idea did not pose a problem for him, Ally might appreciate a roof over her head. "We will stop in upon our return." Liam extended his hand.

"Ah, none of that," Doc said, and put his arms around him.

As they made their way to Constance, Liam noticed spring was beginning to unwind; the first hints of summer were already in the air. The trees were nearly in bloom and the landscape was ever changing. One moment, enormous cedar trees lined either side of the road creating an archway above. Then the forest would thin out and yield to meadows and fields bursting with wildflowers. Not more than a week ago, he had yearned for his life to change. He thought of Ariana's words: *The Lovers Card ... the strongest of romances.* She also predicted a journey and the sword. It appeared she had been correct in all her prophecies.

"Liam," Ally said quietly, "there's something I've wanted to tell you." She hesitated. "I dreamed about all this. Well, not this," she said and motioned around her, "and I don't mean this figuratively, but literally, I dreamed of *you.* I was being chased by a wolf and, when there was nowhere left to run, no chance of escape, I fell off a cliff."

"It is not exactly the vision I hoped to be in," he said.

She laughed and shook her head. "No. You weren't the one chasing me. You were trying to warn me, to save me. Don't you think it's weird that's how I wound up here? I guess what I'm trying to say is, I don't think any of this was an accident. Did you know this was gonna happen? Did you dream about me?"

"I have always dreamed of finding you—"

"You know what I mean."

He sighed. "No. I did not." But why *was* she here? He no longer believed it was without purpose and, whatever the reason, whatever course Fate planned, he made a promise to keep her safe. Her dream, her vision of him, would stay true.

* * *

They rode into Constance late in the afternoon, and the few townspeople in the street eyed them with curious disinterest. Life definitely traveled slower over here, and Ally liked the change.

Ian climbed off Nyx and walked into the feed and grain store. "The town veterinarian is David Sharpe," he said when he returned. "He lives beyond Constance proper."

On the other side of town, they passed a farmhouse where a group of children ran to the edge of the road.

"Aye, lads," Shane shouted and tipped his hat.

"Is this the house of David Sharpe?" Liam asked.

"He is my dad," one of the boys answered.

"He is my dad, too," another added. They looked identical. Twins, Ally assumed.

The first twin nudged the other. "Go."

The boy returned followed by a tall, thin man. "What can I do for you?" he asked.

Liam jumped off Pollux and extended his hand. "I am William Cheveyo of Pembroke. We are passing through on our way to Portsmouth. Doctor Whitman sends his regards. I was told to inform you 'the pig is wearing long johns.'"

The pig is wearing long johns? Ally tried not to show her surprise. *What the heck is he talking about?*

"Ah," the man replied and visibly relaxed. "David Sharpe. Pleased." He took Liam's hand. "How is Rupert?"

"Rupert?" Shane asked and chuckled.

"The doctor is fine," Liam said. "Let me introduce Ally, Shane, Corm, Ian and Oisin. We are in need of a place to spend the night. Could we put up in your barn?"

"Cheveyo, eh? Related to the Cheveyo in the ministry?" David asked.

"Jon Cheveyo is my father."

"He is a good man. Always looks out for our best interests. Of course you are more than welcome to stay, so long as you do not mind sleeping with a few patients." He pointed to a building behind the house.

"I appreciate it, Mr. Sharpe."

"Call me David, please."

"Are you Shayeen?" one of the twins asked.

"And this is my son, Jack, and my other son, James. Please mind your manners boys. The rest of them do not belong to me, thank goodness."

"Yes," Liam replied, answering the boy's question.

"I will inform Jane there will be a few more for dinner."

"It is not necessary to share your table," Oisin said. "We can prepare a meal if you allow us to build a fire."

"I would not hear of it," David said. "Please, make yourselves comfortable before it gets dark."

"Shayeen!" Jack exclaimed and raced ahead of them. "Tell me what each of you is."

"Let us see if you can guess," Corm replied.

"I have a better idea," Shane said. "Once we get settled, we could show you."

Half of the fourteen stalls in the barn were already occupied. More than a few chickens and at least half a dozen cats scattered before their approaching footsteps. Ally was about to remove her bedroll when David joined them, a pretty woman at his side.

"I would like you to meet my wife, Jane," he said.

"Dinner will be ready in an hour. Do you need anything?" Jane asked.

"No, thank you," they replied at once.

"Ally," Jane said, "it would not be proper for you to sleep out here when we have an extra bed in the house. Please, follow me and I will show you to your room."

Ally smiled at Liam and shrugged. *Sometimes being a girl has its benefits.*

She followed Jane up the stone steps and into the house. The smell of baking bread caused her stomach to growl. She really was going to learn how to cook when she got home. Everything here tasted so much better.

Or, maybe everything in this world *was* better.

Jane stopped in front of a closed door. "We might regret this." She opened it a crack and peeked inside. "Not so bad." They stepped into the bedroom. Toys and clothes littered the floor and Ally smiled. It was nice to know, no matter where you were, some things stayed the same.

"It's great," Ally said, "but where will the boys sleep?"

Jane shook her head. "This is not their room, although you would never know it. We have another son, Gabriel. He is a ... special boy. He has been having terrible nightmares for the past week, so we set up a cot in our room. I am sure he will not mind sleeping with us for one more night."

Nightmares? Ally knew how frightening those could be. She followed Jane into the kitchen. "What have they been about?"

"I do not know," Jane answered. "He ..." A boy, older than the twins, was at the table, hunched over a piece of paper, his face hidden by long curly hair. When Jane gently knocked on the table, the boy lifted eyes that were dark brown and framed with lashes that would have cost a small fortune in her world. The smile that began to form was replaced by a look of surprise and, although he no longer looked at what he was drawing, the pencil in his left hand continued to move.

Jane held out her hand. With effort, he gave her the pencil, and she wrote *Ally* on a blank piece of paper.

When his smile returned, Ally had a feeling that "special" was an understatement. He was beautiful. "Hi," she said.

Jane handed the pencil back to Gabriel. "I do not believe he can hear you. We knew, shortly after he was born, that his hearing was limited. Time has not been a kind companion and I fear it will not be long before silence will be all he can detect. His speech never developed properly so, while he could try to communicate, he chooses not to. He can write well enough, can even read lips when they are in plain view. But, what he lacks in those senses, he makes up for in his ability to see things most of us take for granted. He is quite gifted."

Ally caught a glimpse of what he was drawing. "I can see that."

Jane began to pick potatoes from a basket. "At least today he is not focused on the macabre. His recent artwork has been a bit disturbing."

Ally looked at the drawing. A dark horse was running through a meadow, and Gabriel had captured every detail. Maybe all black horses look the same, but the one in his drawing had an uncanny resemblance to Pollux.

Gabriel walked to the window facing the barn and pointed outside.

"He wants to join the others," Jane said, "and I cannot blame him. It is not often we receive such interesting visitors."

"Can I help you with something?" Ally asked. "I know you didn't plan on cooking for six more tonight."

"We have plenty. I started a stew and it is easy to stretch that further."

"Does Gabriel draw in color?"

Jane laughed. "Oh yes, but, since this is what he does most days, black is all we can afford."

There were some special ed students at Alhambra High but they were never allowed to mainstream. Whenever she saw them walking

163

into school or down the hall, Ally had never gone out of her way to be nice, in fact, she'd probably avoided them. Why?

Because I'd say the wrong thing and hurt their feelings.

She looked at Gabriel and realized that probably wasn't the real reason. More likely it was because they were a reminder of how fragile *she* was. A fact, if given the choice, she preferred to ignore. How sad.

Yes, and how selfish.

"You could do something," Jane said. "Would you mind accompanying Gabe outside? He is eager to meet our guests."

"Sure," Ally said, hoping she was ready to confront her fears.

Jane touched his shoulder, pointed to Ally and then out back. He nodded, put his pencil in his pocket and grabbed some paper from the table.

Ally followed him through the barn doors. "Gabriel, wait up."

What an idiot I am.

She caught up to him and put her hand on his shoulder. He swung around and she held up her finger.

While at Stearns', she had picked up something for Liam, as a surprise. But the gift for him was better shared with another. She reached into her bag and pulled out a set of four colored pencils. She returned the blue and the green, she could still give those to Liam, and handed Gabriel the red and the gold. His eyes widened. She patted her chest and pointed to him.

It was a lame attempt at sign language but he seemed to understand. He hesitated and she nodded. "Please." He took them and bowed. "You're welcome," she said. "Come on."

Within the enclosed riding area, one twin was riding atop a white bear while the other was being chased around by a wolf and a panther. Corm sat on the wooden rail fence, and jumped to his feet when he saw them. "Hi, I'm Corm."

But Gabriel was too engrossed to notice. Ally touched his arm and redirected his attention.

"Corm," she said, enunciating each letter.

Gabriel pointed to Corm's neck and Corm revealed the tiny hawk beneath his ear. Gabriel smiled and looked to the sky.

"Why not?" Corm said. "Once we depart the forest, I will leave this part of me behind." He took a few steps and, in an instant, a hawk was in the air. Gabriel stared intently, his fingers tracing

Corm's every move.

The scene reminded Ally of a circus. All that was missing was the ringmaster. Where *was* Liam?

The sound of an axe from behind answered her question. Liam picked up two pieces of split wood and added them to the pile at his feet. He wiped his forehead with his arm and, when he saw her, leaned the axe against the chopping block.

"I trust the accommodations meet with your approval?" he asked with a smirk.

"Hey, it wouldn't have bothered me to sleep in the barn but, yes, they're fine. As a matter of fact, I'm sleeping in Gabriel's room."

Gabriel's eyes stopped following Corm and fell upon Liam. Liam held out his hand. "I am Liam Cheveyo."

Gabriel raised his eyebrows and grabbed Liam's arm, trying to see his neck. When he saw the sword, his mouth dropped. The pencils and paper fell from his hand and he ran to the house.

"Gabriel, wait!" Ally shouted. She started after him but, when he was safely inside, she returned to the others who were standing around Liam.

"That is quite an effect you have on folks," Shane remarked. "What did you say to him?"

"I did not say anything, although I suspect he would not have heard me," Liam answered.

Gabriel returned a moment later, handed Liam a drawing and knelt on the ground. He picked up a blank piece of paper and began to sketch.

Liam smiled, but it was replaced by a look of confusion as he looked at the picture in his hand. "What the…?"

Ally looked over his shoulder. In the center of the picture was a perfect likeness of Liam, a sword in his hand. A hawk was overhead; a bear, a panther and a wolf stood around him.

"When did he draw this?" Corm asked.

"I'm not sure, but he just met Liam. He just met all of you," Ally said. She sat on the ground next to Gabriel. He was drawing the same picture … almost. But next to the hawk, in the air, he sketched … a likeness of her?

Gabriel pulled a knife from his belt, sharpened the gold pencil, and drew a half dozen lines beginning at her outstretched arms and ending on the ground. With his black pencil, he drew another wolf, but this one was more menacing than Oisin. Long teeth protruded from a mouth that seemed to smile. He sharpened the red pencil and brought the animal to life with two large eyes.

Liam took the drawing from Gabriel and touched the gold lines. "What are these?"

Gabriel pointed to Ally.

"It looks as though you are protecting us," Ian said.

Ally stifled a laugh. "Please."

Gabriel grabbed a blank page and began another. He drew Ally peering into a dense thicket. The ends of the branches looked like snakes and then, he sketched two hands reaching through the bushes, toward her.

"That looks like a Gorgon bush," Ian said. "I have seen pictures but they are not found within the forest."

"Gorgon bush?" Ally asked.

"Yes, they are terribly poisonous. Their thorns can incapacitate with a single scratch."

Gabriel got to his feet and pointed to her neck. Ally stood, pulled back her hair and shook her head. "Uh ... sorry?" He picked up the gold pencil and nodded.

"I think he wants to draw something on you," Oisin said.

"Okay." But Ally doubted if the pencil would leave a mark. It tickled as the tip touched the spot beneath her ear. When he finished, he stood back to admire his work.

"What'd he draw? I can't see it," she said.

"You do not need to. You have seen it before," Liam said.

"What is it?"

"It is identical to what I drew on the kite ... the picture of the angel."

"How could he know about that?"

Liam looked at the first picture. "How could he have drawn this?"

Gabriel pointed to the sword in the drawing. "Aye," Liam finally said and went into the barn. He returned with the sword and, when Gabriel reached for it, Liam put it into his hand. The final rays of sunlight reflected off the blade. Gabriel's lips began to move and he closed his eyes. When he opened them, he handed it back to Liam.

"Were you aware that there is writing etched upon the blade?" Ian asked, watching.

"There were symbols, but I do not recall any words," Liam replied.

Shane leaned closer to see. "What does it say?"

"Take me up," Liam said and turned the blade over. "And, 'Cast me away.'"

"Where did your mother get this?" Ally asked.

Liam's eyes didn't meet hers. "Thea did not say. She only told me it was forged many years ago, and that we would recognize it as the sword of Nuada."

"The sword of Nuada? It cannot be," Oisin whispered.

"No, it can't," Ally said, matter-of-fact. "Those are words written on Excalibur."

"Excalibur?" The sword vibrated when Liam said the word.

"Excalibur was the legendary sword of King Arthur," Ally replied. "You know. The Knights of the Round Table? The Holy Grail?" They all stared at her with blank expressions. "Supposedly, King Arthur was the leader of England back in the fifth century."

"How did this King Arthur come about the sword?" Oisin asked.

Ally squinted, thinking, then remembered. "According to legend, it was given to him by the Lady in the Lake."

"Nuada was thought to be a legend as well," Ian said, his eyes still fixed on the sword.

Chapter 23

"Thank you," Liam said when he finished dinner. "If you will excuse me, I need to attend to something in the barn." He wanted to … needed to hold the sword again. It was as if it were calling to him.

He pulled it from beneath the pile of hay in Pollux's stall and drew it from the sheath. The lack of light made it difficult to see the inscription, but he ran his fingers down the blade and felt the engraving, felt the energy that surged through it.

"That is quite a sword," Oisin said from behind.

Liam turned around. "Hold it. Tell me if you feel anything."

Oisin took the sword and assumed a fencing stance. "What exactly am I supposed to be feeling?"

Perhaps it was his imagination. It was a piece of steel, no different from any other.

"Tell me something, Liam," Oisin said as he continued to spar with his invisible partner. "Do you hope Ally will find her way home?" He handed Liam the sword and took a seat on the dusty floor.

"I am no longer sure of what I want. However, if that is what *she* desires, I will do everything in my power to see she does."

"I have to be honest. I have never looked upon a lass in the same manner you gaze at Ally. And, as true, no woman has looked upon me the way she does you."

Aside from Corm, Liam was unaware their feelings for each other were so obvious. He sat beside Oisin and placed the sword on the floor. "I know, before we met, there was something missing from my life. But now, I feel an inner strength I have never felt before. Does that sound crazy?"

"No, my friend." Oisin chuckled. "That is the way it is supposed to be. I sense, if given more time, I might have found such a bond with Ariana." He rested his elbows on his knees and put his head into his hands. "I have not been able to stop thinking about her."

"Am I interrupting?" Ally asked. She was standing just outside the door.

"Not at all. I am going for a run," Oisin replied. He got to his feet and dashed from the barn. A high-pitched howl followed a few seconds later as he disappeared.

Ally walked to her bag and turned to face him. She smiled mysteriously, both hands behind her back. "I know it's not much. Actually, now it's even less. Pick a hand."

His eyes went back and forth and then, he pointed to the right. She put it in front of her and opened it, revealing a blue and a green pencil.

"I now understand how Gabriel came into possession of such fine colors," he said. "Thank you." He pushed her hair back from her shoulder. The outline of the angel was clear. "He sees you as I do. May I?" he whispered and leaned close.

"Yes."

He put his hand on her cheek. His thumb traced her lips and he kissed them gently, then he took her hand and led her to a pile of hay in the corner.

They sat side by side. "I have been curious about something," he said, his fingers entwined in her hair.

"What would that be?" she replied, a slight lilt in her voice.

"What happened that day when you were in the barn with Jade?"

Ally shook her head. "I'm not really sure. I wanted to help. This might sound silly but … she seemed to beg me to touch her. At first there was nothing, but then my hand was drawn to her leg and some sort of … energy traveled between us. It was difficult to break away. Do you know what I mean?"

Liam nodded. He had felt the same when he held the sword.

"Can I tell you something else?" she said. "The night I touched Pilotte, the night he'd been bitten, it was the same thing."

"I think you helped them both."

She looked at him with skepticism. "I couldn't do that at home. Why would I be able to do it here?"

"Perhaps this world is bringing out the magic in you."

The others entered the barn. Liam stood and helped her to her feet. "I will escort you to the house."

When they reached the kitchen door, he put his hands on her shoulders. "I will say goodnight to you here," he said, and kissed her cheek.

"I don't think so." She stood on her toes, wrapped both arms around his neck and kissed him on the lips. "That's more like it," she whispered.

* * *

The light of dawn was greeted by a rooster's cry and the realization that she was starving. Ally hopped out of bed and walked into the empty kitchen. Another of Gabriel's drawings was on the table. She picked it up and looked at it. Her hunger was replaced by a knot that began to form in her stomach.

Gabriel walked in behind her. She held up the picture and he motioned toward the barn. "I know. It's them," she said. He repeatedly pointed to himself, and then to the drawing. What was he trying to say? She finally gave up. "Okay." She nodded, unsure as to what she was agreeing to. "I'll be right back."

Ally walked into the barn where Corm and Ian were rolling up blankets.

"Where's everyone else?" she asked.

"Outside getting the horses ready," Corm said. "What is the matter?"

Ally handed him the drawing. The sketch was from a low perspective. Gabriel had drawn Ian and Oisin on the ground. She touched the paper. "They look ... hurt." Shane stood between them. In the center of the page, Liam was lying face down, and Gabriel had drawn Ally, on her knees, leaning over him.

"Liam discovered a visitor in the chicken coop this morning, Corm," Shane said from behind.

Corm looked up at him, confused. "What are you talking about?"

"It is Raya," Oisin said, joining Shane. "She arrived during the night. Made herself right at home. She carries a mysterious communication." He handed Ally a small piece of paper. She looked at Corm and then, squinting to decipher the tiny print, read the message aloud.

The silence broken, the voice is new
The message speaks of fortune true
For the mute is cloaked within plain sight
The joining of spirits which he drew.

The mutant next will take a hold
Of hearts and souls, his spirit bold
The kindness shown will be returned
With fortitude, his house will hold.

She turned it over and continued reading.

The betrayed exhibits an unkind heart
But a metamorphosis will start
Hope will lie within his hand
Before his body and soul depart.

Your fate will hinge upon these three
Each intertwined with your destiny.

"The mute, the mutant and the metamorphosis," Oisin said. "Gabriel is the mute, but what does he have to do with our destiny?"

Corm showed Oisin the drawing. "Perhaps more than we think."

Liam walked in and smiled when he saw Ally. "The horses are ready," he said. "Why are you looking at me that way?"

"You need to see this," Oisin said.

Ally and Liam walked into the house together. Gabriel was still in the kitchen by himself. Liam put the drawing on the table and placed three gold coins beside it. "Thank you and your family for your hospitality." He bowed and turned toward the door, but before he could walk away, Gabriel jumped up from his chair, nearly knocking the table over. He grabbed Liam by the arm, patted his own chest and picked up a bag on the floor.

"He wants to come with us," Ally said. Had that been what she agreed to earlier? She closed her eyes, furious for misleading him.

"No." Liam shook his head. "You cannot."

Gabriel nodded, tears of disappointment gleaming in his eyes, and he dropped into the chair.

Liam put his hand under the boy's chin, forcing their eyes to meet. "I will see you upon my return," he said, carefully pronouncing each word. "I promise."

"I have to be honest," Ally said, once they were on the road, "Gabriel's drawing has me a little freaked out."

"Freaked out?" Liam said.

"It's bothering me."

"Aye. It has me freaked out as well then. But we are safe as long as we are in the forest."

"What happens when we leave it?" she asked.

"Then we will need to be on our guard."

That statement got her thinking and she took a deep breath. "Liam, are there guns over here?"

"Guns?"

She let out a heavy sigh. Their worlds were *so* different. Was it possible the weapons that existed in her world hadn't made it over here ... yet?

"My world can be really violent, really immoral at times," she said. "We've developed weapons more powerful and deadly than a sword or a bow and arrow." She pointed with her index finger and cocked her thumb. "We have guns, a firearm that shoots a bullet, a small piece of lead, so fast and so hard it can enter here," she pointed to her chest, "and exit through your back. There's chemical ... and nuclear warfare."

His expression was blank at first then turned to surprise.

"I'm glad you don't know what I'm talking about. The truth is, my world has perfected the art of killing one another."

"You cannot be serious."

"Unfortunately, I am. And I'm starting to worry that if I was able to come over, maybe others have as well. Maybe they've brought those kinds of weapons here. Weapons that make what we have," she said, looking at his sword, "useless."

"It might be a bit selfish of me," he said, "but I pray they remain over there. Your world does not sound like a place I would like to visit. So, please tell me, why are you so eager to return?"

That was a good question based on the little she'd told him. "I don't know. I have to believe things will change. Besides, based on what Thea said, maybe we're not totally to blame." There was also another reason. The most important. "I have to go back. My mom is there, and right now she's alone."

"Aye. That, I understand." Liam smiled. "And you were born in that world. It cannot be all bad."

"It's not. Most people there are good."

"So why have they not done something about it? About the killing of each other?"

"They've tried but ..."

"I find that type of indifference difficult to comprehend."

Corm stopped Lightning and waited for them to catch up. "I have been listening to your conversation but feel guilty about eavesdropping. Do you mind if I join you? This discussion is definitely more interesting than that one." He pointed ahead of them.

Shane was arguing, "A bear will always beat a cat or a wolf!"

"Sure," Ally said and touched the heart around her neck. "My dad actually took an interest in trying to improve things. His job wasn't creating weapons, but helping to protect our country against attacks from others. He worked for the Department of Defense."

"As opposed to the Department of Offense?" Corm said.

She nodded her head but, in reality, they were probably the same thing.

"I was never sure what he did. He was never able to talk about it and then one day, my mom got a call. He was in the hospital. The doctors had never seen a virus like it before. What they did know, what they were sure of, was he didn't have long." She'd never told anyone this and it was harder than she imagined.

"We went into his room and it was difficult for him to talk. It was weird, because I'd just seen him two days before and he was fine. He saw how upset we were and he actually tried to smile. Then he whispered, 'Don't cry. It'll be okay. I did my best to ensure that. I love you both more than you'll ever know.' And then he was gone."

She blinked away the tears and looked at the road ahead of her.

"I am sorry about the loss of your father," Liam said quietly.

"Aye, I am as well," said Corm.

"Thanks. They never figured out what happened but that's why I need to get home. I'm kind of a miracle baby. My mom wasn't supposed to be able to have kids and I know losing us both would destroy her."

Chapter 24

Ally glanced around as they rode into Exeter. It was much larger than Pembroke or Constance, and it felt good to be in a town so full of life. Many small shops lined the main street, but there were also roads to the left and right marked with more stores and houses. Children played in the cobblestone streets while adults stood nearby engaged in conversation.

"Should we seek out the local veterinarian?" Oisin asked.

"I think we should discuss our options over an ale and hot meal," Shane replied.

They found a tavern near the center of town. The sign that hung from the front of the two-story brick building read "The Oar."

When they walked in, Ally noticed that half the tables in the pub were already taken; the other half could seat only four, maybe six comfortably. A bald man with a black handlebar mustache stood behind the bar and waved them in. "I can push two tables together, but with the likes of him," he looked at Shane, "you might want to take the table in the back. Norma," he called to a waitress hurrying by, "show them to the table in the bower."

As they began to move behind Norma, Liam put his hand on Ally's lower back, and a shiver traveled down her spine. *Stop it!* She tried to focus instead on the oars and paddles that were mounted on the wall to the right while they were led to an alcove near the kitchen. Before they reached the table, Ally stopped. "Where's the bathroom?" she whispered to Liam. He pointed back to the bar. *Hallelujah!*

When she exited the restroom five minutes later, Ally felt like a new person. She headed back toward the others but could see only Liam and Corm. The rest were out of view behind a narrow wall. Liam stood and pulled out the chair at the head of the table. "What are we all having?" she asked.

"The lovely Norma will give us her recommendation when she returns," Ian said.

A few moments later, Norma placed a mug in front of each of the boys.

"I am sorry," Liam said. "I did not know what to order for you."

"That's okay. Do you have tea?"

"Best sweet tea this side of Big River," Norma said and flashed a crooked smile.

"That sounds great," Ally replied, but the smile wasn't meant for her.

Norma stared at Corm. "Would you like to hear the specials?"

"What do *you* recommend?" Corm asked in return.

She raised an eyebrow and smiled seductively. "Although it is an acquired taste, the lamb will melt in your mouth."

"Then I will try that," Corm said.

"I believe Norma is taken with you, Corm," Shane said when the waitress was out of earshot.

"Do you think?" Ally replied, stifling a giggle.

"Only if necessary," Shane answered. "But I am curious about something. Do tell, Ally. You are a lass." He ignored the exasperated look from Ian and continued. "Perhaps you could provide insight on this matter. What are women in search of when it comes to romance?"

"Well, that depends on the girl."

"Do you see?" Shane said, and took a drink. "This is exactly what I am talking about. I can never get a straight answer. It is no wonder I have yet to attract the girl of my dreams."

"She has a point, Shane," Oisin said.

"And what do you think they are looking for, my esteemed friend?" Shane asked.

"The same thing we are all in search of," Oisin replied. "Someone who sees and accepts us for who we are."

Shane belched loudly. "Then, perhaps it might take me a while. Though you must admit, in our little corner of the forest, the odds are against the perfect person dropping into your lap. Except for Liam, that is."

"Yes, I am lucky in that respect," Liam said. He took Ally's hand and kissed her cheek.

Wow. He was *so* different from any boy she'd ever met.

"Would you gentlemen care for another pint?" Norma asked on her way back to the kitchen. "Your food should be out in a minute."

Liam and Corm shook their heads, but Oisin, Ian and Shane nodded.

"I take it there's no legal drinking age here," Ally said to no one in particular.

"What do you mean by legal?" Ian asked.

"I mean, where I'm from, you're not allowed to drink until you're twenty-one."

"Twenty-one?" Oisin cried.

"There are a lot of rules meant to protect us … from ourselves, I guess."

"But twenty-one seems a bit much, no?" Oisin said. "I mean, it is not as if someone his age could get a drink." He pointed to a boy bussing a table.

His back was to them, so Ally couldn't tell how old he was, but he looked too young to be working. She was about to add there were also rules about child labor in her world, but bit her tongue.

Norma put plates in front of her, Liam and Corm. "I will be right back," she said.

Ally looked back at the boy. He was placing dirty dishes into a wooden bucket. When he finished, he lifted it with his right hand and straddled it on his hip. The maneuver looked awkward, but she didn't know why. When he turned and shuffled toward them, the answer was clear. He had only one arm.

He couldn't have been more than ten or eleven and was struggling with the weight of the dishes, but his arm wasn't the only disfigurement. The entire left side of his face was covered with scars.

"Get out of the way, Adam," Norma said roughly, as he limped past. He backed against the wall and she placed the remaining dinners on the table. "Can I get you anything else?" she asked, and smiled warmly at Corm.

Corm shook his head in disgust. "No, thank you."

Shane looked up from his plate. "What do you suppose happened to him?"

"Looks like he was in a fire," Oisin replied. "Poor kid."

"He is too young to be working, especially in a place like this," Liam said.

The front door slammed and laughter drifted their way. Three boys walked in and something in their swagger caused Ally to inwardly groan. *Punks.*

The restaurant was almost empty now, and half a dozen tables needed to be cleared. "So where are we going to stay tonight?" Shane asked.

"I have a suggestion," Oisin said. "We could camp outside of town. It is—" He put his nose into the air.

"What is it?" Corm asked.

"I smell trouble," Oisin answered in a low voice.

Ally glanced at the bartender, who eyed the newcomers with a look of annoyance. "Marcus, please, sit at a table that is clean," he said when the boys were about to sit at one still covered with dirty dishes.

"Bernard, is that any way to talk to your best customers?" the boy, Marcus, said loudly. He laughed and looked at his two friends.

"I am simply stating a fact. Sit wherever you like," Bernard replied.

Adam hurried to the front of the restaurant, bucket in hand. He filled it and began to walk toward the kitchen. The three boys looked at each other and grinned. She knew that look, had seen it before, and put her fork down. *Please, let me be wrong.*

Adam moved past the trio, and Ally watched in horror as Marcus put his foot directly in his path. Adam tripped, fell to the floor and the sound of smashing dishes filled the air.

Ally leaped to her feet and rushed to Adam's side. She glared at Marcus. "What are you? An asshole? What's the matter with you?" Adam was trying hard not to cry as he got to his knees and began to pick up the broken pieces. "Let me help you with that," she said.

Marcus squatted beside her, his face inches from her own. "What if I am? What are you going to do about it, bitch?"

"Marcus," one of his friends said in a low but urgent tone. Marcus got to his feet and took a step back.

Ally turned around. Standing behind her were Liam and the others.

"That is not the proper way to address a lady," Liam said, his hands clenched into fists at his side. "Never mind the way you treated this boy. You have a choice. First, and this is not a choice, you will apologize to both of them for your rude behavior. Second, and this is where you do have a decision to make, you can take your leave or

177

deal with me."

One of the boys looked at Shane. "Let us go, Marcus. The food here is only fit for *animals* anyway."

Marcus hesitated and gritted his teeth. "Shayeen trash," he finally said. "You think you are better than the rest of us. Well, you are wrong. I am sorry," he said to Adam and looked at Ally. "You, too." He pushed his friends out of the way, marched through the restaurant and out the front door.

"Are you all right?" Ally asked Adam. She expected to see the boy she'd seen earlier, the one who was on the verge of tears, but instead he was beaming.

"Yeah, I'm okay." His black hair reached his shoulders. The left side of his face was definitely worse than the right. But his brown eyes were full of life.

"Adam, please bring the broken dishes into the kitchen," Bernard said. Adam hoisted the bucket onto his hip and skipped from view.

"It wasn't his fault, you know," Ally said.

Bernard nodded. "I know. It is one thing when Marcus picks on Norma or any of the other help I manage to keep," he said, "but it is with Adam he gets the most pleasure."

"Why don't you just stop him from coming in here?" she asked.

"It is not that simple. His father owns this building and, in turn, my livelihood … a price I must pay to do business. But, if you noticed, I was not going to stop your friends from mopping the floor with them."

"What about Adam?" Liam asked.

"Unfortunate, I have to admit. But I am trying to help him. I gave him a job, a place to live. I cannot babysit as well. He needs to learn how to take care of himself. I have been meaning to seek out another living arrangement. This is no place for a child. Thank you for stepping in today. I would like to offer your meals as a token of my appreciation—" The door opened and two couples walked in. "Excuse me."

Liam helped her to her feet. "You are going to keep me busy, are you not?"

"Well, what would you've done?"

"I was actually about to do the same but could not move quickly enough. It is one of your many qualities that I admire."

One of her many qualities? Please. "I guess you bring out the best in me," she said. "Besides, it's always good to pay it forward."

"Pay it what?"

"*Pay It Forward*. It was a movie where ..." She saw the confused look on his face. "*Argh*, a story where the pictures move. Never mind. The idea is, if you do something good for someone, they in turn will do something good for someone else and so on and so on."

"But what if something bad is done to someone?" Liam asked. "Does that 'pay it forward' as well?"

She'd never thought of it like that, and remembered Adam's eyes. They still had a shine in them. "I hope not."

Adam walked over to the table. "Thanks," he said.

"It does not mean he will not return tomorrow," Shane answered, eating the balance of Corm's meal.

"Nah. His da's back. Don't see too much of him when he's round. Surprised he's here today. Shayeen." He said the word with reverence and looked at Ally. "What're you?"

Corm smiled. "She is our conscience. We should settle up and determine where we are going to camp."

"The meals are compliments of Bernard," Liam said. "It is his way of saying thank you for a situation beyond his control."

"Where you camping?" Adam asked.

"Not sure," Ian said, "Do you have any suggestions?"

"Abandoned farm right outside town. Don't think anyone would mind. Barn would be okay for horses, and there's an open field right behind it, be perfect for camping."

"That does sound ideal," Liam said. "What time are you finished here?"

* * *

Bernard agreed to let Adam camp with them, and he rode on Pollux in front of Liam.

"This horse is something," Adam said. "Can we ride fast?"

Liam grinned. "Oh, yes. Are you ready?"

They sped down the road and reached the barn ahead of the others. Liam dismounted Pollux and lifted Adam from the saddle.

"The barn will work for the horses," Liam said. "They will not mind sharing their quarters with a few mice and bats." He walked through the door, which hung loosely on a well-worn hinge.

"Do you have a tent big enough for all of us?" Adam asked.

The others walked in behind them. "No, and that is probably a good thing," Ian said.

"Who'll I sleep with?"

"Well, you do not want to sleep with Shane," Oisin said. "He snores like a bear and there is no room in his tent for anyone but him."

"You can sleep with me, if you do not mind," Corm said. "My tent is big enough for two."

"Ian," Oisin said, "If you agree to keep me company, I promise to behave like a gentleman."

Ian grinned and shook his head. "It would make sense to pitch as few as possible to get an early start tomorrow. So, if I have your word, I agree."

"Then, I suppose, Ally will join me," Liam said.

Ally smirked. "Taking one for the team, huh Liam?"

"What?"

She shook her head. "Never mind."

They brought the horses to the pasture behind the barn, which was overgrown with smooth brome grass and red clover, and began to remove their belongings. Adam at his side, Liam retrieved his roll and placed it on the ground a short distance from where the others were preparing their sites. "Let us ready the barn before we set this up."

"I'll take care of the tent," Ally said.

"I am not sure that you will—"

"I used to go camping with my dad and a tent is a tent, no matter where you are."

"Please, do not feel—"

"I've got this," she said and held up her hand.

Liam smiled. "As you wish," he said and turned his attention to the barn. Although it was not falling down, he doubted it would survive another harsh winter. It would, though, stand one more night and provide adequate shelter for the horses. Ten large stalls, five on either side, lined the center aisle. The front corner of each was marked by a wrought-iron post which held a swinging door. The lower half was made of wood, the top half constructed with metal bars with an opening in the middle that allowed the horses to hang their heads outside their confinement. Whoever built this had spared no expense.

"What you think?" Adam asked.

"I think it will be fine. To whom does this barn belong?"

"Don't know. Has been here as long as I remember, and has always been empty."

Liam whistled for Pollux, who lifted his head and began to walk in their direction, followed by the other horses.

"How you do that?" Adam asked.

"Magic," Liam replied and grinned. "We can bring that hay over for bedding," he said, spotting a pile in the far corner, and pointed to four buckets on the floor. "And they will have to share, but we can use those for water. Do you know how to take a saddle off a horse?"

"Nah, never had a horse," Adam replied and stroked Pollux's nose.

"I am going to show you then."

Liam pulled at the cinch. "I will hold this. Now, unhook the clasp." Adam reached under Pollux and released it with little effort. "You are strong."

"Do everything with this arm," Adam replied matter-of-factly.

Liam lifted the saddle from Pollux and placed it over Adam's outstretched arm. "There is a saddle rack over there," he said and pointed to the stand just inside the back door.   Liam peeked out at Ally. She had properly unfolded the tent and was attempting to secure the corner stakes. Why was he so surprised? Of course, she would be capable of setting up a tent.

"Why are you living with Bernard?" Liam asked.

"Got no parents. Mr. Bernard's been takin' care of me for a while now," Adam replied. He returned empty handed and nuzzled up to Pollux.

"He likes you," Liam said. Pollux *was* an amazing animal but could be a bit unpredictable with strangers. However, he showed no sign of it with Adam.

"How long has Marcus been picking on you?"

"Long time. Got used to it, just don't like it."

Liam had been miserable not more than a week ago, but now understood he had no idea of the word's meaning. He had family that loved him, friends that supported him ... not to mention all of his limbs, and he felt the need to, as Ally said, pay it forward.

"I have a suggestion. When we are done here, we could give you instruction on how to protect yourself." But he was actually thinking of a different way in which to help Adam.

They finished with the horses and began to carry hay to the stalls. "Liam, look what I found," Adam said after half a dozen trips. In his hand was a quiver.

As Liam examined it, he realized it looked older than the barn. The leather was so dry, he was afraid it might crack and disintegrate if not handled properly, and inside were eight timeworn arrows.

"Can you use 'em?" Adam asked.

"Oisin is the archer among us."

"Can I give it to him then?"

Liam doubted whether the arrows would withstand being pulled in a bow, but also knew it did not matter. "I think he would be happy to accept them."

"Oisin! I have something for you," Adam shouted as he ran from the barn. Liam followed him outside. Ally had properly set the tent. It had taken him numerous attempts the first time, while his father shouted instruction, before he was able to do it correctly.

"You continue to amaze me," he said.

"It should be okay as long as the wind doesn't pick up," she replied. "Otherwise it might fall down. You guys haven't discovered pop-ups yet, I see."

"Pop-ups?"

She smiled and shook her head. "Never mind."

Oisin gently removed the arrows from the quiver. "I am afraid this will no longer serve its purpose, but one can never have too many arrows. I will place these with my own. Thank you."

"I told Adam we would give him a lesson in self-defense," Liam said.

Shane got to his feet. "I believe Ally could give him some instruction in that regard. I remember a move she executed not too long ago."

"What was that?" Adam asked.

"I kicked someone," Ally replied.

"So?"

"I kicked him right there," she said and pointed between Adam's legs.

"*Ow!*" he said. "What he do?"

"He went down rather quickly," Ian answered.

"Remember, he also got up rather quickly," Ally added.

"Who was he?" Adam asked.

Oisin spit the piece of the grass he was chewing on the ground. "Someone we met in a rather unpleasant circumstance."

"And someone who, I am certain, will always remember Ally," Shane said with a laugh.

Chapter 25

Caleb easily found the ruins the Master described, less than a kilometer beyond the forest. His task did not require great effort. He was on his hands and knees, familiarizing himself with the tunnels and committing the passages to memory. It was dark and damp, but he was at ease with his surroundings. He would rest for a while. And then what? He was not sure but the unknown was not cause for concern. These types of situations always worked themselves out.

Caleb was born in Riddlesby, a hamlet located within the forest, and was the eldest of three. His father disappeared when he was thirteen and, although his mother tried, she could not accept life's challenges on her own. Her attempts to find the perfect mate resulted in attracting men who saw her as she saw herself, with little worth. Once they realized the effort of raising three children, each man vanished, leaving her with unanswered questions and broken promises.

He was sixteen when he discovered he carried the power of the Araneae, the ability to change into a spider. It was not long before he put that talent to use.

One afternoon, he returned home to find his mother on the front steps of their rundown cottage. Her eyes were red from crying. Her lower lip was split and bleeding; a purple bruise was visible on her cheek.

Caleb ran into the house and found his brothers hiding in a corner of the bedroom they shared. "Where is he?"

His youngest brother pointed to the outbuilding behind the house. When Caleb peered through its window, he saw his mother's most recent suitor, at the workbench, a bottle of spirits in his hand. Caleb's repulsion and anger grew with each passing second. He changed into his spider form and crept in, unnoticed. He climbed up the man's pant leg and then to his neck, where he planted his fangs and released the venom.

Caleb crawled to the floor and watched the man's discomfort grow. When he changed into his human form, the shock upon the man's face quickly changed to something else: fear, as Caleb picked up a spade from the room's corner and raised it over his head.

The gratitude he expected from his mother never materialized. In fact, she seemed afraid of him, and soon, her familiar pattern reestablished itself. He considered leaving home but knew his brothers needed his protection. So he spent more and more time alone … and lonely.

One day, while picking through the trash behind the local tavern, looking for food, he heard someone whisper his name. He turned to see a peculiar-looking man. He smiled at Caleb but his dark eyes contained no warmth. They were lined with deep creases and set into a face the color of burnt wheat; black hair reached the middle of his back. His white shirt and black pants were made of fine materials, the stitching intricate.

"Come. Let us share a meal, Caleb," the man said and held out his hand. "It appears you are in need of a good meal and some sympathetic company." The nails on his fingers were long and dark, claw-like.

How did this stranger know his name? Did it matter? He was hungry, and could not remember the last time his mother cooked anything other than soup. Caleb nodded and, together, they walked into the pub.

"Order whatever pleases you. A boy who has been through as much as you deserves it." The waitress walked to their table and, when the man raised his eyes, she took a step back.

"Bring us a couple of pints," he ordered. "May I suggest the lamb?" he said to Caleb. "I understand it is simply divine."

Caleb nodded.

They sat in silence until the server returned with their ale. "A toast," the man said and held up his glass, "to new friends."

Caleb raised his in return and took a sip. The taste was bitter.

The man eyed him for a moment. "I understand you have a special talent."

Caleb lifted his eyes, confused. "I do not know what you are talking about."

"I think you do. You have the passion to stand against those who threaten the ones you love, regardless of the consequence."

How could this man know about that?

"Do not be concerned. Your secret is safe with me, Caleb. Others might not appreciate what you did, but I do. I travel great distances in search of those who possess a spirit such as yours. Is it not unfair that the more fortunate, the more powerful, take advantage of you? Why is it you struggle to have food on your table, while others toss theirs away? Why is it so difficult for you to survive?

"I will tell you the answer," he said and leaned close, his voice barely a whisper. "Because they have taken your voice, have stolen your hope. They think you will not fight to regain what is yours. They are wrong. The situation in this world is becoming desperate. When the prophecies are fulfilled and the lines are drawn, you must decide on which side you will stand."

Caleb could barely breathe. "How do you know these things? How do you know about me?"

"I have been given a special gift from the gods. And I cannot ignore their message when someone as important as you is shown to me. I possess great magic and soon, great power. I promise you this: Once I have what I need, you will be richer than you ever imagined. You will be able to care for your family in the proper manner. The time for the change will soon be upon us. Tell me, Caleb ..." He looked him directly in the eye. "What did it feel like when *you* transformed?"

Caleb was uncertain if he was referring to his spider counterpart, or the killer within that had recently been revealed. "I became something more than what I am. Something more powerful," he said, answering both.

"Smart boy. After you finish your meal, I would like you to accompany me as I travel east and join with the forces that will change this world forever. All I ask in return is your loyalty. A small price to make all your dreams come true, no?" He smiled. A cold smile.

"I would like to," Caleb replied. "But my family ... my brothers need me."

"I will see to it personally your family is taken care of. You have my word."

"If you can promise me that, I agree."

"It is settled then."

"I just need to go home and pack my things."

"Time is important, my boy. We need to depart immediately. I will provide all you require."

"I should say goodbye so they know where I am."

"I fear your mother, yet again, would not have your best interests at heart. I will send a message to make her aware of your intention."

Caleb nodded. Of courses he would leave his family for a short time, especially for a cause as worthy as this. Perhaps he would finally be appreciated, be accepted. And he knew, at that moment, he would have done anything this man asked him to.

* * *

The fire was nearly out and she leaned over the hearth. Where was Caleb? He should be doing this.

"Boys!" she called to her youngest sons. "Bring some wood."

They ran in, each carrying a bundle of dry sticks. They tossed them into the fireplace and she blew on the cinders trying to create a spark, but succeeded only in displacing the ashes in the firebox. She closed her eyes against the swirling soot. When she opened them, the embers had caught and the flames reached toward her. She stepped back, spun around and tripped over the boys, falling to the floor, trapping them beneath her. The fiery blaze licked at her clothing. She struggled to get to her feet but an unseen hand held her down. She turned her head to look at the fire. Where was Caleb?

"He is with me." The voice came from the hearth. "And sends his warmest regards."

* * *

Caleb was given his own room within the castle but Crooks, as it was called, was actually a fortress that loomed above the mountainous terrain. There was only one approach road, and it was nearly impossible for anyone to reach the castle undetected. How it came to be or who was responsible for its construction was a mystery, but it had been no easy feat. To reach the entrance, one had to maneuver through a complex labyrinth of bridges erected over deep pits. He was certain the desperate wailing that reached his ears when he traveled across those catwalks would haunt him to the grave.

From time to time, the castle's inhabitants, traitors, he was told, disappeared and Caleb suspected they had discovered the horror that lay beneath. He hoped, for their sake, the fall had killed them before they met what lurked in the darkness.

His days were spent perfecting his skills and watching others display theirs. There were many at the castle like him, but also those who possessed far greater powers. He watched with fascination as great warriors defeated men and beasts twice their size. Some relied only on their hands, while others used strange weapons, but he was most captivated by those who used magic: a black magic more powerful than anything he imagined.

When he was finally summoned to the Master's private chambers, he was delighted.

"You have been specifically chosen for an important task, Caleb," the Master's witch said, her one eye staring at him with intensity. "Your success is crucial to our future. You must not fail."

Where is the Master?

"He is not able to join us at the present time," she said, reading his thoughts. "I am speaking on his behalf. You need to journey to the forest of Gilgamesh and retrieve a valuable object. The Master has risked much to secure it but, despite all the gifts the gods have bestowed upon him, the dark forces within the forest prevent him from doing this himself. Are you ready for your worth to be realized?"

"Of course," Caleb said without hesitation.

"Good." The witch smiled. "He cannot accompany you, but requests to be with you, here," she pointed to her eye, "to protect you: to ensure you do not fall victim to the evil consuming Gilgamesh. It is a special honor extended to few. It will hurt a bit, but you would do this for him, would you not?"

"Anything," Caleb agreed but, he soon found out, it hurt more than a bit.

The tattoos on his face and arms were the result of challenges successfully completed. They were a symbol of status and rank and, like war paint, he displayed them proudly. The process was uncomfortable but the time for them to heal was quick. His eyes were a different matter. When the tip of the dagger touched his pupil, he lost consciousness and, when he woke, his vision was swimming in red, as if he opened his eyes in a bloody pool. Maelyn had used the

Master's blood to mark his eyes, and Caleb felt the difference, the power, immediately.

He stopped reflecting on the past and returned to the task at hand. The Master needed the girl. *She holds the key to our future, Caleb. You need to bring her to me. Once I have what I need, you can do with her what you wish.*

After the humiliation at the gypsy tent, he looked forward to that.

Chapter 26

"Let us move beyond Ally's method of self-defense," Oisin said. "If the situation presents itself, you already know how to do that." He leaped to his feet and shuffled from side to side, his arms out in front of him.

Liam pulled Shane aside. "Bernard told me he was seeking an alternative living arrangement for Adam. I would like to offer him the opportunity to live with us— well, with Thea and Meg for now. He needs a more stable environment, someone to look after him. Bernard is not able to do that while running his business. When Raya arrives again, I will send a note making Thea aware of my intentions, but I need someone to accompany him to Pembroke."

"Ask Thea to communicate with my family," Shane said. "Brian and Joseph would not let an opportunity to travel to Exeter escape them, especially given the circumstance."

"Thank you." Although neither of Shane's older brothers was born with the mark, they were large, and quite capable of delivering Adam safely to Pembroke. Yet before speaking with Bernard, Liam needed to ensure Adam was agreeable to the idea.

* * *

"Before it gets too dark," Ally said, "you need a bath."

"Really?" Oisin replied. "I did not think I smelled that foul."

"Not you," she said exasperated, and looked at Adam. "You."

"She does have a point, buddy," Shane said. "Allow me to accompany you to the stream."

"I'd rather have Ally," Adam said, glancing at what remained of his left arm.

Was he embarrassed that the boys would see the extent of his scars?

"Must be something about your maternal nature," Ian said.

Maybe, but the reason didn't really matter. "Let me grab my bag and we'll take a walk," Ally said.

At the edge of the stream, Adam removed his shoes, socks and shirt and put his toe into the water. She pulled the lavender soap from her bag and handed it to him. "Go ahead. I'll turn around."

"It smells girly," Adam said.

"There are worse things you could smell like," she said. "Did you get a whiff of Shane?"

Adam laughed, and before Ally turned away, she saw the stump that had once been his arm, the burns that covered most of his body. And the words in Meg's note occurred to her: *The mutant next will take a hold, of hearts and souls, his spirit bold.* She couldn't remember the rest but, was Adam the mutant? If so, the predictions were coming true ... again.

She heard splashing sounds, and said, "What happened to your arm, if you don't mind me asking?"

"Don't mind. House caught on fire. The rest of my family didn't make it. By the time they found me ... they had to cut off my arm to save my life. Mister Bernard took me in."

"I'm sorry it's been so hard for you—"

She saw Liam pushing his way through the brush, a shirt in his hand. "Aye, I am sorry about that as well," he said. "But I would like to change that. How would you feel about moving to Pembroke, with me and my family? I am headed beyond the forest right now, and my sister and our grandmother could use your help until I return."

The splashing stopped. "Ally, you be coming back, too?"

"No," she replied.

"Why not?"

"Liam, can I talk to Adam alone?"

He tossed the shirt to her. "Sure. It might be big, but at least it is clean."

"I think you'll like living at Liam's," she said when they were alone. "They took me in when I needed a place to stay, so I can tell you they're really nice. His sister, Meg, is terrific and his grandmother is amazing."

"What about you?"

"Liam is helping me get home and, once there, I'm not sure if I'll be able to come back."

"Why not?"

"Because it's really far away and ... no matter how much I like it here, it's not where I belong. I miss my family."

"Know how that feels."

"So what do you think?"

"I think this is the best day of my life! I'm ready for a towel."

She held her towel, along with Liam's shirt, behind her back.

"Done," he said a few minutes later.

She turned around and eyed him from head to toe. "You look really handsome in Liam's shirt."

"Really? Well maybe except for this." He held up his empty left sleeve.

"Let me roll that up."

"I can't wait to go to Liam's, but I'm afraid."

"Afraid?"

"What if my brother comes lookin' for me? He won't know where I am."

"I thought your family died in the fire."

"They did, but I have another brother. He went missing before it happened. Don't remember much about him now. There's one thing, though. He never thought I knew, but I saw. He could change, like the rest of 'em." He pointed to the field. "Except he changed into a spider."

"Well, Bernard could tell him where you are if he shows up." Ally picked up Adam's shirt and placed it inside her bag. "What's your brother's name?"

"Come on, Adam!" Shane shouted. "The sun is going down."

Adam turned and began to run back toward the others.

"Hey, what's his name?" Ally asked again.

"Caleb!" Adam called over his shoulder.

* * *

Adam's laughter reached Ally's ears and Liam put his arm around her. "Whatever you did made him very happy."

Ally shook her head. "It's what you did that made him happy. I just insisted on a little soap and water."

"Speaking of which." Liam pinched his nose.

She gently pushed him away. "Oh, stop. I'll jump in tomorrow before we leave. I'm sure we'll be up at the crack of dawn."

Liam smiled. "There is nothing wrong with rising with the sun," he said. "Was Adam agreeable to the idea?"

"He is, but I can't believe you're willing to do that for him."

"I am sure you would do the same, if given the opportunity."

"I would, but things are really complicated where I come from. There's this thing called Child Protective Services and— Oh, forget it. I know he's excited, but he's nervous. He told me something quite interest—"

Adam ran over and pulled her arm. "We're gonna tell stories and look at the stars. Come on."

Moments later, they were all on their backs in a circle. The sun had set and the stars were bright overhead.

"It is an exceptionally clear night," Ian said. "I cannot see a cloud anywhere." He pointed out the constellations and told the stories surrounding their origin. Liam found her hand and held it. At some point, she looked over to see Adam asleep.

"We should put him to bed," she whispered.

"I will take care of that," Shane said and picked him up. "I am ready as well. I will see you in the morning."

Oisin got to his feet. "I am right behind you."

"Actually, I'm going to bed too," Ally said, and removed her hand from Liam's. "Have to be up early and take that bath. Good night." She leaned over and kissed Liam's cheek.

"I will be there in a moment," Liam said. "I need to discuss something with Ian and Corm."

She crawled into the tent. Two sets of blankets were side by side. Liam must have laid them out earlier and she began to feel a little nervous. She knew he would act like a perfect gentleman, but ... was that what she really wanted?

Before Liam, there'd been only one boy in her life. She and Scott had started off as friends, but that progressed to holding hands and a strong shoulder to rest her head on during a pair of slow dances at the last homecoming event. And then his father had accepted a job in Cincinnati. End of story. Would this end just as abruptly?

Twenty minutes later, Liam entered the tent, crawled in beside her and saw she was awake. "I hope I am doing the right thing with Adam."

"You're giving him a chance, more than what he has here. By

the way, I found out what happened with his arm."

She relayed what Adam had told her. "And there's something else. He has another brother, one who didn't die in the fire. You'll never guess what his name is."

"If I will never guess, then I will not try."

"Ha, ha. It's Caleb. You don't think it's the same person, do you?"

"Caleb is not an uncommon name and two people *are* allowed to have the same one in this world."

"Really," she said, rolling her eyes. "He also told me Caleb could change like you guys, but his twin is a spider. Meg and I saw a weird one at Olivia's, and then you saw one at your house. I think it was the same spider that showed up while I was taking a bath that morning. You said you'd never seen one like it. I was honestly beginning to think it was following me around."

His face showed its first uncertainty. "Perhaps your theory holds merit."

"I know, right?" She propped herself up on her left elbow. "Liam, why do you think I'm here?"

He sat up and wound his fingers through hers. "Among other things, you are making my somewhat meaningless life, complete." He hesitated. "Although we have never shared the same world, the same reality, it is clear we share the same soul. There is a bond between us I cannot deny." He brought her hand to his lips.

"Oh," she said softly and exhaled. *My god. Scott who?* It was then she knew. She'd never met anyone like him before … nor would she ever again. She gently pushed him to his back, her breath coming in shallow gasps. His arms were around her and, with the help of the moon, she looked into his eyes. He was … beautiful and she covered his face with tender kisses.

* * *

He caressed her back while she kissed his cheek, his ear, his neck. When she looked down upon him, he reached for her, his tongue tracing the outline of her lips, sweeter than any fruit he had ever tasted, and he yearned for her to be closer. He moved on top of her, his weight on his hands, and he stared at her with such longing, it hurt.

194

He slowly lowered his body. His heart exploded in his chest while her touch sent shivers throughout his body. She lifted her head so that their lips could meet again.

"You are bringing out feelings I never knew I could possess," he said. "Feelings, I am afraid, are without control." He rolled off her, onto his side. His fingers trembled as he touched her face. She untied the leather strip that held his hair; it fell loose to his shoulders. He closed his eyes and wrapped his arms around her.

"Can I ask you something?" he finally said.

She nodded.

"I was wondering if, in your world, you have a beau or sweetheart."

She laughed. "I did once, but he moved away. Long-distance relationships never work. And, even if I had a boyfriend before, I wouldn't now … not after meeting you. And speaking of past romances, you never told me what happened between you and Olivia."

He felt the corner of his mouth turn up.

"Oh yeah, I'm going there," she said.

"Honestly? When I met you, I felt something very different than I ever experienced with Olivia, even before I knew you well." He took her hand. "This," he said, "is how it is supposed to feel. Do you not agree?"

"Yes."

How far did her 'boyfriend' move to cause the relationship to fall apart? Certainly not the distance they would be from each other if she found her way home. If possible, would he go with her? Not if it meant leaving his family behind. She felt the same, and he did not blame her. Theirs was a hopeless situation. His arms tightened around her. He had never felt so happy and, at the same time, so scared in his life.

* * *

Adam walked into the house with his brother. They threw the sticks into the hearth. His mother leaned over the fire, trying to get it started.

The kindling caught; flames leaped out at them. His mother tripped and fell. He smelled something burning and realized it was

195

her clothes… her. She would not get off them and he struggled to free himself. She was smothering him and screaming, and then … she stopped. But he could still smell the fire.

Adam opened his eyes. This was not the first time he dreamed about that day, but this time it seemed so … so *real*. He sat up. Corm was asleep beside him. Yes, just a dream. As he lay back down, he took a deep breath. His eyes flew open.

"Fire!" he yelled and shook Corm. "Fire, Corm, Fire!"

Chapter 27

"Fire!" Corm yelled from outside. "Sweet mother of Athena! Wake up! Fire!" he screamed. Liam threw on his boots, scrambled from the tent, and saw the barn consumed in flame. Corm had ripped his shirt off and was using it to pull the door open. Dense smoke billowed through, struggling to make its escape. The horses whinnied from inside and Corm rushed into the burning building.

Liam followed, but paused after crossing the threshold. The light from the fire was bright but the thick smoke burned his eyes, rendering him blind. He took a deep breath, but the acrid fumes filled his lungs and he began to choke.

Breathe slowly, calm down. You will not be able to help Corm free the horses if you cannot focus.

He cleared the panic from his consciousness and visualized the barn's interior. If he could not use his eyes, he would use his mind to set him in the proper direction.

"Liam, I cannot open the stalls!" Corm cried.

"They are secured with a latch. Lift it and slide it to the left. Three of the horses are on the right. Take care of them, I will free the others!"

"Liam! Corm!" Shane's voice exploded from behind.

"Do not come in! Corm and I can handle it." Liam raised his arm to shield his face. "Round them up when we send them out!"

"Ian and Oisin can do that. I will get the saddles!"

Liam made his way deeper into the inferno. *Should be ten steps in this direction.* He had counted off eight when he tripped over something on the floor, something that had not been there earlier. His foot dropped heavily as he attempted to regain his balance. "What the—?"

"Help," a voice gasped.

"Corm?" Liam fell to his knees.

"Over here, Liam! Once I free them, I pray they have enough sense to do the rest!"

If Corm was near the horses, then who was this?

He leaned close to the floor and made out a familiar face: Marcus, the boy from the pub.

Liam's only thought had been to save the horses but, as he looked upon Marcus, he felt sick. This fire had not started without intention.

"Help me, it got out of control, could not find my way out," Marcus mumbled.

"*He-ya!*" Corm yelled. Chestnut bolted past only inches away. "*Ahhhhh!*" Marcus screamed as his legs were trampled under the fleeing horse. Liam pulled him out of the way, only seconds before Beowulf and Lightning raced by.

"Liam, where are you?" Corm said. "Are you all right?"

"Aye! That was not me. Free the others!"

"Get out!" Corm shouted. The floor trembled beneath Liam as two more horses fought to be free of this nightmare. Was one of them Pollux?

"Pollux!" Corm screamed.

Apparently not. Liam tried to whistle, but a whisper was all that escaped. He struggled to see his horse but could not.

"Please. I do not want to die," Marcus said. "We need to get out of here *now*."

The fire had started in the front of the barn but was quickly moving to the back, and it would not be long before it surrounded them. "Pollux," Liam said softly.

"Adam!" Ally cried from outside. Her voice gave him strength. He looked to the fire and then to the floor, and made a heart-wrenching decision.

"You son of a bitch," Liam said. He put his arms under Marcus and, balancing the boy's weight in his arms, stood carefully. Nyx bolted past, nearly knocking them both over. He followed the sound of horse's hooves, toward what he hoped was the door.

"Corm! Forget Pollux!" Something crashed to the floor behind him. It was a beam that had supported the loft. Soon, the entire building would collapse.

"Corm! Get out now!" He stepped forward, and finally felt rain upon his face.

Shane took Marcus from his arms. "What the hell was he doing in there?" he asked, and placed him on the ground a short distance away. Despite the rain, sparks flew through the air like manic fireflies.

Liam ignored the question and began to stagger toward the barn, but stopped as his legs threatened to betray him. Oisin grabbed him by the arm. "Where do you think you are going?"

"I need … get Corm," Liam answered. He tried to free himself from Oisin's hold but the earth began to sway and he fell to his knees.

"I will get him," Shane said. "I thought you said you two were all right." He started in the direction of the burning barn and was nearly at its door when Corm ran into him.

"Corm!" Shane put an arm around his shoulder and led him away.

Corm wiped tears that filled his eyes and said through choked breaths, "I could not get him, Liam. He was not in the stall. He got free of it somehow. I tried, but he kept backing away from me." He put his hands on his knees, lowered his head and gagged.

Liam looked at Marcus, saw him dragging himself away from the barn, his eyes wide, as if fearful the flames would reach out and pull him back inside.

"Pollux!" Adam shouted from a distance.

Liam looked around for Adam. *His voice cannot be coming from*
…

A horrible truth descended upon him. "Where are Adam and Ally?" he screamed.

* * *

Standing outside the tent, Ally stared at the barn, at the flames that were about to engulf it. Dark smoke filled the sky. *The horses!*

Seeming to make the same connection, Adam began to run after Corm and Liam.

Ally followed and reached for his shirt. "No!"

Ian grabbed them both. "Stay here," he said. "It is too dangerous." He caught up to Shane and Oisin, who were nearly inside the barn.

Her thoughts were desperate. Of course there was no fire extinguisher, no blanket large enough to smother this. There would also be no fire department coming, sirens wailing.

Chestnut bolted from the barn, the end of her tail on fire. Ian threw his arms around the horse's neck and used his shirt to put out the flame.

"Oh, please hurry up," she moaned.

"Where is Pollux?" Adam asked.

She shook her head. More important, where were Corm and Liam?

"Pollux!" Adam rushed to the front of the barn. She followed and felt the heat of the fire, heard the wood crackle and pop.

"Adam! Stop!" But it was too late. He had run through the hole that had once been the front door.

"Adam, please!" She entered the barn, struggled to see him, and began to cough as the smoke filled her lungs.

"Ally, there he is," he shouted. His voice came from the right.

The memory came: *Stop, drop and roll.*

"Adam, get on the floor!" She fell onto her hands and knees and began to crawl toward the sound of his voice.

"He's over here. In the corner."

But which corner? It was hard to breathe, never mind see where she was going. A piece of the roof gave way to her left and fear began to take hold. *I might find him, but we'll never get out of here alive.*

"Easy boy," Adam said.

His voice was directly in front of her. She reached out and found his pant leg.

"Ally, he won't listen. He's scared."

He wasn't the only one. "Adam, get on the floor. There's more air down here." She slowly began to stand knowing, if she lost him now, she'd never find him again.

"But ..." he said, and then fell at her feet. She could see Pollux, but there was no time now to deal with a terrified horse.

She knelt down. "Adam!" He didn't respond. "Oh, please ..." She tried to lift him but he was too heavy. She put her arms around his waist and began to walk backwards, dragging him in the direction of the door. She glanced behind her.

"What ...?" Ally was looking at a beautiful woman standing

inches away. The smoke, which surrounded and threatened to suffocate them a moment before, had disappeared. The apparition stood with her arms out. Her brown dress floated eerily behind her. Her long hair was the color of gold, and wrapped around her head was a wreath made of silver branches. She smiled, and Ally was no longer afraid. Maybe this was what happened when you died. No white light, just a woman to guide you to the other side.

"You are not going to die, Malakai," the woman whispered.

"Who're you?" Ally asked, still holding onto Adam.

"As you inspire and watch over others, I do the same for you. *Hatcha!*" she said.

Pollux walked obediently to her, and she stroked his nose. "You will do anything to ensure I come back and visit, eh, my love?" Then she looked at Ally. "There is not much time. Heed what I have to tell you. You have been given a powerful gift. Guard it carefully and use it wisely. There are those who would stop at nothing to take it from you, but, while I am able, I will help you. *Sta ya.*" Pollux knelt. "Take the boy and go. I will see you out of here safely."

Was she dreaming? There was only one way to find out. She dragged Adam onto Pollux and got on behind him.

"Here is something else," the woman said. She opened Ally's hand and placed a smooth, flat stone inside. "This will help find your way home. It will deliver hope when you need it most." She closed Ally's fingers around it. "*Bet ya.*" Pollux stood. "I have missed you," she whispered into the horse's ear. "Continue to serve him well."

Then, the woman returned her eyes to Ally. "We will be watching. The magic of the forest still exists … for now."

"Thank you," was all Ally could manage.

"Hold on tightly."

Ally wrapped her arms around Pollux's neck and he galloped to the back of the barn. *Wouldn't it be easier to go out the front?* It was certainly closer. But the flames and smoke stayed clear of them, as if they were in a protective tunnel. She put her head down and closed her eyes.

"Praise Artemis," she heard Oisin call.

Pollux stopped. And then there were arms around her, trying to pull her off. "Let go. You are safe." Shane's voice.

"Adam is under me. Be careful." Sobs of relief overtook her. She released her grip and fell into Shane's arms. He, in turn, placed her in

Liam's.

"Got him," Shane said.

"Are you okay?" Liam whispered and held her tight.

She nodded through tears.

He kissed her cheek and lowered her onto the ground. Shane placed Adam beside her.

"Something is wrong with him," Ian said.

"Adam?" His lips were blue. "Adam!" Ally began to shake him.

He didn't respond.

She straddled his body, lifted his neck and pinched his nose. She blew three quick breaths into his open mouth and then, with her hands together, pushed firmly at the base of his rib cage. "Come on," she whispered and repeated the exercise. She was about to start her fifth series when he began to cough.

"Yes!" she screamed as he gasped for air. His eyes fluttered open.

But he shouted "No!" and began thrashing about. She rolled off him and put her hand on his shoulder. "Adam. Stop. You're okay."

"Make him go away! Don't go with him!"

"Adam, look at me. It's Ally. No one's going anywhere. You're here … with your friends, look—" He bolted to a sitting position and, when he recognized her at last, threw his arm around her. "You're going to be okay," she said.

"What did you do to him?" said a strange voice. She looked up. It was Marcus, the boy from the pub. He was sitting on the ground not far away. *What's he doing here?*

He eyed her with suspicion. "I asked, what did you *do?* You are a witch."

"Be quiet," Liam said and then turned his attention to the three riders approaching from the road.

It was Bernard and two other men. They jumped from their horses. "What happened?" Bernard asked. "I saw the flames from town as I was closing up."

"Barn caught on fire, Mister Bernard," Adam replied.

"I can see that. Is everyone safe?" Before anyone could answer, the walls of the barn collapsed, sending a flurry of sparks into the air.

"We are satisfactory given the situation," Liam answered.

Bernard looked at Marcus. "Why are you here?"

"I believe he started it," Liam said.

Bernard shook his head. "I should have known something like this would happen eventually." He looked at Marcus with contempt. "Do you understand what could have happened? No, I suppose you do not. Your father will not be happy about this."

"His father might want to know Liam saved his son's life," Shane said.

"I will accompany Marcus home and explain what happened," Bernard said. "His father will not take this lightly, and will be grateful for what you have done. He is a wealthy man. You should think about that."

Liam glanced at Adam, and then walked to Bernard. "I wanted to talk to you about something," he said, and led him away from the others.

"I cannot believe I did not smell it," Oisin said and looked at Ally. "And I did not see you run inside. It must have been when we were rounding up the horses. I thought you had more sense."

"I had no choice," she answered. "Adam ran in to save Pollux."

"Your breath kept Death away." Ian shook his head. "I have never seen that kind of magic before."

"Nothing magical about it," she replied. "It's CPR." She turned to Adam. "Don't do anything like that again. You could've gotten yourself killed."

"But it was Pollux. He couldn't get out—"

"Well done," Corm said, and put his arm around the boy. "I know Liam is grateful, but I also know he would not want you to risk your life for that of his horse."

"We weren't gonna get hurt," Adam replied. "The forest lady was there ... protectin' us from the fire ... and from the bad man."

"Who?" Corm asked.

"The forest lady. Ally was talkin' to her and then the bad man showed up. He wanted me and Ally to go with him."

Corm looked at her. "What happened in there?"

"I need something to drink," she said.

"I will get a canteen," Ian replied.

Ally looked into the sky. "Thank you," she said, and opened her hand.

Liam and Bernard walked back in their direction. "Your kindness and generosity are admirable," Bernard said. "I know Mason will be agreeable to your proposal. In fact, he will want to do more, but I will ensure he takes care of it. You have my word."

"I live only a short distance up the road," one of the other men said. "You are more than welcome to come to the house. Rain started just in time. Funny, there was not a cloud in the sky. Seems to have stopped as quickly. James Hawthorne," he said and removed his hat.

"That is kind of you, sir," Ian said, "but we should stay here. The fire might still breathe life."

"What about you?" Bernard said to Adam. "Perhaps you should let these kids be."

"But I want to stay."

"Actually, sir," Corm said, "if not for Adam, this could have turned out quite differently. He was the first to wake and warn us. I would be honored if you would allow him to spend the rest of the night."

"I will not argue then," Bernard said.

"If I cannot persuade you to come tonight," James said, "please stop by in the morning for breakfast. My wife makes wonderful flapjacks."

"That is an offer I will accept," Shane replied.

* * *

Liam and Corm retrieved the horses, which had been secured to the trees surrounding the field. "Corm," Liam said, "when Ally was trapped within the barn, I could not bear the thought of losing her. What if she did not make it out safely?"

"Life is full of what-ifs," Corm replied. "The only thing you have is what is. She did make it, but I cannot say with certainty you will not lose her in the future."

"There is a difference, though, between those two things—" *A big difference.*

Corm placed his hand on Liam's shoulder. "Remember, I know how special she is. Liam … there is something you should know. There were two others in the barn with them."

"What? Who?"

"You will not believe it."

Chapter 28

Guess I'm not the only one in need of a bath now. Ally took a sip of water and looked around. Between the rain, the fire and the mud, everyone was filthy.

Liam wrapped his arms around Adam. "Thank you for saving Pollux."

Adam beamed. "Ally helped too."

"I have something for her as well." Liam knelt and kissed her lips. "But," he said, and looked back to Adam, "you do realize you put not only your own, but Ally's life in danger. That was not a wise choice."

"Aye, was not smart but very brave," Oisin said, "especially given the scars you bear."

"Pollux needed me," Adam said. "And if I had to again? I would do the same. Besides, like I told you, the forest lady was there."

"Aye, Corm mentioned that. I think we are all interested to hear what happened."

"She appeared out of nowhere. She was tall and really pretty, huh Ally?"

Ally took a deep breath. "Yes, she was beautiful. It happened so fast and, at the same time, so slow. I ran in after Adam, but the fire was intense, I couldn't see anything. I was struggling to breathe. Adam was on the floor, Pollux was in the corner frightened, and then … she was standing behind me. The fire and the smoke didn't bother her. She talked to Pollux, calmed him so Adam and I could get on him, and she protected us on the way out. It was like a dream. And she gave me this."

She held out her hand and showed them the red triangular stone. An outline of a dagger was etched in black on its center.

"That was no dream. That was the goddess Tellervo," Ian said.

Ally looked at him. "Who?"

"Impossible," Shane said. "She does not allow herself to be seen.

Ally, what did she look like?"

"She was tall, dressed in brown. And her hair … long and gold-colored. And she wore a wreath of silver branches."

"Well, perhaps she makes an exception every thousand years," Shane said.

"You know her?"

"We know *of* her," Corm answered. "Do you remember our conversation about the magic within the forest?"

She nodded.

"Tellervo *is* the goddess of the forest—the protector of the wild animals—but she has not been seen in a very long time."

"She is a powerful spirit," Ian said, "and one who has taken an interest in you, it seems. May I hold the stone she gave you?"

Ally handed it to him. "She said it would help us find hope when we needed it."

"I have never seen anything like this but, if it was given to you by Tellervo, it is very valuable."

"Adam mentioned a man was in the barn with you as well," Oisin said.

"I never saw a man. I'm actually surprised he saw, ah, Tellervo. She showed up after he passed out."

"I saw her even though my eyes was closed," Adam said. "But I wasn't paying attention once I saw him walk in. I seen him before. He came to get Mom and Mikey, but this time he wanted me … and Ally."

"What did he look like?" Corm asked.

"Never can see his face, but he's dressed in black. He got real close this time, he almost had his hands on us, but he went away."

"Who do you think it was?" Ally asked, afraid of the answer.

"Death," Corm said. "But he will need to wait another day to take anyone here."

* * *

"They should leave the forest tomorrow," Caleb said as he looked at his underground prison.

I will arrive early. Take her and wait for me to join you.

"You are coming?"

I cannot entrust this task to another. It is too important.

"You have my word, Master."

* * *

The early morning light filtered into the tent. Ally grabbed her bag and slipped outside. She heard Ian say, "I am surprised the saddles are dry, given the rain we received last night."

"Aye, I am as well." It was Liam.

Shane walked from the direction of the stream and shook his wet head from side to side. "Hey, Ally, wait," he said as she hurried past.

"No time," she replied. She needed to take a bath, now. She headed down the embankment and began to yank her shirt over head.

"Ally, stop!"

She pulled it down. Oisin was standing waist-deep in the stream. "Sorry," she said. "I didn't know you were down here."

"I thought Shane would have told you."

"I think he tried but I wasn't listening."

"Ally?"

"Yes?"

"I am getting out now, so it does not matter to me but you might want to," he twirled his finger in the air.

"Oh! Sorry." She spun around and put her face into her hands. *What an idiot you are!*

He dressed, walked past her and then turned around. "I have never met anyone like you," he said. "I do not believe any of us has. Understand, as painful as it might be, you are one of us now." He smiled and shook his head. "Poor thing."

"Could you make sure everyone else knows I'm down here?"

"I have your back, I promise."

You're one of us now. The words made her smile.

* * *

When they rode into the yard, James Hawthorne appeared at the door.

"Tie the horses on the side of the house and come on in. There is someone here who would like to meet you."

They walked into the kitchen. A woman was at the stove. "Please, take a seat. Juice is on the table," she said.

"I would like you to meet Mason Black." James pointed to a tall man in the corner.

"Pleased," Mason replied, "but I am already familiar with some of you."

"How so?" asked Ian.

"I was present at the games this year. The stake of Pembroke was well represented. I apologize for making your acquaintance under this circumstance."

Mrs. Hawthorne brought a plate of pancakes to the table. "Please, help yourself." She turned back to the stove and poured more batter into a skillet.

"Let me begin by saying how grateful I am that you saved my son from the fire," Mason said. "I apologize for the trouble he caused. Bernard mentioned there is something I can do for you in return."

Adam was piling pancakes onto his plate, not paying attention to the conversation. "I will see to it he gets to Pembroke posthaste. Two men will arrive shortly to take the trip, but I need to know where to deliver him."

Liam nodded. "I will prepare a set of directions—"

"What is he referring to, Liam?" Oisin asked.

"Adam," Liam said, "when we finish breakfast, we will take you to Bernard's, and then you will be leaving for Pembroke today."

"You mean it?" Adam asked.

"I do, but you must do something for me in return."

They stood in front of the pub and Liam handed Adam a letter. "I need you to give this to Thea," he said.

"I will," Adam replied. He began to unbutton the shirt. "This be yours, Liam."

"Keep it for now."

Adam put the paper in his breast pocket. "Thanks. See ya soon. See y'all soon ... well, except you, Ally." He hugged each of them and disappeared inside The Oar.

"We need to get on the road if we hope to reach Berwick before nightfall," Ian said.

"Aye," Liam replied, but at the present he was more concerned about something else. He prayed the letter would reach Thea before they left the forest. He was beginning to think their safety would depend on it.

Chapter 29

"Liam," Ally said as they rode side by side. "I didn't tell you everything that happened with Tellervo last night."

"What do you mean?"

"Has Pollux always been your horse?"

He looked at her. "Yes and no. Shortly after my mother died, I found him. It was as if he was waiting for me. He was the most beautiful animal I had ever seen. It took a while but, eventually, he allowed me on his back. Riding him is what I imagine it feels like to fly upon the winds. It was one of the happiest moments of my life … until I met you." He cleared his throat. "Why do you ask?"

"Tellervo said she missed him and, when she spoke, Pollux understood her. I think he belongs to her. If that's true, Pollux is every bit as magical as she is."

He shook his head and sighed. "I am not surprised. He is an extraordinary animal. It would make sense, given the nature of Tellervo's magic, they are acquainted. But I have to admit, until today, I thought she was a myth."

"I still can't believe I met a goddess."

"Yesterday the gods looked upon us with favor but, if they should turn away, know I will do anything to keep you safe. I fear my world is nothing without you."

They began to pass small groups traveling in the same direction, and Ally overheard a bit of the conversation between four women riding in a wagon.

"I wonder about her dress," one said.

"She could wear a brown sack and still look good," another answered, "but, with the money her father has, I would wager it is a bit fancier than that on this special day."

"What are they discussing?" Corm asked after they passed them.

"Sounds like wedding talk," Ally replied.

"Ah," Oisin said and rolled his eyes. "Then I have no interest in eavesdropping on that conversation."

"Why not?"Ally said.

"Because it is difficult just to live with one's self, never mind another. Marriage is a huge commitment, and one I do not intend to enter into lightly."

"And," Ian added, "if you need to sample the fruit on every tree while looking for the perfect peach, all the better. But, I recall at the tavern, you thought there was someone out there for all of us."

"I know what I said," Oisin said. "I was simply trying to make Shane feel better."

"Oisin, I can hear you," Shane said.

"Ah, look." Oisin pointed. "Ally was right."

Shane shook his head. "And your attempt to change the subject is pathetic, my friend."

They rode into Berwick, where decorated banners were strung between the shops and streamers hung from the trees. The street was full of people, all holding flowers. Liam dismounted Pollux and helped Ally from Chestnut.

"We will catch up with you when this madness is over," Oisin said before he, Ian and Shane disappeared into the crowd. She stood between Liam and Corm in front of the bakery.

"They are coming at last," said a woman beside her. Ally leaned out to see what she could. A procession was headed in their direction. The quartet in the common across the street began to play a familiar tune as the entourage approached.

The wedding party rode into town, two by two. In the lead were a young girl and boy. They each rode a small pony and smiled wide. The crowd began to cheer and throw flowers into the street.

"Liam?"

Liam turned around to see who had spoken. "Mr. Hargreaves. It is good to see you, sir."

"And you as well. I did not realize you knew Elizabeth and Joshua."

"Actually, I do not. We are passing through. Our good luck, it seems."

"I should say so. How is your father? I have not seen Jon in a while. No reason for me to visit the ministry, which is always a good thing." He chuckled.

"My father is well. We are on our way to meet him in Portsmouth."

"Portsmouth?"

"Yes, he needed to attend to a business matter."

"Ah, well, it never ends, does it not?"

"Let me introduce Ally Ashworth and Corm Jeuter," Liam said.

"I am pleased to meet you," he said and smiled. "There is my daughter. She is one of the bride's attendants." Mr. Hargreaves waved to a pretty girl riding sidesaddle upon a white horse.

The bride and groom made their appearance, at last, in a horse-drawn carriage. Liam leaned over and kissed Ally's cheek. She looked into his eyes and smiled, then returned her attention to the parade. Odd. The bride was staring at her and then picked up the wreath in her lap. She tossed it in the air. Ally overcame being startled in time to catch it. It was covered with flowers and long purple ribbons hung from the back.

"It's beautiful, but why did she give it to me?" Ally asked.

"My dear, do not tell me this is your first wedding," Mr. Hargreaves replied.

"I don't get out much."

Mr. Hargreaves put his hand upon her shoulder. "You have received the laurels of love. The scent of the flowers is believed to ward away evil spirits, allowing love to bloom. It is unusual, though, for it to be given to a stranger. Elizabeth must have noticed something special in both of you."

Her cheeks began to burn and, rather than look at Liam, Ally stared at the wreath. He took it from her hand and placed it on her head.

"It fits you perfectly," he said.

"The celebration is just outside town, at the Fournier farm," Mr. Hargreaves said. "Please join us. Or are you leaving immediately?"

"We are actually going to remain the night and depart tomorrow," Liam replied.

"It is settled then." He stepped into the street. "I will see you at the celebration!" he shouted and followed the procession winding its way out of town.

Liam looked around. "What do you think, Corm? Where are the others?"

"Corm pointed to the street. "They are enjoying the festivities."

The top of Shane's head bounced up and down as he danced behind the wedding party. "But I think it is a good idea, and I do not expect much argument from them."

"We weren't invited," Ally said. "I mean, not by the bride and groom. Is it okay if we just show up? We don't even have a gift."

Liam looked at her as if she'd suddenly sprouted horns. "Weddings are a celebration. There is no invitation required and, not to sound egocentric, but your gift is your presence. Making the time to share an important day is not to be taken lightly. Why? What are they like in your world?"

* * *

Caleb stood in front of the town common, glancing at the group directly across the street. He had arrived just as the procession was moving through, and was able to blend into the crowd. He watched the boy place the wreath upon the girl's head. True love. *Too bad it will not last another day.* And the Shayeen hawk, who would never fly again. He smiled. *Soon ... very soon.*

The old man indicated he would see them at the celebration where there would be food ... and drink ... and Caleb had an idea. One that might ensure the boys could not interfere with his plan. He slipped out of town and headed west where he had seen a cluster of pink flowers.

* * *

"We thought we might attend the festivities," Corm said when they rejoined the others.

Shane nodded. "I believe a bit of nourishment for body and soul is in order."

Oisin pointed to Ally's head. "The laurels of love. Impressive."

"Yeah, right," Ally replied.

"We should locate a campsite before it gets dark," Ian said and looked at Oisin. "If the opportunity for, ah, better accommodation presents itself, we need to be aware of our departure point in the morning."

"I have no intention of separating from your fine company," Oisin replied.

213

"Would you care to place a wager on that?" Shane asked, grinning.

Just outside town, a large white tent was in the center of an open field. Torches and lanterns were lit, awaiting the darkness that would soon be upon them. *How different this is.* Ally had never really thought about her wedding day but, now ...

Don't even go there.

She touched the wreath. If she ever did get married, she wanted a wedding just like this.

"Ally," Corm said loudly.

"Huh?"

"Where are you right now?"

She shook her head. "Nowhere. Why?"

"I asked if you would mind sleeping under the stars. It would save a lot of time if we did not have to set up and take down tents."

"Sure ... whatever," she said, wanting to get back to her daydream.

They traveled a short distance beyond the field, and the forest closed in on them again. Shane, in the lead, followed a narrow road that forked to the left. "This is the perfect spot," he said.

Ian pulled out his map. "I believe we are still within the forest. I have not seen the pillars or the stake of Argus, marking its end."

"Then it is indeed perfect," Liam said, eyeing the pond in front of them, which was surrounded by tall pines, the ground carpeted in soft needles. They returned to the reception and tied up the horses with the hundred or so already grazing in the long grass.

Beneath the tent were wooden barrels supporting long planks of wood, nearly every inch covered with food. A pig hung from a spit in a nearby fire pit, turning slowly over the coals.

Liam handed her a plate. "Are you hungry?"

"I still feel a little like I'm intruding. Are you sure no one will mind?"

"Does it look like anyone will?"

"Ah, cornbread, baked beans, roasted quail and curried sausage," Shane said. He began to pile massive quantities onto his plate.

"All right." She helped herself to chicken, sweet potatoes, applesauce and fresh bread.

Oisin spotted three girls at one table eyeing him, and not discreetly. He smiled. "Shane, follow me. This might be your lucky day."

"Aye, I am fortunate to have such an irresistible friend," Shane replied. "But I have not forgotten our wager."

She, Liam and Corm found three seats at another table.

"Would you care for a pint?" Corm asked before he sat down.

She looked at Liam, who shrugged. "Why not?" she answered and began to dig in.

The darkness settled in and the torches provided a romantic glow. She took a deep breath and closed her eyes. *Click.* She would remember this forever.

"The first night of the double moon," Corm said. "Rather fitting to celebrate a wedding, eh?"

"Double moon," Ally murmured.

"Yes," Corm answered. "Every quarter year, the two moons, Pegasus and Chimera, appear before dawn's light. Do you not have two moons in your sky?"

"No," she said and looked overhead, "but I only see one. Is that Pegasus or Chimera?"

"That is Pegasus, the flying horse. He is the one seen on most nights, but tonight he will be joined by Chimera, the dragon. Legend has it Chimera is chasing Pegasus, but the horse drives him away. They signify the struggle between good and evil ... much like marriage," Corm said and smiled.

"Oh, ha ha. Very funny, Corm," she said. "I don't care what they signify. I agree it's romantic to get married when they're both in the sky—"

She looked toward a familiar sound. A short distance away, a man was tuning a fiddle and another was turning the pegs on a guitar. Standing behind them was a boy in front of four wooden drums. They were joined by a woman carrying a flute and a young girl holding a tambourine. When the band began to play, the field came alive with people swinging each other around the makeshift dance floor. Ally caught sight of the bride and groom walking in their direction.

Liam smiled. "Oh, there is a tradition that we have. Perhaps I forgot to mention it."

Ally grabbed his hand. "What is it?"

Too late.

"Hello, I am Elizabeth Connors and this is my husband, Joshua."

Liam stood. "I am Liam Cheveyo and this is Ally Ashworth and Cormac Jeuter. Congratulations."

"Thank you. I could not be happier," Joshua replied.

Elizabeth laughed. "He has not tasted my cooking yet. Although we were not acquainted, it was obvious you should receive the laurels. Are you ready to join us after this song?"

What was she talking about? The apprehension Ally felt a moment earlier began to develop into a full-blown panic attack.

"We are," Liam said. He put his arm around Ally and led her away from the table.

"Good luck," Corm said.

"Liam, what are we doing?" The band finished to a rousing applause. Elizabeth looked at the fiddle player and nodded.

"Will the wedding attendants please join the bride and groom for the valza," he shouted. The guests stepped aside and the wedding party made their way through the crowd.

"Liam …" He held her hand and, together, they walked onto the dance floor.

"Just follow me." He directed her to stand beside the girls, and took his place opposite her. As if on cue, the boys bowed to their partner. A panic attack would be a blessing at this point. The girls curtseyed and, when Ally tried to do the same, she nearly fell.

"I'm going to kill you," she said between clenched teeth. The music began, and Liam held his right arm high. She looked at the others and put her left hand inside his. He put his other arm around her waist and brought her close. Scott was the only boy she'd ever danced with, and they'd simply put their heads on each other's shoulders … nothing like this. She shuffled her feet, trying not to step on his toes.

"I know it might be difficult for you," Liam whispered and smiled, "but allow me to lead."

"I thought I was." She closed her eyes. *Feel the music.* The song was a waltz. She should be able to figure it out. She followed him, trying to forget about everything else, and found herself moving around the field. He removed his hand from her waist and, slowly, twirled her around. They repeated it twice and were back in each other's arms. She couldn't take her eyes from his and their bodies moved gracefully as one. When the music stopped, he released her and bowed.

"You did very well," he said and grabbed her hand as she was about to walk away.

"Ally, do not leave just yet," Elizabeth said. "I would be honored if you would join the band."

"You're killing me," Ally said to Liam. "When did you …?"

Oh, what the heck, I'll never see any of these people again. Well, most of them anyway.

"She carries her own instrument," Liam said, "if you would allow me to retrieve it." He ran toward the horses and, when he returned, handed her his mother's fiddle.

"You brought this?" she said, astonished.

"I thought you might enjoy the distraction. It appears I was correct."

"What song would you care to play?" the guitarist asked.

"I'm sure I don't know anything you do. Just start and I'll figure it out."

"All right then," he said, and looked at the others with skepticism. "'Juniper Jump' … in the key of G."

She followed the changes and began to play. It was a lively piece and, at one point, she and the fiddle player took turns with the lead. She smiled. *Dueling fiddles.* Everyone, including the other musicians, stared at her with mouths open. She pulled the bow across the strings, signaling the end of the song, and the field erupted.

"Bravo," the guitarist said and patted her back. She bowed and began to laugh. This really was a perfect night.

"Very nicely done," Corm said. He was on his feet, still applauding, when she joined he and Liam at the table.

"I've never danced like that in my life," she said. "I can't believe I didn't knock anyone over."

"I meant the music, but the dancing was good as well."

"Thanks." She was about to sit down when someone tugged at her sleeve. A little boy stood beside her.

"Hi," she said.

He held up a wooden recorder. "Look, I can make music, too." He put his mouth to the wooden block and began to blow while his fingers pressed the tiny holes. It was a tune she recognized: "Twinkle, Twinkle, Little Star." He finished and looked up at her proudly.

"That was very good," she said.

A woman walked over to them. "Joseph. There you are. Please do not wander off again and stop bothering these guests."

"He is no bother," Liam replied.

"He has been doing this all day. I need an additional set of eyes and arms to keep him close. Your music was inspirational," she said to Ally. "I cannot tell you how much I enjoyed it. My husband never dances with me, but today he made an exception."

"I'm glad. Thank you."

"No, thank you. Joseph, come with me." She took his hand. "And do not do that again."

Liam couldn't conceal a yawn. "Would you care to leave?" he asked.

"It's up to you."

"I have to admit, I am tired. What about you, Corm?"

"I was tired when we arrived. I am more than ready."

"We just need to tell the others," Liam said.

They found Oisin, Ian and Shane at the far end of the field, around a fire with the three girls. "I am very impressed, Ally," Oisin said. "You are gifted in more ways than I imagined."

"Thank you," she replied.

"We are going to take our leave," Liam said. "Do you remember where we are staying?"

Shane smiled. "Yes, but I would not wait up."

* * *

Caleb had returned while the girl was playing the fiddle. When the two boys stepped away from the table, he had slipped a hefty dose of valerian into their ale. The effect of the plant would not take long. He found the girl's horse and concealed himself under the saddle blanket. He had no idea where they were headed but, when the three of them set off in the direction of the ruins, he smiled.

* * *

Liam lit a lantern and Ally spread out the blankets. "Do you think we need a fire?" Corm asked as he took off his boots.

"No, and I am too tired to get one started," Liam replied. He removed the sword and hung it from Pollux's saddle. The soothing sound of crickets and tree frogs was interrupted by a high-pitched screech.

Ally grimaced. "What's that?"

"That," Liam replied and looked at Corm with dread, "is the cry of the great horned owl."

Chapter 30

Timing was crucial. Chimera was not yet visible on the eastern horizon and Pegasus was beginning its descent behind the trees at the far end of the pond. The glowing beam of soft blue light that spilled from the half-hemisphere was losing the battle to the growing shadows. In fewer than fifteen minutes, all light would be lost for a short time. When this happened, the girl would be unlikely to venture from her spot. Caleb stood a short distance away, hidden from view by the trunk of a large oak. Maelyn had cloaked the pillar marking the end of the forest, and this spot was a good half kilometer beyond its boundaries. Here the Shayeen would be helpless. But, courtesy of the Master, Caleb could still transform.

Tonight, he could not believe his good luck. The three had unwittingly chosen a spot no more than two hundred meters from the prison where he was instructed to hold the girl. All he needed to do was lure her away from her companions. He would get her out of the way, and then present the two boys with their ugly fates ... a moment he wanted to savor and enjoy.

* * *

As soon as Liam lay down, he began to drift to sleep. Corm's steady breathing a short distance away indicated he had already surrendered to exhaustion. Liam rolled to his side and put his arm around Ally. She moved closer and nestled her head into his chest.

"Good night," he whispered.

"Night," she mumbled. "Love you."

He smiled and looked to the heavens. "Thank you." His thoughts danced to the rhythm of her heart and he fell into a deep and immediate sleep.

* * *

Now!

It was divine intervention, it must be. Caleb pulled the wooden instrument from his back pocket, the one he had picked up when the lad set it down. At the time, he was unsure as to why. But now, he knew. He walked half the distance to the sleeping three and placed it on the ground, transformed into his spider form and crept to where they lay.

He crawled onto the girl's arm and then to her neck. His legs played with the thin short hairs on her throat. When she stirred, he leaped off and scurried into the woods, changed back and picked up the recorder. Softly, he began to play the same tune the boy played earlier. Was it coincidence that Caleb knew how to play this stupid instrument? Was it luck the song the boy kept playing was one of four he actually knew? No, he decided, it was Destiny, working to fulfill the Master's promise to him.

He worked the recorder with his lips and fingers and moved back toward the trees.

* * *

"*Eyck!*" Ally sat up and brushed away whatever bug or, worse, spider was on her throat. Her eyes darted around but the intruder had disappeared. She was about to lay back down when she heard a familiar sound from the woods: a recorder, playing the song the little boy had played earlier. Had he wandered away again, at this hour?

She caught a glimpse of a silhouette moving awkwardly through the trees. She reached beside her. "Liam, wake up." But he remained asleep ... and snoring. She smiled. *I'll point that out to him in the morning.* She got on her knees and crawled between Liam and Corm. "Hey, hey!" she said, giving them each a shove. But exhaustion, or perhaps one too many beers, had taken over. They didn't stir.

I can do this. Who knows? It might be nothing, but when the song began again, she doubted it. The moon was bright and would provide all the light needed. It didn't sound like he was very far away. "Joseph?" she called out, her feet already moving her into the woods.

* * *

Caleb's lips broke into a sadistic smile as her voice moved up behind him. He didn't have to turn around to know his plan was working. Her voice was not accompanied by another, and he sensed the leaves behind him were stirring from a single pair of feet. The drug had done its part, and the other two were still asleep. She had willingly moved away from her friends, eager to help a stranger. Continuing to play, he walked deeper into the woods.

The bushes with the thorny vines began to fill in the space between the trees. Although a vine occasionally crossed his path, the leather riding pants he wore protected his legs from nature's tiny daggers. He reached the oak tree whose dead form he had committed to memory. Bushes encircled the tree, and vines gripped its lower limbs, as if trying to pull the skeletal remains down.

His retreat reached a dead end. He fell to his knees, dropped the recorder and, after he transformed, crept onto one of the vines growing from the center of the bush. It moved like the head of a viper in search of a tree branch to cling to. He scrambled to the other side and changed back, knowing he was now completely concealed.

* * *

"Joseph," she called, continuing to follow the music. Something was weird about the way he ran and she began to get nervous. She envisioned the Pied Piper, calling Ireland's children to their doom. *Stop it.* This wasn't some grotesque fairy tale. It was simply a little boy. She turned around, no longer able to see where Liam and Corm were sleeping, and hoped she wouldn't regret her decision to leave the camp. *I'll find him and then get lost myself.*

She avoided the fallen branches and bushes that dove at her ankles until something bit into her lower legs ... something long enough to cut through her jeans. A vine had attached itself to the front of her pants. She tried to remove it and winced.

"Joseph!" She held her hand to her eye. A thorn protruded from her fingertip. *If he's in here, he's probably stuck on these.* She pulled it out and flicked it away. As it dropped, she looked at her leg. Half a dozen of the prickly barbs protruded from her jeans.

A sound came from the tall bushes directly ahead of her. The dense thicket looked alive. Dead, twisted branches waved in the breeze, inviting her closer.

She began moving again. "Joseph, don't run away from me." A vine whipped across her path and cut into her right leg. The ground began to spin. Off-balance, she reached out and gripped one of the vines. Its thorns pierced her palm. "*Ooww!*" She made a fist and blood dripped from her hand, trickled onto the leaves at her feet. The sound sent a chill through her.

She looked at the moving branches again and lifted her head, realizing they danced in silence. There was no wind. So why were they moving? A weird sense of déjà vu, and fear, began to consume her.

The dream she'd had on her second night here … the bush Gabriel drew and Ian's warning: *That is a Gorgon bush. Their thorns incapacitate with a single scratch.* Her inner voice screamed, *It's a trap!*

The warning, the recognition came too late. Weak in the knees, she began to fall to the ground. Two gloved hands grasped her wrists and roughly pulled her through the bushes. The image of the old oak being suffocated by the vines was the last thing she remembered.

* * *

Caleb threw the leather gloves on the ground and picked her up. But after only a short distance, he began to struggle. He put her down and began to walk backwards, dragging her the twenty-five meters to the tunnel entrance.

The subterranean labyrinth stretched two hundred meters to the south and almost four hundred meters to the north. It was nearly invisible to those not aware of its existence. The main passageway was concealed in a small hill adjacent to the ancient gardens. Two life-size statues, hidden by the untended overgrowth, were the only clues that, at one time, this was the home of Minos, the ancient king. One of the sculptures bore the head of a bull and the body of a man, the Minotaur, and the other was a frightening likeness of Medusa.

The ceilings in the underground maze were surprisingly high, and he pulled her down a series of narrow hallways, keeping track of the number of openings he passed before changing course. He navigated a series of switchbacks and finally reached his destination:

a four-meter by three-meter room. There was no door to confine her, but that would not be necessary.

He placed her body in the corner and picked up the sticky webbing he had spun the day before, while in spider form. Once he wrapped it around her and was confident she was adequately restrained, he reached for one of several vines. He had removed the thorns from the last thirty centimeters of their length and used them to bind her legs, securing the thorn-free ends. If she regained consciousness earlier than anticipated, she could stay perfectly still and respect her situation or find herself returning to the darkness.

Exhaustion made it hard to think, but he knew the Master would be pleased. Just one more minor detail.

He returned to where the two boys slept. He needed to inject as much poison as possible with a single bite. The drug would be wearing off and, if they realized what was happening, he might lose his advantage.

In spider form, he crawled inside the boy named Liam's pant leg. He sunk his fangs into the fleshy part of the calf, allowing the poison to flow freely. He did not want to wake him. Not until he was sure the venom had taken effect. After a moment, he let go and quickly scurried toward the other.

Once done, Caleb waited at their feet and looked at their four horses. The large black stallion stared at him and began to whinny, fighting to be free of his tether. He would take that one when it was time to leave. That horse was clearly the strongest.

* * *

"Pollux?" Liam sat up slowly and rubbed his leg where something had bitten him. He assumed it was the consequence of sleeping near a pond on a warm night and looked beside him.

"Ally?" he called out, and waited.

"Ally!" Again, the answer was silence. "Corm!"

"What is it?" Corm asked, groggy.

"Where is Ally?" Liam tried to stand, but his legs buckled and he fell to his knees. Sweat broke out on his forehead. His breathing became heavy. He looked around but his vision was blurred, his surroundings distorted.

He tried to get to his feet a second time, but a violent pain exploded in his chest and intense cramps erupted in his abdomen. He lay on his side and held his stomach. "*Aaah!*" he shouted when the pain became unbearable.

Corm began to moan as well. Liam saw him try to get up, then flop back down to his blanket.

"Corm," he groaned between clenched teeth. He heard his friend violently retch on the ground beside him.

What is happening? He looked around and saw multiple images of the same thing. And then, the distorted shape of a boy floated at his feet.

Chapter 31

Oisin offered to refill their mugs and walked to the firkin, but stopped midstride. Apprehension ran through him like a dagger, and he looked in the direction of the camp. The feeling of dread was impossible to deny. He nearly collided with Ian and Shane as they ran past.

"Something is wrong!" Shane said.

"I sensed it as well." Oisin dropped the flagons and they raced toward the horses.

"Wait. Where are you going?" one of the girls cried out, but the question went unanswered as the boys disappeared into the night.

* * *

"Help us," Liam begged as a wave of nausea rolled over him.

"We meet again, although this time it is I who controls your Fate."

Despite his impaired vision, Liam saw the malicious smile that played upon the boy's lips, and hope was replaced with despair when he realized who it was.

"I believe the poison is taking effect. I will enjoy watching you suffer. This is for you." Caleb drew back his foot and kicked Liam sharply in the stomach. "How does that feel? Not very good I imagine, given your present state."

Liam could not even utter a scream as he writhed in pain.

"On a happier note," Caleb continued, "know that Ally is in my capable hands. I will certainly take better care of her than you were able to. I promise."

* * *

Their bodies wrenched with spasms. It would not be long now. Caleb doubted they could still hear him but he went on.

"You underestimated me, a grievous mistake. It is regrettable your precious forest and its magic cannot save you. We are stronger. Remember that. However," he picked up Ally's bag, "I do not believe we will meet again."

He attempted to communicate with the Master but, for the first time since he departed Crooks, he could not. No matter. He would arrive soon enough.

It was two hours until sunup when he made his way back to the labyrinth ... to his prisoner. She held the key to his future, among other things, and he smiled. *Once the Master obtains what he needs, you belong to me.*

* * *

The two riders raced through the night. The glowing eyes of the demon horses they rode upon were the only features that distinguished them from their surroundings. The thunder of hoof beats was deafening as they roared by. The birds of the night took flight, fearful the malignant spirits within these beasts would reach out and turn them to stone. Their fiery breath, which hung in the air, was the only indication they passed at all as they continued to gallop toward their destination.

Cepheus gazed into the talisman, monitoring the progress of the two warriors, while he stroked the two-headed raven on the perch beside him. His promise to Caleb was necessary, but he never intended to make the journey. He could not risk leaving the castle until the girl was firmly within his grasp. The boy would be disappointed but might live to return—if only to meet his fate. A pity.

Caleb, without hesitation, had extinguished the lives of the two from Gilgamesh. And then the connection between he and Caleb had been severed. Maelyn had no explanation for the separation and, although it caused unease, he knew there was no need for concern. Askari and Sukata were two of his finest, the magic within them as powerful as any in the castle. Nothing or no one was capable of standing between them and the girl. Of that, he was sure.

* * *

Oisin directed Nemesis off the road, Ian and Shane close behind. He jumped from the saddle before the horse came to a stop and rushed to the spot where his friends were on the ground, their bodies still. "Liam! Corm!" He fell to his knees and attempted to turn Liam onto his back and break him from the fetal position he had assumed.

"What in the name of Hades happened?" Shane shouted.

Ian looked wildly around. "I do not know, but we must act quickly! Where is Ally?"

"Liam, what or who did this to you?" Oisin put his ear to Liam's gray-white lips and prayed there was still a breath of life inside.

* * *

Where is Ally? The question broke through the cobwebs that filled Liam's mind and the intense throbbing that pushed on his eyes. He gathered all his energy, tapped into the last trace of life within and slowly, opened his mouth. "'Pider bite," was all he managed before the darkness began to choke him.

* * *

"Corm, stay with me my friend!" But Shane's command received no response.

"They are inflicted with a spider bite!" Oisin cried.

Ian grabbed Liam's bag and dumped Thea's potions on the ground. "Will one of these treat a spider bite? None of them bear a label!"

Oisin cradled Liam's head. "I do not know, but you need to make a choice!"

"It is useless unless we know where they were bitten!" Ian picked up a bottle that contained a clear liquid.

"Quickly," Oisin said. "I hear the singing of the spirits! They are coming to take them—"

The light from the second moon shone on the saber that hung from Pollux. Through the sheath, the blade erupted in brilliance. The ground around Liam and Corm glowed.

"That is not the spirits we hear," Ian said. "It is the sword." He withdrew it and, as he looked at the blade, the writing shifted and changed.

Put me near Achilles and the two-headed diamond.

"Oisin! Shane! Roll up their pants! "

Ian looked at Liam's calf. The sword directed itself to the red welt that was now visible, and the tip penetrated Liam's flesh.

* * *

Liam's voice was lost to the fire that burned through his body. He saw a specter in the distance. It floated toward him and he recognized the hair, the face.

"Liam, go back," his mother whispered, but the ghost's lips did not move. "I will not let you pass. You have missed the second of Time's markers. There is a tomorrow and the survival of everything around you dictates it be the path you follow. You must return and fulfill your destiny."

She was inches from him now, and he could see through her.

"The evil hidden for centuries will soon be revealed. You carry a great weight, but it is one you cannot bear alone. Together, you have the power to defeat it. Always remember what lies within your heart," she whispered and put a ghost-like hand upon his chest.

"Do not leave me." But his silent plea could not keep the spirit from fading.

"The angel needs you. You must save her. Her strength will inspire and unite. Return to her, Liam."

Ally! Her face appeared in front of him, and he fought to be free. With effort, he opened his eyes. A face, inches from his own, stared down at him.

"Ally," Liam moaned.

"No. It is I, Shane."

Oisin pushed him away. "I am sure he is not confusing you with Ally."

"Oisin?" Liam gasped. His mouth was dry, his throat tight.

"Yes," Oisin replied. "Shane, please bring water."

Oisin helped him to a sitting position and placed the pouch to his lips. He took only a sip but it cooled the fire that burned in his throat.

The pounding in his head was another matter and his body continued to shake.

"Corm," Liam said and looked to his left. Ian held the sword to Corm's lower leg and, when he lifted it, blood dripped from the tip. Corm slowly opened his eyes.

"What are you doing?" Liam asked.

"What the sword told me to," Ian answered. "We did not have much time, did not even know where you had been bitten when your sword began to … sing."

"How ever did you decipher the meaning of the words?" Shane asked Ian.

"You really need to read more," Ian answered.

Liam slowly got to his feet and took the sword from Ian. The writing on the blade was as he remembered and, as he held it, he felt renewed strength. "We must get Ally."

"Where is she?" Oisin said.

"He has her. We need to go."

Shane's brow furrowed. "Who?"

"Caleb. When I awoke, she was gone but he was here. He poisoned us. He is an arachnid and … Ally believes he might be Adam's brother."

"Did they leave on horseback?" Oisin asked.

"I cannot be sure," Liam replied, and picked up the wreath on the ground. He touched the flowers, which were beginning to wilt and discolor. "But we need to hurry."

"Are you strong enough to give pursuit?" Shane asked.

"Aye," Liam replied.

"I am, as well," Corm said. "I will look from the sky. Perhaps I can determine their location."

"When we rode in," Ian said, "I noticed the pillars marking the end of the forest. We are currently beyond Gilgamesh."

"What?" Liam asked in disbelief.

"Aye," Ian answered and took a deep breath. "I assure you, they were not visible yesterday—"

Corm closed his eyes and rose into the air.

Oisin stood still. "I cannot change. Can either of you?"

Ian and Shane shook their heads as Corm flew out of sight.

"Caleb was able to transform," Liam said. "Perhaps his venom contains black magic of its own. Perhaps that is the reason Corm is

230

able to assume his form and you are not."

Corm appeared on the ground beside them. "There is no sign of them in the immediate area."

"Head east," Liam said, "and continue to search from above. We will follow on horseback."

"What makes you think they traveled in that direction?" Shane asked.

"Caleb went to great lengths to ensure we were out of the forest," Liam replied. "He will not reenter it. At most, they are a few hours ahead of us. They could not have gotten very far."

* * *

Ally saw her surroundings in the faint glow from a lantern. She tried to move but her body was captive in heavy gauze, her ankles tied with thorny vines. The air was damp and reeked of mold. Where was she? Her eyes adjusted and she saw a shadow not far away. She tried to free herself, but it was useless, and claustrophobia began to creep into her consciousness. *Relax. Breathe. Think.* An image of a warm summer's night, a lifetime ago now, appeared in front of her.

She and her father were on their deck, gazing at the stars, when a lunar moth flew into a spider's web in the corner. Its wings fluttered madly as it tried to free itself. "It does not realize the more it struggles, the more entangled it becomes," her father said. "Panic is only making the situation worse but," he continued as he tore down the web and freed the moth, "it does not know any better."

"There is plenty of room down here for both of us." His voice startled her. It *was* him ... Caleb. "You are not going anywhere," he said. "Not yet."

"Liam! Corm! Help!" she shouted.

"The darkness will steal the sound of your screams, and your cries for help will go unanswered. You are in the labyrinth of Minos. There is at least one meter of clay above you and a half meter of topsoil above that. The Gorgon bushes that surround this hiding place succeed in discouraging undesired company. Your friends cannot hear you, I guarantee that. But, if you persist, I will gag you as well."

"What do you want with me?" She needed to come up with a plan but for now, she also needed to be the patient moth, the one that didn't panic.

"You have something we need," he said and inched closer. He ripped away the cobwebs at her neck. She cringed when his fingers touched her throat. He smiled. "I will not bite." He held her necklace in his hands. "This is very important."

"Well, then, just take it." She regretted the words as soon she said them.

"It does not work that way. For whatever reason, he needs you as well."

"He?"

Caleb stared at her and smiled. "The Master. He will be here soon enough."

It was time to think about pulling her trump card. "Your name is Caleb, isn't it?"

He didn't answer.

"Do you come from a family of assholes, or are you the only one?"

He snickered, but remained silent.

"A few days ago we met a little boy … an orphan, whose face was badly scarred from a fire. He had only one arm, but considered himself lucky because both his mother and brother had died in it."

He glared at her. "I am not interested in any little boys you met."

"We tried to help him." She began to talk fast. She needed to know the truth. "And he's actually going to live with Liam and his family. But do you know what he was worried about? He was afraid his older brother might come back and not be able to find him. Do you know what his name is?"

"No, nor do I care."

She laid her ace on the table. "His name is Adam, and I think you're his brother."

"I have no idea what you are talking about," he said, but it was too late. Even in the dim light, she saw his expression change, soften for just an instant.

"I don't believe you," she said. "Do me a favor, though. Stay away from him. He's better off without you. I don't know why he cared so much."

Caleb looked at her with narrowed eyes. How could she prove she was telling the truth? Adam's shirt! "If you don't believe me, check my bag."

* * *

How could she have known his brother's name? Was she using some trickery, trying to deceive him? He did not think so. Something inside told him she was speaking the truth. He picked up her bag, grabbed the lantern, and left her alone in the compartment.

He placed the lamp just inside the tunnel and stepped outside, opened her bag and began to remove its contents. A folded piece of material … a flyer, like the one they had played with at the lake. He tossed it aside. Her clothing, a bottle of water. There was nothing here that spoke to him of Adam. He started to shove her garments back inside and stopped. His eyes rested on a well-worn blue shirt.

His fingers touched the buttons sewed upon the front. The letter "C" was carved into each. He looked at the uneven stitching and recognized the sloppy seam work. It was one of his own. How had she come into possession of one of his shirts? It did not confirm her words, but he could not rid himself of the feeling he had been betrayed. The anger within him swelled as tremors erupted beneath his feet.

Had the Master deceived him and taken the only thing he cared about? The answer seemed obvious. "You told me they would be safe!" he shouted to the empty garden and paced back and forth. *I have what he desires. I need to get the boy's horse and take her—*

The thought was interrupted by another tremor, but his eyes saw nothing as he looked around. He picked up her bag and began to make his way back toward their camp. Ten steps later, the ground dissolved beneath his feet.

* * *

Ally moved her arms, gingerly at first, and the webbing that held her hostage began to loosen. She clawed at it and, a few moments later, her upper body was free. She cautiously untied the vines that bound her legs, careful to avoid the thorns. Slowly, she stood. What was she going to do now? Caleb had taken the only source of light, and was still lurking around somewhere. Chances were, she wouldn't get very far. Could she persuade him he was playing for the wrong side? She didn't know, but was sure that waiting for him to return would be a mistake.

The light couldn't penetrate where she was being held. How had she gotten here? He must've carried or dragged her. She got on her knees and felt the dirt floor. Her fingers came upon two ridges in the earth. She reached behind and touched the heels of her shoes. They were caked with dirt. *Those ridges ... they're my heel marks!* She crawled forward, focused on following the slight indentations in the ground.

Twenty minutes later, she heard the sound of wind around the corner. "Freedom," she whispered and stepped outside, but the word was lost amidst shouting not far away. She couldn't see him, but heard Caleb as he cursed. Loudly.

* * *

Caleb dropped through the air but managed to land on his feet. His head slammed into a limestone column and it pounded with each heartbeat as he looked around. The second moon was above the western horizon. He had fallen into an underground room on the site of the ruins. "Damn it!"

He approached the steep embankment that marked his entrance into this chasm. It was no more than four meters in height, but near vertical. He tried to climb out but the earth was too soft to support his weight. The rich, black dirt under his feet returned to the marble floor with him. He tried morphing. As a spider he would be lighter. He closed his eyes and concentrated but knew, before he opened them, his attempt had failed. What was wrong?

Only one answer made sense. The Master had deserted him.

He would think about that later. He needed to get out of here—now. He inspected the boundaries of his new predicament. Behind him, two limestone columns supported most of the earthen slab that separated the heavens from this underworld. The walls to the left and right were unbroken, except for an open doorway in the center of each. There were three choices. He could venture down one of the two dark hallways, at the risk of entering an unfamiliar section of the labyrinth, or try to climb up the wall again. That was it.

No. There was more. He could no longer change, or return to the girl who was his bargaining chit. "*Aaah!*" he screamed, and screamed once more and again.

Chapter 32

Be careful. She followed the sound of his cries and stepped over a stone wall. Cautiously, she approached an opening in the ground and peered over the edge. It was at least twelve feet deep, and two emotions surged through her simultaneously: relief and terror.

A few truths became clear. Caleb couldn't get out the same way he got in, and whomever he kept calling "the Master" wasn't here, not yet. But Caleb wasn't alone. On the ground were three snakes, each at least twenty feet in length. They didn't try to bite him, but seemed intent on taking turns trying to trip him up. And they seemed to be succeeding in wearing him down. He continued to jump around their coiling bodies, too busy to notice she was there.

Run while you have the chance.

It was the voice of reason. She was about to turn away, convinced this time that voice was right, but found she couldn't.

What's the matter with you? Go!

Maybe, in another time, she'd have listened, but something inside her had changed. There was a boy down there. A boy who was Adam's brother. She had to at least try to help him.

"Caleb, Give me your hand!" She got on her stomach and leaned over the edge as far as she could.

He looked up at her, surprised, and hesitated a moment. Then he ran and leaped into the air. She had a flash of catching his hand, only to be pulled in with him, but the closest he came was a good four feet away. She looked around for something to help pull him out.

"Caleb, throw me my bag!" she cried, spotting it on the floor of the open room.

He looked at her suspiciously, but then jumped over one of the snakes. He snatched her bag with his right hand and, while his eyes remained on the two serpents in the corner, threw it in her direction. It sailed over her head. She retrieved it and looked back into the hole. Caleb was running toward the left column in the pit, but there were now eight snakes keeping him company, impeding his progress.

He leaned weakly against the pillar and paused to catch his breath. In seconds, the snakes would be on him again. Looking for anything that might help, she pulled out her clothes piece by piece. *Aha!*

She didn't know if it would be long enough, but it had to do. She tied the sleeves of Adam's shirt and her blouse together, and pulled on either end of her makeshift rope. They easily came apart. Remembering something she'd seen on TV, she retied the shirts and reached into her bag. She found the bottle of water from Lake Lorwyn and poured some over the knots, to make them stronger. The water dried instantly. She thought back to how strong she'd felt after swallowing only a sip, and drained the last of it into her mouth. She pulled on the knots. They held. She looped and tied one of the sleeves to the handle of her bag and wrapped her arms through the straps.

She leaned over the edge and hung her line over the side. "Caleb, grab hold of this!"

He ran and managed to grasp onto it. His feet scrambled along the soft wall of dirt. She grunted and clutched the bag's straps. He was holding on, but she couldn't lift him more than a few inches.

The water's power must be confined to the lake. A cool breeze caressed her face while the clouds stole the moon's light. She felt a cold presence beside her and looked around.

"No!" she screamed. "You can't have him!"

The drops of water at last settled in her stomach and began to ignite a fire. She yanked the strap around her wrist and sat back, legs in front of her, and began to propel herself away from the edge.

* * *

Who was she talking to, and why was she fighting so hard to save him? It did not matter, he decided. If the Master was close, he needed to hurry.

He dug his feet into the loose slope. His arms were forced to take most of the weight, but he did not have the strength to pull himself up. Was his only hope beyond one of those doorways? No. His fate rested with the gods, who he hoped would spare him from the twelve serpents now at his feet. His strength was renewed and his spirit lifted his body. His eyes, though, reached for her, and he noticed she was still alone.

* * *

Ally stopped her backward progress and looked between her legs. Caleb pulled himself up the last foot and stood for a second before he collapsed onto his hands.

Gasping, he looked at her. "It appears the snakes of Medusa are not a myth," he said. "Who were you talking to?"

"Death," she answered.

"I see. You managed to free yourself of the labyrinth, yet you chose to jeopardize that freedom to rescue me. Why?"

She hesitated. It was a stupid answer but it was the only one that made sense. "Because I could."

The sounds of approaching horses made her turn. Her heart lifted. *Liam!*

"Well, you should not have saved me," Caleb replied. He got to his feet and grabbed her roughly by the arm. He twisted it behind her as two giant horses crashed through the brush and stopped short of where they were standing.

Chapter 33

Neither of the horses was the height of Pollux or the size of Beowulf, but something in their confident nature made her uneasy. Their eyes never left her, but she finally managed to break free of their spell. Unfortunately, the men upon their backs only notched her anxiety higher. Each man wore black silk pants reaching just below their knees. That was it. No shirt, no shoes ... nothing. Even their heads were without hair.

Caleb looked from one to the other, but his words were for Ally. "You say you spoke to Death? Well, these are his half brothers. Sukata, let me introduce you to the Master's prize. I am surprised to see you. I was led to believe he would be meeting me."

Despite Caleb's tone, she could tell he was nervous. His eyes remained on the blank faces of the men, which were as smooth as stone. Their eyes contained no emotion; their expressions showed only icy calm.

"The plans have changed, young man," Sukata, the one closest to her, said. On his chest was the tattoo of a two-headed dragon. The heads stared at each other, but the bright red eye visible on each, looked at her. An orange flame curled from their mouths and ended on the man's throat. The dragon's body covered his stomach, its tail wrapped behind him. He smiled, displaying perfect white teeth, and she shivered.

"Sukata," the other said to his fellow rider, "you promote him to young man? He is but a foolish boy." A drawing of a cobra flowed between this man's muscles, defining his chest. The snake's hood was open, and revealed a bright red rhombus. "What of the Shayeen hawk and the young man who keeps him company?"

"Askari, you have more respect for the dead than you do for me," Caleb replied. He looked at them with suspicion. "You will find

238

their bodies a few hundred meters away."

"They're dead? What? No!" She fought to be free of Caleb's grasp. He pulled on her right wrist and forced it toward her left shoulder. She fell to her knees and then to her chest. His knee found her lower back while he slid her wrist a little higher.

"*Aaah!* Oh, God, please stop!" she screamed when the pain became unbearable.

"Caleb, release her," Askari said.

When he did, the snake man signaled for her to rise. She got to her feet. Her knees were weak, not only from Caleb's abuse, but from his words.

"Caleb, you will ride with me," Sukata said, "and the girl with Askari."

Askari leaped from his horse and landed beside her. The snake on his chest stared at her. "Let me help you find your place atop Mayhem," he said with a twisted smile.

"No!"

"Now." He dug his fingers into her upper arm and pushed her forward.

Her shaking hands grasped the pommel. She was able to put her left foot in the stirrup, but didn't have the strength to do anything else. Askari grabbed the waist of her pants and lifted her onto the saddle.

"Their horses are tethered where their bodies lie," Caleb said. "They have a stallion worthy of the Master's collection. I would like to present it to him as a gift. We can take what life remains in them if I am wrong."

"That will not be necessary," Sukata replied. "Time is now the precious jewel. On the back of Catastrophe, there is more than enough room for you." He lowered his hand and effortlessly lifted Caleb onto the back of the horse.

Is it true? Did she lose not only Liam ... and Corm, but also any hope of finding her way home? Weeping, her head dropped back and she looked into the sky.

A lone shape flew in front of the moon's silhouette. It disappeared but returned a moment later, screeching loudly.

* * *

At Liam's shout to stop, Shane pulled on Beowulf's reins. "What is your concern?"

Liam pointed to the sky. Corm circled an area not far from the campsite. "It appears he has found something of worth."

"Perhaps we should exchange progress for possibilities," Oisin said.

"I believe Pollux would like that. He is determined to go back the way we came," Liam said, struggling to keep his horse under control.

"How can there be possibilities in what we have already seen?" Shane asked.

Liam wondered that as well, until a thought came to him. Perhaps Pollux's behavior meant that Ally and Caleb had not gotten far at all. Perhaps they never left.

Liam turned Pollux about. "We need to return!"

* * *

Ally looked to the sky. Was that Corm?

"You say you killed him," Sukata said, following her gaze. "The soul touching Chimera's light indicates you have failed."

"I did kill him," Caleb replied.

"You believe that to be so, but you are mistaken." Sukata glanced at Askari, who pulled the single arrow from the quiver hanging from his horse's saddle. To Ally in the brown-red light of the moon, the tip appeared covered in blood. "Chimera often plays tricks with one's eyes," Sukata said as if reading her mind. "What you see is not a lie but, rather, a premonition jumping in time."

Askari held the arrow near its tip with his right hand and pressed his thumb against one of its flat sides. The snake tattoo on his chest began to writhe, and the head of the cobra broke free from his flesh. There was no blood, only blackness and bone that filled the space left behind. The serpent's head hovered inches from Askari's right ear, its tongue darting in and out of its mouth.

The repulsive sight was more than Ally could take. She slipped from Mayhem's back and hit the ground, hard. The pain in the left side of her head and shoulder nearly blinded her, and she fought to remain conscious. She looked above her, and saw Askari's left hand take hold of the snake's head, his fingers wrapped around its neck and his thumb pushed down between the snake's eyes. Drops of poison oozed from the fangs and landed on the arrow's point. His lower ribs and pelvis were exposed now, the bones clean. No flesh except for that of the snake clung to his skeleton. *Death's half brothers* ... The world faded again, but she fought to hold on as long as she could.

Corm moved from right to left over the tops of the trees, and Askari faced him while he loaded the arrow into the bow and directed it toward the sky.

Corm came into view again. "Now the Shayeen will come to know night," Askari said to Ally.

"No!" she screamed.

The cobra curled around Askari's extended arm, its head cocked in an odd way near his fingers as he traced the path of his prey. The arrow jumped into the night; the air shifted as it went on its way.

"Corm!" she screamed. He had to see it coming but remained directly in its path. *Why isn't he flying away?* A sickening screech met her ears as the arrow found its mark. Her friend hung in the air for a moment, and then tumbled from the sky.

Strength from a supernatural source made her scramble to her feet and begin a stumbling run in the direction he went down. In her side vision, she saw Caleb jump from the horse. He dove at her and succeeded in pulling her to the ground.

"Let go of me!" she screamed. As they struggled to their feet, she summoned all her rage. Her right fist smashed against his chin. She'd taken only a step when a hand grabbed her hair and yanked her back.

"My dear girl, my brother and I insist you stay close," Askari said. He held her by the hair and dragged her back to his horse.

"Perhaps the other is still alive as well," Sukata said. Askari forced her to look at his brother. "Is this true? Is your friend still alive?"

Tears spilled from her eyes. Askari turned her around and held her at arm's length. He looked at her slowly, head to toe. His eyes paused on the necklace, and he fingered it with his free hand.

"Don't touch me," she screeched and tried to swat his hand away. With blinding speed, he grabbed her by the jaw. The rage that had strengthened her receded, and she grimaced in pain and revulsion.

"Be careful, I sense the core of me is hungry," Askari said while he bound her hands in front of her. "We were told to bring you back alive, but nothing else."

"It appears this trip might be more enjoyable than originally anticipated," Sukata said.

Askari picked her up and tossed her over his shoulder. His flesh had returned but she could see where the snake still moved beneath his skin. Her face came within inches of the bizarre parade of glistening diamonds on his back.

"Caleb," Sukata called. "So which is it? Did you complete the task the Master gave you?"

"They were given more than enough poison to kill them," Caleb said. He walked slowly toward Sukata. "If both or either are still alive, it is not because I failed. Something, or someone, is protecting them."

"Then it was up to you to find their weakness," Askari said.

As Caleb moved past, his eyes stayed on her. "Not everyone's vulnerability is worn on their chest ... marked in red."

"It is not wise to play games in the company of Death," Askari replied. His skin turned gray for a moment, and then the arrow appeared in his hands, dripping in blood.

If Corm is ... was alive ... then maybe Liam was, too. *Please.* She closed her eyes. *Liam, where are you?*

I am near, he answered.

Her eyes flew open. *You're alive!*

Yes. Where are you?

She looked around. *I'm at some ruins, not far from the camp with Caleb and two really dangerous men but ... something tells me they think you're alone. They don't know about the others. We're about to leave. They got C—*

She felt him slip away.

* * *

"Wait!" Liam shouted. He brought Pollux about. "Two others have joined Ally and Caleb, but they have made the erroneous assumption Corm and I are traveling alone. I believe she is no more than a kilometer northwest of where we are."

"And how do you know this, my friend?" Oisin asked.

"She is with me in here," he said, touching his heart, "and here." He pointed to his head. "I have an idea." Could it work? He reached out, to let her know her message was received, but she was gone.

"Where exactly is she?" Oisin asked.

"I am not sure—"

"What is that?" Shane asked. A white shape clung to the top of a tree not far from where Corm disappeared.

Ian squinted. "It looks like … a kite."

Chapter 34

Sukata looked to the road. "I hear a horse approaching and there is desperation in its speed. Caleb, join me!"

Askari returned the arrow to his quiver and flipped Ally from his shoulder. She landed rough, snug against the horn of the saddle. Before she could move to a better position, he took his place behind her. His chest pressed against her back and she cringed.

It will deliver hope when you need it most. The stone Tellervo gave her! It was in the zippered compartment of her bag so she wouldn't lose it. *Stupid! Stupid! Stupid!*

"Wait!" she cried. "I forgot my—"

"Silence," Sukata ordered.

They stopped a short distance from the road and remained hidden in the woods. Sukata held up his hand. "Wait until he passes."

She drew in her breath to scream, but Askari covered her mouth and whispered in her ear, "If you make a sound, you will only succeed in alerting whoever is passing to our position, nothing more. If you remain silent, you will allow them to live … a bit longer."

Through the trees, Pollux's blurred shape raced by, a cloud of dust in his wake.

"That is the horse I mentioned earlier," Caleb said, shifting nervously behind Sukata.

Askari held her around the waist, and they left the cover of the forest. She hoped to see Liam ahead of them, but all she saw was Pollux's hindquarters as he disappeared around another bend in the road. The dust was burning her eyes and tickling her throat. Where was Liam going? Pollux was fast, but he couldn't outrun these horses forever. The road finally opened up and then, she noticed it. They all did.

Pollux was without a rider.

A whistle came from the bushes at the side of the road. Pollux skidded to a stop and spun around to face them.

"*Seisahdus!*" Sukata shouted and pulled on Catastrophe's reins. Askari pulled Mayhem to a stop. His left arm held Ally tighter while his right hand released the reins and he reached behind him for his arrow.

Pollux swished the branch tied to his tail while he shook his head from side to side, and began to walk toward them. With each step forward, the two great horses took a step back. Ally's mind scrambled. *I need to get off this horse ... now.* But how?

That question was answered when Mayhem reared onto his hind legs. She tried to grab the horn, but instead tumbled backwards and hit the ground, landing on top of Askari. He released his grip, and that second was all she needed to roll away and get to her feet. As she did, Oisin ran in from the right, Ian from the left, and galloping up from behind were Shane—and Liam.

* * *

Liam recognized their adversaries. They were Shenfo, descendants of the serpents, and legend told of their powerful black magic. Ally's message didn't reveal their identity, though he was sure they did not exist in her world. But what were warriors of this caliber doing here? He jumped off Nyx, drew the sword and ran to where Ally stood in the road.

"Ally, hold out your hands!" he called out as he ran.

She put them in front of her but he could see she was shaking. "Do not move!" he shouted. He prayed he would not wound her in his haste but the motion was instinctive, as if the sword was leading him, and he sliced the ropes around her wrists.

She put a trembling hand to her face. "Corm—"

"*Please*, stay here." He could not be worried about her safety, or concern himself with Corm's whereabouts, not if they hoped to get out of this alive.

Oisin raised his bow, his target was to be whoever was closest to Ally, and released an arrow. It sped through the air and entered the Shenfo's chest to the left of the snake's head, but it met no resistance. It was as if it had torn through a piece of parchment, nothing more, and exited through his back.

Unheeding of the attempt on his life, the Shenfo looked to the sky. His flesh turned gray, and then disappeared above his waist, exposing his skeleton. The specter now before Liam was the image born from nightmares, and he recoiled when the snake unwrapped itself from the demon's ribs and slid into the air. A foul odor reached his nose: the stench of decay, the smell of Death. He looked to the other Shenfo. A two-headed dragon had revealed itself.

Shane released his arrow, but, as quick as it was, it did not possess the speed of the dragon's heads. They parted, and the arrow passed cleanly through the blackness between the man's ribs. "Ian!" Shane shouted. Ian leaped into the air, but lacked the time or space to react to the arrow that burst through the Shenfo; the missile found its place in his upper thigh.

Crying out, Ian fell to the ground. The Shenfo met Shane with a steady gaze. "My great friend, you have picked the wrong day for an ambush."

"*Aaah!*" Oisin shouted, and charged the dragon.

"Is the wolf's courage any match for the dragon's fire?" the Shenfo asked in a gravelly voice. The dragon left the man's flesh and became many times larger than the painted image. With one claw-like hand, the creature grabbed Oisin and lifted him into the air.

Liam's gift was strategy, but the time for rational thought, for tactics, was over. He held the sword in front of him and rushed forward. He gripped the hilt tight and brought the blade up through the air, managing to cut the dragon's flapping wing. Certainly not life threatening, but enough to free Oisin from its crushing grip, and he landed hard on the ground.

With an agility that rivaled Ian's, the dragon turned itself around. Liam stopped, heart pounding against his ribs. The Shenfo narrowed his eyes and looked at the sword. "You are full of surprises, boy."

* * *

Oisin's scream pulled Ally from her stupor in time to see him smash against the road. When he sat up, his left shoulder was nonexistent, and his arm hung at an odd angle in front of him. With his right hand he picked up his bow and scrambled in her direction. *Could this get any worse?*

"Ian! Oisin!" Shane cried as he rushed toward Sukata. The dragon began to shriek. Its left wing hung limp, as if broken, and its smooth, leather-like skin merged with the scales that shielded the beast's torso.

"Shane! Do not look into its eyes," Ian shouted. It was too late. Shane had stopped his retreat, his body turned to stone.

Yes, it could, thought Ally in despair.

But then the dragon lowered its heads. Sukata winced and covered his ears with his hands. His jaw contorted unnaturally while he glared at the sword in Liam's hand. "Brother! Get the sword!" he cried. "Caleb! Get the girl!" He fell to his knees.

The arrow in Askari's hand changed into a long black sword. He advanced on Liam, and the clanging of metal on metal reached Ally's ears. Her rage renewed itself, twined around frustration. It was up to her. There was no one else. Before Caleb could get to her, she ran to Oisin.

"Give me the bow!"

Oisin handed it to her. "My arrows are useless against him," he gasped.

"I don't care. I have to try." But even if the arrow traveled that far, she didn't have a clear shot. Liam stood between her and Askari.

"The Shenfo have only one weakness, an Achilles heel," Ian said, his hands around the arrow in his leg, the front of his pants soaked with blood.

"What is it?" she cried. Her hands were shaking as she tried to thread the arrow into the bow. And then, she remembered Caleb's words: *Not everyone wears their vulnerability marked in red.*

The mark on the snake's throat!

Caleb was headed in her direction. Behind him, Sukata removed one of the dragon's long, sharp claws. His eyes followed Liam as he drew his arm back.

When he was nearly upon her, Caleb glanced over his shoulder. When he saw Sukata get to his feet, he changed course and ran toward Liam.

"No!" she screamed.

"Now, Ally!" Caleb shouted as he rushed past. The dagger-sharp claw flew end over end, through the air, and disappeared into Caleb's back as he pulled Liam to the ground.

The bow was tight and she struggled to pull it back. She straightened her left arm and released the arrow. It fell to the ground a few feet away. *No!*

Oisin handed her another arrow. "I beg you, make this one count."

* * *

Someone tackled him from behind and Liam fell, face first, onto the packed earth. The sword flew from his hand. He freed himself from Caleb's grasp, rolled over and blindly reached behind him.

A bony knee crushed his hand.

"The sword of Nuada. The Master will be pleased," the Shenfo said in a low voice. He held his saber with both hands over his head, the tip of the blade centered over Liam's chest.

The Shenfo's black eyes penetrated his. "You will now meet Death, my —"

Whatever else he might have said never found voice. The Shenfo's body now seemed frozen.

Liam turned his head. Oisin was handing Ally an arrow, but they too looked like Shane, as if they had turned to stone. Sukata was on his knees, his mouth open in a silent scream. Liam was about to slide his body from under the black blade when a cold unwelcomed chill ran down his spine.

"Stay where you are."

The man's voice defied the unnatural silence. Liam looked to see who was addressing him, but the man advancing on him was as unfamiliar as the voice. His coat was black and, if not for the purple threads woven into the high collar or the silver buttons on his sleeve, he would have created a bottomless hole of the space he occupied. His piercing blue eyes sought to penetrate Liam's soul.

"Askari was correct. You are meeting Death," the man said, looking at the Shenfo, "but not in the way he imagined. Remain still. Any move on your part might put you in contact with that blade. That would not be good for you. Or me, for that matter."

The man reached into his coat and pulled out a dagger. Despite his compromised position, Liam did not fear the action.

The man turned the dagger over in his hand and held it out for Liam to see. Miniature skulls were etched into one side of the blade in excruciating detail. "Over the ages, this knife and I have sorted through the aftermath of many wars together," he said. "I have had more than my share of ugly business, but I manage affairs of the flesh fairly. If I did not, those atop the likes of Catastrophe and Mayhem would rule the day. I am not able to take their lives, but I can choose to save yours. If I do not, I will be very busy indeed. The universe is infinite with possibilities, but there is only one certainty: There is no cheating Death.

"You have been trusted with a most difficult task," the man went on, "one that spans two worlds. And it is one that has caught you unprepared. My half-brothers," he motioned to the Shenfo, "have aligned themselves with a dark but powerful force whose purpose is to conquer and control these realms. Take this." He handed Liam a small silver shield imprinted with a coat of arms ... a human skull with a sundial in its center. "Without this, the girl's arrow will arrive too late to save you."

Liam took the shield and slid it under his shirt, centering it under the tip of the black blade.

"I am sure you realize the sword you carry is a powerful weapon. It was forged, in fact, to do away with me. But do not let the sword define the warrior. It has happened before with this blade."

Liam blinked, and time had, once again, resumed.

"— half-brother," the Shenfo finally finished his sentence.

Liam looked into the Shenfo's eyes and smiled as the sword plunged toward his chest.

* * *

Ally set the arrow and pulled back the bow. "Please-please-please," she begged. "Hit the red spot.... *Kill* that son-of-a-bitch!"

"Wait!" Oisin shouted. "Do not use that arrow! It is one that Adam ga— "

"What?" she cried as the arrow ripped through her fingers and tore through the air.

"Praise Artemis," Oisin said in awe.

* * *

The tip of the blade pierced Liam's shirt and struck the metal plate. The Shenfo had not expected the sword to meet resistance, and the vibration that traveled back to his hand rattled his teeth. He looked at Liam in shock.

"I have already met your half-brother," Liam said, "and he sends his regards."

The Shenfo looked at Liam, confused, until the whistling sound from behind stole his attention. He turned his head and his eyes widened in surprise when an arrow tore into the throat of the snake on his chest. "No!" he screamed, and staggered to his feet. The snake writhed from his chest and began an unearthly hissing.

The Shenfo collapsed to the ground, his flesh and bone crumbled as he disintegrated before Liam's eyes. The pile of ash that remained was lifted into the air, then swirled into a funnel cloud and disappeared.

Ally took another arrow from Oisin and turned toward the other Shenfo. "This one has your name on it, you piece of ..."

"My brother's death *will* be avenged," he roared. Pollux stepped aside, and the two dark horses began to run down the road. "Make no mistake about that!" He leaped upon the back of one as it passed. "*Tulla!*" he cried, and then, he too was gone.

When the Shenfo disappeared, so did the spell that held Shane captive. He ran to Ian and Oisin and knelt between them. "I am so sorry, Ian," he said. "Your warning was too late. I could hear, I could see what was happening, but was unable to move."

An eerie feeling of familiarity came over Liam. He had seen the scene in front of him before, but where and how?

His jaw dropped. Gabriel's drawing. The boy had seen all of this, but it had been through Liam's eyes. The body he had drawn face-down was not, was never Liam. It was Caleb.

* * *

Ally whispered into Caleb's ear. "Thank you." She wiped her tear-washed face with her shirtsleeve, then leaned forward and put her face close to his. With effort, he opened his eyes.

"Tell Adam ... I love him, and ... I am sorry. Please. Tell him ... I did the right thing ... in the end."

She looked at the blood that had soaked though his shirt and formed a pool in the dirt. "You can tell him yourself. You have to stay al—"

"Please." Something cold moved past her, and Caleb's body jerked.

"No!" A spider crawled across her hand. She fell backwards and got to her feet. The ground around her was alive with them and they swarmed onto Caleb's body.

Horrified, she took a step back and bumped into Liam. "Where did all these come from?"

"His spirit is being taken by his own, but he does not deserve your tears. Where is Corm?"

* * *

Ally sat in front of Liam on Pollux. Four great hawks were overhead, flying in the direction Corm went down. They kept the birds in their sights as they veered off the road and raced through the brush. *Please, let him be alive.* She refused to allow her mind to accept any other reality, refused to allow doubt to drown the hope she clung to.

At the spot where the birds circled overhead, they jumped from Pollux. There, in a pile of dead leaves, was the lifeless body of a hawk. Dried blood matted the feathers on its chest. Ally fell at Corm's side. "Can't he change back?"

"Not if he was injured in this form," Liam said, dropping to his knees. "Corm, can you hear me?" But Corm's body didn't move. Liam looked at Ally but quickly turned his head.

"Why didn't he get out of the way?" She tenderly touched the feathers on his chest. Her emotions swelled up like waves, and the barrier that had kept them back finally succumbed to the weight. She drew breaths in short gasps, her throat became tight, and she began to sob. "He saw ... the arrow ... coming ... but didn't move. Why?"

"I think he wanted to stay in the air as long as he could, to ensure we found you." Liam put his head into his hands.

It was her fault. She wrapped her arms around her stomach and rocked back and forth. "I wish ... Corm, don't ... you ... dare ..." She couldn't say it. She leaned close as the tears flowed freely. She wiped them away and put her hand on his chest.

"Please," she begged and closed her eyes.

Chapter 35

"Huh?" Her hand moved and, through her pain, she heard a gasp. Liam expressing grief over the loss of his best friend, surely.

She opened her eyes. Her fingers no longer rested upon the torn and bloodied feathers of a bird, but on a human chest that moved in easy rhythm with each breath. Before she could fully process the change, Corm sat up, threw his arms around her neck and held her tight.

Liam lifted his head. "Corm?"

"Oh," Ally cried, "you ... you're alive!"

"It is as the legend promised," Corm whispered. "The tears of the Phoenix have reunited my body with my spirit."

"I'm *from* Phoenix," she replied, and hiccoughed a laugh. "I'm not *the* Phoenix."

"I believe you are mistaken," he said, and buried his face in her shoulder.

The wound in Corm's stomach was ugly, but already beginning to heal. Death had, once again, left them alone. Would they continue to be so lucky? There was still a two-day journey ahead. But Ally now possessed something she never had before: Belief that, together, they could defeat anything—or anyone—that stood in their way.

* * *

Ally by his side, Liam wiped his hands and looked at the shallow grave. The others were back at the campsite, tending to their wounds. He had decided to keep his own encounter with Death to himself. But the spirit had been correct. He was not prepared for the task at hand. Liam knew the traits the others had inherited were instinctive, but his strength was one that came from experience … and he had little of it. The most important element of strategy was to know your enemy, and he had entered into this journey blind. Perhaps he had been wrong when he thought Caleb deserved to die. Perhaps the boy was merely a pawn in this game of chess. But who were the other players, and who was the king controlling their moves?

Ally placed her wreath of flowers on the mound of dirt near the pond, and they rejoined the others.

"Brothers," Shane said, "and sister." He put out his hand and one by one, they placed theirs on top of his. "Our diversity is what makes us strong. To friends, and to the journey ahead."

Liam joined in, but the ritual did little to lighten the weight in his chest. He did not know what lay ahead. There were dark forces that threatened what was important to him … to all of them. He prayed that Thea would send an answer to his message and soon.

Ascencia, he implored in silence and looked to the heavens, *I will do everything within my power to ensure your light remains in the sky, but you must continue to help us as well—*

"Look," Ian said, and Liam followed his pointing finger.

Although the sun was up, a shooting star traveled across the eastern horizon. And, despite all the uncertainty, all the unknowns they would face tomorrow, Liam smiled.

Chapter 36

"How?" Cepheus screamed in disbelief. "How did a girl, a boy, and a Shayeen hawk defeat two Shenfo?" In the talisman, he had seen Sukata returning alone, but it did not reveal what led to this unexpected and incomprehensible turn of events.

Sukata pointed his finger at him. *"Your* carelessness caused my brother to fall."

Cepheus stilled his pacing feet. "My carelessness?"

"Where are the arrows of Golan ... of your father?"

Cepheus remained silent.

"The girl could barely hold a bow yet, when she prayed for the arrow to strike Askari, it found his one weakness. There is something else ... she is traveling with five Shayeen, not one as we were told."

"Where *is* Caleb?"

"He betrayed us and took a dragon's claw intended for the boy, Liam, who is not only marked with the sword but carries one as well."

"We all have swords. What of it?" Cepheus asked with impatience.

"No, my lord, he is in possession of *the* sword."

Cepheus hid his shock, though barely. "How can you be certain?"

"It brought me to my knees and caused an immeasurable amount of pain."

"Indeed? The sword has found its way back? You say there were five?"

"The girl makes six, but Askari's arrow found the hawk."

"Is it dead?"

"I cannot be sure, but the arrow pierced its soul."

Cepheus went to the glass orb. When the answer to his question came, he raised his eyes to Sukata. "The spirit guides returned alone.

The hawk is still alive. If the prophecy is to hold, two more must join them. We need to break the circle before the eight is formed."

Sukata gave him a twisted smile. "I will ensure *all* their lives are extinguished."

"You will have your revenge." They carried the arrows of Golan, the sword and the necklace? *Ahhh, but I possess something valuable as well.* "Bring the two prisoners to my chambers, and summon Maelyn. We need to have a word."

When Cepheus was alone, he pulled the chain holding his charms from inside his shirt. "You will not defeat me again, Ascencia. I will make sure of that." And, when his fingers found the tiny heart-shaped ruby within the curved outline of the swan's neck, he smiled.

Gallery of Illustrations

Ian

Shane

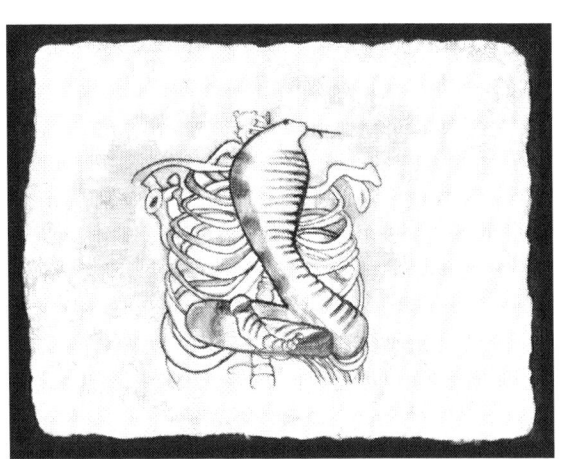

Acknowledgements

It's been four years since I sat down and wrote the sentence that started this journey and I still have no idea what led me to hit that first keystroke. What I do know is that I couldn't have completed this without the support of my family and friends. I am very lucky to have so many wonderful people in my life who took the time to read Double Star and provide me with valuable feedback. I know I put you all in a precarious position. Thanks for being honest.

Thanks to my mom: my tireless cheerleader, my proofreader and a constant source of optimism. I love you.

Thanks to brother, Ned: your words inspire me, your depth enlightens me and your support lifts me. I hope you'll have my back again with Double Star II. You will definitely make it a better read.

To my kids: I had no idea writing was such a lonely business. Thanks for being patient and eating many frozen pizza's for dinner.

To Andrea: my wonderful sister. It's great to have a lawyer in the family.

To my independent readers who read the book, sometimes more than once: Beth, Randy, Cal, Joe, Kate, Andrea, Laural, Laurie, Laura, Steph and MaryAnn. Thanks for keeping me focused.

To Arlene and Terry: my editors, my new friends and, most definitely, my harshest critics. They helped me transform a 203,000 word beast into an 85,000 word novel ... painful but necessary.

To Tammy: thanks for creating the website and Facebook page.

To Laurie: my illustrator. Thanks for putting up with me.

And to those of you who like Double Star: your encouragement will help me see this through to the end so please, share your feedback on www.dblstar.com and like us on Facebook.

Until next time ... find your light, explore the possibilities and ... believe.